The Witness Must Die

Alex R Carver

Published by ARC Books, 2023.

THE WITNESS MUST DIE

First edition. November 1, 2023.

Copyright © 2023 Alex R Carver.

ISBN: 979-8223873495

Written by Alex R Carver.

AFRICA

The night-vision goggles gave everything a green glow, but Luke Caldwell was used to that and paid it no mind as he scanned the grounds of the estate across the road.

For a week he had hidden in the abandoned warehouse where he had made his perch as he studied the lush, green, and well-kept grounds, which contrasted sharply with the parched lands around it, and the house that sat in the middle. During that time he had learned the habits and movements of the occupants, becoming familiar with their routines, and identifying any dangers.

He could have made his move at any time during the past seven days, but he was a patient and cautious man, not prone to rushing things without good cause. That was how he had become so successful in his chosen career — professional assassin.

Everything at the estate had seemed normal during his observations, but he knew how little it could take for things to go catastrophically wrong, and he wasn't about to chance that.

When he was certain that nothing had changed, and there were no surprises waiting for him, he set aside the goggles and took out the suppressed rifle from the case by his feet. With the rifle tight against his shoulder, he sighted on the first of the guards patrolling the grounds of the estate. He made a few adjustments as he tracked the man, and then he squeezed the trigger. Half a pound of pressure was all it took to end the man's life. A small exertion for such a large result.

Luke watched for a moment to be sure he hadn't missed, he would have been surprised if he had, and then he shifted aim. There were two more guards patrolling the estate, both of whom he dropped as quickly and as quietly as the first. Though he was sure there were no other guards to worry about, he made a last sweep of the grounds, searching them through the scope, to be certain.

When he was satisfied the grounds were empty of threats, he packed the rifle away. Ready at the side of the rifle case was a crossbow, which he took up and aimed at the wall surrounding the estate. A loud twang sounded as the bolt leapt from the weapon to fly through the night and bury itself in the wall just below the top. It quivered there for a few moments before becoming still.

Attached to the tail of the bolt was a lightweight but strong length of rope. He untied the end he had secured to the leg of a nearby machine to stop it following the bolt out of the window, pulled it tight, and then redid the knot. He tested the rope to be sure it would hold his weight and the machine wouldn't move, and then he made a final check of his weapons.

He had a pair of suppressed pistols, one in a shoulder holster and the other tucked into the waistband at the back of his trousers, a seven-inch combat knife with a black, carbon steel blade, and a MP5 submachine gun with a suppressor attached, which he slung over his shoulder and pulled tight against his chest.

A last look out the window assured him there was no traffic on the long and dusty road that led from the nearest city, two miles distant, to the nearest town, many miles away, and no-one to observe him. Satisfied that he wasn't going to be witnessed, he climbed out the third-floor window and made his way, hand over hand, along the rope until he was able to pull himself up onto the top of the wall surrounding the estate. Swinging himself over, he dropped down to land lightly in Philip Mbokani's estate.

He remained by the wall for almost a minute as he scanned the darkness with his night-vision goggles to be sure there were no surprises waiting for him.

When he saw nothing, he straightened and made for the nearest of the guards he had killed, his finger on the trigger of his MP5, ready to react at the first sign of trouble. From the guard's pocket he took out a swipe card, which he used to unlock the kitchen door at the rear of the house.

The house was silent as he crossed the kitchen and crept down the passage to the small security room, where the cameras that monitored the estate for intruders were watched. The positioning of the cameras had been poorly thought out, and he was confident that he had made it that far without appearing on any of them since no alarm had been raised, but he wasn't about to take any chances.

It took him barely two minutes to deal with the guard watching the cameras and remove the hard drives on which the footage was stored, and after finishing there he made for the first floor, where he found the master bedroom without difficulty.

Even if he hadn't known where it was located, he would have been able to find it easily for there was a guard seated outside. Unfortunately for Philip Mbokani, the guard was asleep, not that it would have done any good for him to be awake for a single shot from the suppressed MP5 in Luke's hand killed him before he could have known anyone was there.

Ignoring the bloody smear that stained the wall behind the guard, Luke moved quickly down the passage and slipped through the door into the bedroom. The room was darker than the rest of the house and he paused after closing the door to let his night-vision goggles adjust. Once he could see well enough, he crossed to the bed and moved around it until he was standing over Philip Mbokani.

The fifty-eight-year-old looked like a grandfather, sleeping peacefully next to his wife of many years. He appeared a little worn by a hard life providing for his family, but other than that he looked good for his age. Luke knew the truth, however. Philip Mbokani was about as far from a kindly, hardworking grandfather as it was possible to be. He was a murderous arms dealer, who sold weapons to dictators, rebels, terrorists, drug lords, and criminal gangs around the world. Through the weapons he had sold he was responsible for the deaths of tens of thousands of people.

Luke knew that and didn't care. He was not there because of Mbokani's business, nor because of the deaths he was responsible for, not even those he was personally responsible for. He was there because someone disliked Mbokani enough to pay for his death. He didn't know who they were or why they wanted Mbokani dead, and he wasn't interested in knowing. The only thing that mattered to him was that they were prepared to pay for his services, which didn't come cheap.

Without a thought for the fact that he was ending a man's life, he raised his gun and placed the muzzle an inch from Mbokani's temple. He fired once and blood stained the pillow beneath the arms dealer's head. He stayed where he was for a moment in case Mbokani was somehow still alive, and then he turned away from the bed.

He was almost at the door when he heard movement behind him. He spun back, gun at the ready, and saw the woman who had been sleeping next to Mbokani stirring. He waited, his finger on the trigger of his MP5, silently urging the woman to settle and go back to sleep. She was Mbokani's personal assistant as well as his lover, and deeply involved in his business, which made her almost as guilty as him, but he wasn't being paid for her death and he was reluctant to kill her if it wasn't necessary. Luck was not on his side, however, or hers.

1

BARCELONA, SPAIN

• • • •

THE GUNFIRE ENDED WITH shocking suddenness, as did the screams and shouts, but Sofia Torres stayed where she was, huddled in the bottom of the wardrobe. Through the door she could hear her employer, Tomas Abrantes, his wife, and their bodyguard, her uncle, Miguel. She wanted to go to her uncle, she always felt safe around him, but the concern in the voices of those she could hear kept her in hiding.

Her decision to remain in the wardrobe soon proved to be the right one. Her hiding place shook as the crashing sound of an explosion, followed by a fresh burst of gunfire, came from the room beyond.

"Hello, Tomas."

There was something about the voice that spoke those two words that frightened Sofia more than the gunfire had. In her hiding place, she trembled violently.

"Y-you murdering b-bastard. Why? They n-never hurt anyone."

Sofia had never heard her employer stammer before, and it surprised her to realise that he was as frightened as she was. She couldn't blame him, though. She didn't know exactly what had happened, or why, but she was sure that all the gunfire meant that many, if not all, of the people she worked with and for were dead.

Laughter, sharp and humourless, answered Tomas Abrantes' question.

"You're really asking why," the mystery man said when he stopped laughing. "You want to know why I did this. You know why. You invaded my territory and killed my men when they tried to stop you, and you ask why I did this. I warned you what would happen if you didn't back off and stick to your side of the border, but you didn't listen. This is on you."

"You di-didn't have to kill the kids. They were innocent."

There was another burst of laughter. "You think I'm going to leave someone alive who might come after me when they grow up? I'm not stupid. I told you what would happen if you kept trying to muscle in on my territory. I made it very clear what I would do. You promised to back off. You lied. You lied, but I'm a man of my word, so now it's time for you to see what I do to people who lie to me."

· · · ·

CHOKING, SOFIA SHOVED open the burning hot wardrobe door and stumbled out into the bedroom. She made for the door, desperate to escape the horror that surrounded her, but got turned around in the smoke that filled the room and her lungs and made her cough and gasp for air. She tripped over a figure on the floor, who it was she didn't know, and fell onto the massive bed that dominated the room. She sprawled across the body that was tied to it and felt flames jump to her clothes from the covers.

With a scream that became a hacking cough, she pushed herself up. She could taste the smoke as it filled her mouth again and tickled the back of her throat. It had an acrid taste, like burnt meat, that made her gag and want to throw up.

Her hands outstretched, she turned to where she thought the door was and groped her way forward. She found the wall and moved sideways until she located the door and pulled it open. The handle burned her, provoking another strangled scream, and a fresh wave of smoke and flames billowed around her.

Sofia staggered from the bedroom, leaving one fire for another, and made her way down the stairs, a hand on the wall to support and guide her. The front door was closer, but she automatically made for the kitchen door at the rear of the house when she reached the ground floor. The habit of entering and leaving the house through the kitchen was too ingrained in her. Not even her injuries, or the fact that the house was on fire, could break her of it. As fast as her injured legs allowed, she stumbled through the swirling smoke that filled the house to the kitchen.

She fell to her knees, retching, the moment she pushed through the door. It wasn't just the heat and the smoke that sent her to her knees. The kitchen resembled a scene from a horror movie, with bodies strewn all about and blood coating nearly every surface that could be seen through the smoke.

What she had heard while hidden in the wardrobe had been bad enough. What she saw now was worse, much worse. The bodies of the people she had worked with, people she had been friends with, lay wherever she looked.

When there was nothing left in her stomach, Sofia forced herself back to her feet. She did her best to keep her eyes averted from the bodies as she made for the back door. It wasn't easy, though, for there were bodies all around the kitchen. She stumbled and tripped over the body of the head cook as she dodged around the body of one of her fellow maids, cutting herself on the corner of a counter, but didn't stop. She didn't think anything would have made her stop and stay in that room, surrounded by bodies and blood.

The moment she was outside she sucked in fresh air to clear her lungs of smoke. All she succeeded in doing, however, was to bring on a fresh fit of coughing that sent her back to her knees.

It took her a short while to recover, and once she did she made her way around the side of the house, her eyes on her feet so she didn't have to see the horror that surrounded her.

When she reached the gates, which stood open, she started down the road towards the city. Her pace was slow; she struggled for breath and her legs hurt where they had been burned and cut, making walking difficult, but she determinedly kept going.

How long she had been walking for when she saw the car in the distance, Sofia didn't know, but the sight of it sent her into a panic. It was the killers, come back for her, she was sure of it. The thought sent her stumbling across the road in a desperate bid to get away and find somewhere to hide.

She tripped over a rock, hidden by the grass, and fell. A cry of pain escaped her as she landed heavily but she didn't stop, her flight was too desperate for pain or blood to stop her. She struggled to get back to her feet, and when she failed to do so she began crawling.

2

Reluctantly, Cortez pushed away from the wall where he had been lounging and straightened up. He took a last pull on his cigarette and flipped the butt away before approaching the car that had pulled up.

"What's the situation, Sergeant?" Detective Sergeant Pizarro asked the moment he was out of the car.

"Nice to see you too, Francisco," Cortez said, wondering what bad luck had resulted in his former partner being sent out there. "The situation isn't clear yet. They're still trying to put out the fire and determine what happened. Hopefully, we'll have a better idea in an hour or so." His eyes went to the burning house, where smoke poured from the windows while several teams of firefighters trained hoses on the property as they fought to get the fire under control.

"Tell me what you do know," Pizarro instructed, as unhappy with the discovery that Miguel Cortez was not only there but the officer in charge, prior to his arrival, as Cortez was with his presence.

Cortez watched the firefighters for a few moments more and then returned his attention to Pizarro. "An hour and a half ago a young woman was found at the side of the road, injured and in distress, and babbling about dead bodies and a fire. She was still babbling about them when I got there. I couldn't get any sense out of her, but the smoke from the fire was visible, so I was able to figure out where the maid had come from."

"The maid?" Pizarro asked.

"The young woman, Francisco, she's a maid."

"How do you know that?"

Cortez sighed. "Because she's wearing a maid's uniform. As I was saying, the smoke from the fire was visible, so I came up here while the paramedics dealt with the woman. Firefighters were dispatched as soon as I reported in. They got here within about fifteen minutes and got to work." Without thinking about what he was doing, he reached into his pocket for a cigarette, which he lit, ignoring the disapproving look from Pizarro. "By that time, I'd been able to look around."

"And?" Pizarro prompted when Cortez smoked his cigarette instead of continuing.

"And this case should be given to someone better than you," Cortez said. He enjoyed the look of annoyance that crossed his former partner's face at his comment. "There's a lot of bodies here. I have no idea how many, but it's a massacre. I found a guard with his throat cut over there in the gatehouse," he pointed to the small hut just inside the gates. "The place looks like it's been painted with his blood. There's two more guards on the South side of the house, they've been shot and run over, and another at the rear of the house who's been shot, that's in addition to those you can see from here. I also saw several bodies in the kitchen through the window. No idea how they died, I couldn't get in there to check them out, the fire was too strong when I tried."

"Do you know whose place this is?" Pizarro asked. "Or have any clue who is responsible, or why they did this?"

"You're the detective, it's your job to figure that out," Cortez said, though he didn't have high hopes that Pizarro would manage to do so, at least not without help.

Pizarro was silent for several long moments, during which he scowled at Cortez. Finally, he said, "Yes, it is, so why don't you go and do whatever it is you do now you're in uniform, while I get this investigation underway."

· · · ·

"WHY DIDN'T YOU TELL Pizarro about this?" Officer Santos wanted to know as he trailed after his partner.

"I could have given Francisco the people responsible for this on a silver platter and he wouldn't have taken it," Cortez said over his shoulder as he strode down the road, following the trail of bloody footprints that led from the gatehouse, out of the estate, and away from the city. "If he bothers to do his job, he'll be heading this way himself soon enough. And if he doesn't, it won't matter because we're doing it. Besides, it's obvious that whoever made this trail is responsible for at least one of the murders back there. Don't you think it will look good on your record to have a hand in catching the killers? This is going to be all over the news in a few hours. Catching one of the people responsible might just get you promoted."

"You mean it will look good on your record," Santos said. "I know what you're thinking, you think if you follow this trail and catch one of the killers, you'll get your old job back as a detective, and show up Pizarro as a bonus. Don't try and pretend that isn't what you're thinking," he said before Cortez could say anything.

"Sure," Cortez admitted, abandoning what he had been going to say. "This is a golden opportunity for me to show up Francisco. He's made it where he is by trading on his connections and other people's work. He's no detective, and if Meteiros has any sense he'll take him off this case before he can balls it up. If I can get my old job back at the same time, so much the better."

The footsteps gradually faded, but they persisted long enough for them to reach a petrol station a kilometre and a half from the estate. They led into the shop and then back out again before disappearing abruptly. Cortez and Santos looked all around the forecourt but could find no further sign of the bloody footprints.

"He must have had a car here, or been picked up by someone," Cortez observed after giving up the search.

"Why would he have parked here and walked all the way to the estate to kill someone, only to walk back again?" Santos asked. "Maybe he, assuming it's a man who left the footprints, isn't one of the killers but someone from the estate who was injured and got away. He could have come here to try and get away from the killers and find some help."

"Maybe, but I doubt it. For one thing, if he was injured and looking for help, he'd have headed towards the city, not away from it, and for another, the footsteps are too steady for someone who was either injured or trying to get away from a group of killers. Come on." Cortez strode across the forecourt to the shop, while Santos stood there, wondering what his partner was up to.

"Can I help you?" the young man behind the counter asked when Cortez reached him.

Cortez noted the look of guilt on the cashier's face and filed it away in case it should prove important. He doubted it would. He suspected it was just the ordinary guilt of someone unexpectedly confronted by a police officer, but he was experienced enough to know that anything could prove relevant in a case.

"Yes, you can, Jorge, is it?" he asked, reading the nametag the young man was wearing. When he received a nod, he went on, "Some time ago a man came here. He would have arrived on foot from that direction," he pointed up the road towards the burning estate, "and left in a vehicle. Did you see him?"

"Yeah, I saw him," Jorge said with a nod. "Must have been about two hours ago. I wouldn't have paid much attention, but we don't get many people walking in here — too far from the city. Plus, his car was parked here when I started. I wondered whose it was, so I was kind of keeping an eye on it. He came in, bought himself a Snickers and a bottle of Coke, got in the car and left. He drove off back the way he came, heading towards the city."

"Can you describe him? Him and his car?" Cortez pulled out a notepad and pen, so he could write down what he was told.

"I can do better than that. He's on camera," Jorge said, pointing behind and above him to where a camera watched the cash register. "And there's more cameras outside that will have caught his car."

That was a stroke of luck that Cortez hadn't anticipated.

• • • •

STRIDING UP TO THE door, Cortez knocked loudly and then stepped back. "What?" he demanded when he saw the uncertainty on his partner's face.

"Shouldn't we tell Detective Pizarro about this?" Santos asked. "We followed the bloody trail and got a name. Surely it's up to the investigating officers to follow up on what we've found."

Cortez gave his partner a hard look and then turned to knock again. "It's the police," he called out. "Open up, Mr Tevez."

"Come on, Miguel, he's not home," Santos said when there had been no response after a couple of minutes. "It's time to pass this on to Pizarro. He can have people look for Mr Tevez." He started down the hallway but was stopped by a heavy thud from behind him. "What the hell are you doing?" he asked, looking back in time to see Cortez kick the apartment door a second time. "You can't do this," he said, hurrying back to take Cortez by the arm so he could pull him away from the door. "We don't have a warrant or anything."

Cortez pulled free from Santos' grasp and kicked the door again, making it shiver in its frame. "Sod getting a warrant." He kicked the door for a third time. "It'll take too bloody long, and so will convincing Francisco to do anything about what we've discovered." A fourth kick caused the door to fly open and crash into the wall behind it. He was through in an instant, his eyes darting everywhere as he moved down the passage, searching for Rafael Tevez.

"Shit!" he swore when he saw the arm on the floor behind the sofa. As he moved further into the living room more of the body came into view. "You'd better call this in," he told Santos, kneeling beside the body so he could feel for a pulse.

His actions were instinctive, nothing more. It was clear that Rafael Tevez was dead, the deep, dark mark on his neck told the story of what had happened to him, part of it at least.

3

Cortez had just settled himself with a plate of Bolognese and a glass of wine when a knock sounded on the door of his apartment. Grumbling, he put the plate down and got to his feet.

"What d'you want, Diego?" he asked irritably when he saw who was at the door.

"Do you mind if I come in?" the man at the door, who could not have looked more out of place in the hallway of the old and disreputable apartment building Cortez lived in if he had been wearing a clown costume rather than the expensive and tailored suit he had on, asked. "We have some things to discuss, and I don't think it's a good idea for us to discuss them in your doorway." Without waiting for an answer, Diego Vega brushed past Cortez and entered the apartment.

Unsurprised by the rudeness, Cortez closed the door and followed his visitor into the living room.

"So, what brings Roberto Abrantes' number one man here?" he asked, returning to the chair he had left to answer the door, and the dinner he had been about to eat.

An envelope tossed into his lap answered his question.

Accepting that his dinner was almost certainly going to get cold, he picked up the envelope. It had a nice weight and thickness to it, and he tore it open to count the wad of Euros it contained. He was pleased with the figure he came up with — five thousand.

"A small thank you from Mr Abrantes for the information you provided this afternoon," Vega told him.

"I thought he might prefer to hear about his brother's murder before Francisco arrested him for it," Cortez said. "I assume he had nothing to do with it."

Vega gave Cortez a hard look. "Of course not. Mr Abrantes and his brother may have had their disagreements, but he would never have done anything to hurt his niece or her sons."

"Okay. If Roberto didn't kill his brother, who did?" Cortez asked. "Who would be stupid enough to kill Tomas? I wouldn't have thought there was anyone in the city, other than Roberto, with the men or the balls to try something like that, let alone succeed."

"We don't know," Vega admitted, "but we are making inquiries. Mr Abrantes would like you to keep close to the investigation and keep him up to date with any developments Detective Sergeant Pizarro uncovers."

"That's not likely to be easy," Cortez said, sipping at his wine. "Since I'm not a detective anymore, I'm not likely to be let near the investigation, especially when it's in Francisco's hands."

"There's more where that came from, if you can manage it." Vega indicated the envelope Cortez had put on the table next to his plate of Bolognese. "Mr Abrantes wants to know everything you can find out. You told me earlier there is a witness, a maid. Mr Abrantes wants you to find out what she saw and heard. And, if she is able to identify someone, he wants to know who that person is."

Though he liked the idea of earning more money to put towards his private retirement fund, Cortez couldn't help thinking that Roberto Abrantes was asking a lot of him.

"The only way I'm going to get close to the investigation is if I can bring something to it, and right now I have nothing. Unless you can give me something."

• • • •

"EVENING, IZZY," CORTEZ greeted the woman who answered the door.

"Miguel." Isobel Pizarro's voice was cold. "What are you doing here?"

"I need to see Francisco," Cortez told her. "I take it he's home."

"Can't it wait until tomorrow, at the office? Surely whatever you need to see him about isn't that important."

"Who is it dear?" a voice called from the living room.

"I guess you had better come in," Isobel said reluctantly.

"Thanks." Once inside, Cortez made straight for the living room. Having been to the house before, in better times, he knew where he was going. "Evening, Francisco," he said cheerfully the moment he saw his former partner.

Pizarro looked up from the television, distaste on his face. "What are you doing here?" he echoed his wife's question.

"I've come to do you a favour," Cortez told him, ignoring how he had been spoken to.

"I can manage without any favours from you," Pizarro said. "So, whatever it is you are here for you can just leave again."

"Oh, I think you want this favour, Francisco," Cortez said, sitting without invitation. "I know how much you want promotion. You're desperate to be the youngest DI in the city, but you know you can't manage that without something big on your record. Izzy's father can't get you that promotion, no matter how much you'd like him to. This case, the massacre of Tomas Abrantes and his family, and everyone else at his estate, is your golden opportunity. If you solve this case, you're a shoo-in for promotion to DI the next time there's an opening."

"I don't need your help to solve this case," Pizarro said confidently. "I already have a suspect. It's just a matter of getting the evidence, and that shouldn't take long."

Even knowing Pizarro as he did, Cortez couldn't believe he thought the case was going to be that easy.

"If you think Roberto Abrantes is responsible for the massacre of his brother's family, then you're even stupider than I thought."

"I think you should listen to him, Francisco," Isobel said from the doorway. "If he knows anything that might help you solve the case and get that promotion, it will be worth your time."

Pizarro looked from his wife to his former partner and then back before nodding reluctantly. "Okay, what is it you know?" he asked, not the least bit happy with the thought of getting help from the man who had almost cost him his career. "Why do you think someone other than Roberto Abrantes is responsible for the massacre?"

"As you know, I have a number of sources, and they've proved useful over the years," Cortez said. "Well, I put the word out to them earlier, letting them know I'm interested in anything they might know about what happened. One of them got back to me a while ago. It seems that Tomas Abrantes has made a number of trips around the country, and even to France, over the past year, looking to expand his operations. He must have upset someone because according to my source, Tomas increased the security at his estate — extra guards, upgraded security systems, that kind of thing."

"I take it you don't know who he upset."

"No," Cortez shook his head, "but my source is trying to find out. I know it's not much, but it's a starting place. The moment I find out more, I'll let you know."

4

With the door open, Marc rested one foot on the map compartment while he waited. When he finally heard the lorry pull up outside the unit, he stubbed out the remains of his cigarette and took the key from the ignition. The unit was plunged into silence as he crossed to the loading bay's roller door, which he opened with a swift pull on the chain at the side of it.

"You're late," he said abruptly when the door was high enough for him to see the man outside.

Carlos, whose name was just visible on a tag stitched onto his dirty overalls, shrugged aside the complaint. "I had to deal with the old lady. She's got a thing about knowing where I'm going when I leave the house at night. Are the vehicles in there?" he asked, nodding in the direction of the darkness behind Marc.

"Yes. Turn the truck around and I'll bring the first one out."

It took a little over twenty minutes to load all four vehicles onto the transporter, and when it was done Marc climbed into the cab while the last of them was secured.

"Money?" Carlos said when he joined Marc, his hand held out expectantly.

"I told you, you can trust me," Marc said. "Here it is. Twenty-five thousand Euros, as agreed." He handed over the envelope he took from the inside pocket of his jacket.

Carlos practically snatched the envelope in his eagerness to check the contents. He not only counted the notes he examined a random selection of them to be sure he wasn't being cheated, either with forged notes or in some other way. Only when he was satisfied did he stuff the envelope into a pocket and start the engine.

The drive to the scrapyard where Carlos worked, and which he used for his side-line of disposing of vehicles used by criminals, passed in silence. Neither man was interested in knowing more about the other than they already did.

"You start taking the vehicles off the back," Carlos said after parking the transporter by the vehicle crusher that was to be used to get rid of three of the four vehicles on the back. "I'll turn the lights and the crusher on and get the keys to the crane."

"What the hell is this?" Carlos demanded when he returned and got a good look at the vehicles he was being paid to dispose of in the light from the spotlights he had turned on. He hadn't been able to see them clearly when they were being loaded onto the transporter.

"Two vans and a car, like I told you," Marc said. "What's the matter? You can get rid of them, can't you? The crusher can handle them."

"Yeah, I can crush 'em. That's not the problem. The problem is you led me to believe they were used in something simple. Something simple doesn't leave bullet holes." He looked at the two vans in concern. "You were involved in that massacre, weren't you!"

Though he showed no outward reaction to the accusation, Marc swore to himself. The bullet holes in the vans were the one concern he had had, but there had been no way for him to know how Carlos was going to react to them until then. His mind raced as he considered his options.

"Does it really matter what the vehicles were used for?" he asked finally.

"Yeah, it does. Just because I'm a crook doesn't mean I don't have a conscience. The reports on the news said a lot of people were killed in that massacre, including women and kids. I have kids of my own, for God's sake."

Marc looked shrewdly at Carlos. He was sure he knew what the man was really thinking. "Why don't I give you an extra twenty-five thousand," he said. "Will that salve your conscience enough for you to do the job?"

"What kind of man d'you think I am?" Carlos demanded in an outraged tone, though he immediately answered the question himself. "Fifty thousand. An extra fifty thousand and I'll keep my mouth shut."

"Fair enough," Marc said after a moment, during which he appeared to consider the matter. "But you'd better make sure no-one asks questions about these vehicles."

"Unless you've led them here, there's no need to worry. Nobody's asked questions about the other vehicles I've disposed of. There's an extra half dozen crushed up vehicles around here, and I don't think anyone's noticed. And that includes an armoured transport van from a bank job," Carlos bragged about the vehicles he had disposed of. "Do you have the extra money here? I'm not doing nothing till I get the money."

"I've got it, don't worry. You start crushing and I'll be right back." Marc made his way around to the boot of his hire car.

With an eye on Carlos to be sure he couldn't see what he was doing, Marc removed five bundles of cash from the case he had taken from Rafael Tevez after killing him and then made for the crane. He was sure Carlos knew what he was doing, nonetheless he circled wide around the area so as not to be in any danger should the van fall or something else went wrong.

He climbed to the cab when he reached the crane and passed the money to Carlos. He then stepped back outside, so he wouldn't distract the man while he was working. His position afforded him a good view of the van as it was lowered into the crusher, while also enabling him to see what Carlos was doing as he manoeuvred the magnet out of the way and then descended to the ground so he could operate the crusher.

Marc was surprised when no blood sprayed out as the van was compressed into a cube of metal that didn't look large enough to have once been a medium-sized vehicle. He had expected and worried that the bodies hidden in the van would give themselves away when subjected to pressure. Fortunately, that didn't happen, so there was no way for Carlos to know that he was disposing of more than just vehicles.

• • • •

IT WAS FORTY MINUTES before the two vans had been dealt with and the car had been lifted into the crusher. The remains of the vans had been stacked with other, equally unrecognisable vehicles, where they would soon be joined by the car and, hopefully, wouldn't be noticed.

While Carlos headed for the crusher controls to deal with the car, Marc made for his hire car. From under the passenger seat, he retrieved an extendible baton, and with it in hand he stalked towards Carlos. When he was close enough to strike, he gave a quick flick of his wrist to extend the baton and then raised his arm to bring the weapon down on Carlos' head. Unfortunately, things didn't go as planned.

As if sensing the danger, Carlos turned and twisted out of the way at the last second. The baton clanged against the crusher's control box, jarring his arm, but Marc didn't let that stop him. Ignoring the shock of the impact he swung the baton a second time. This time he hit Carlos on the left arm, breaking the bone on the waistline of a hula girl he had tattooed there.

Carlos showed no sign of the pain he must have been feeling, beyond a grunt and a tight compression of his lips. He didn't even pause to take a breath. Instead, he retaliated immediately, swinging his right fist at Marc's head.

Marc reeled back from the blow and lashed out with a foot. The kick landed squarely on Carlos' left knee, yet he showed no more concern over that blow than he had the one that broke his arm. His only reaction was to take a step back to steady himself.

Having been in numerous fights over the years, with people of all sizes, Marc wasn't intimidated by how much bigger than him Carlos was. He knew that the key to winning a fight, especially against someone larger than him, was to keep his opponent on the defensive until he could land a finishing blow. The bigger man's apparent indifference to either injuries or pain did concern him, however.

Marc followed up the kick with a blow from the baton that shattered Carlos' jaw, which produced the first audible reaction from the big man. Carlos tried to call out in pain but the only sound he was able to make was a prolonged moan as his jaw failed to work as it was meant to.

Marc's next blow struck Carlos on the side of the knee, causing him to stumble. He then doubled him up with a jab to the stomach, before finishing him off with an overhand swing that brought the baton crashing down on Carlos' head. He put all his strength into the blow and there was a loud crunching sound, audible over the noise made by the crusher, as the skull fractured.

Carlos slumped to the ground and Marc bent to check the big man for signs of life, while holding the baton ready in case he needed to hit him again. There was no pulse, though the body did twitch several times before finally becoming still.

Rummaging in the man's pockets, he retrieved the money he had given him. He shoved the money into his own pocket and then set about finishing up the work of getting rid of the vehicles used in the attack on Tomas Abrantes' estate. Carlos' body went into the boot of his own car, which was then crushed and stacked with the other vehicles.

When he was done, Marc parked the vehicle transporter in the vacant spot where it belonged, with the keys in the ignition, as though someone had forgot to remove them. He then left the yard so he could head back to his hotel and collect his things for his return to France. He had been in Spain for more than a fortnight, organising things for his employer, and that was as long as he liked to be away from home.

5

"Good afternoon, Miss Torres, I'm Detective Sergeant Pizarro, and this is Detective Diaz," Pizarro introduced himself and his partner as they entered the private hospital room Sofia Torres had been placed in. "We'd like to talk to you about the events that took place at the Abrantes' estate yesterday morning." He collected a chair from the corner of the room and moved it to by the bed so he could sit. "I hope you don't mind answering a few questions for us."

"Do I have a choice?" Sofia asked, uncomfortable with the thought of recounting the previous day's events, which ran through her mind every time she closed her eyes.

"Of course you have a choice."

Pizarro's head snapped around as he asked sharply, "What are you doing here?"

"I'm here to check on the officer on duty here," Cortez said from the doorway. "And since I'm here, I thought I'd see if Miss Torres is alright." It amused him that his presence alone was enough to annoy Pizarro. "Is everything okay?" he asked of Sofia.

Sofia was surprised to hear someone ask that with sincerity and was grateful for it. The nurses treated her well, but she could tell that their inquiries were duty rather than genuine interest in her as a person.

"The doctor tells me I'll be here for a while. How long depends on how well my legs heal. And they want me to see a psychologist because they're worried about PTSD." She paused for a moment and then went on, despite it feeling odd to be talking to a complete stranger about her situation, "It wouldn't be so bad, but I'm stuck here and there's no-one to talk to. There isn't even a television to watch. I'm going to be bored out of my mind by the time I get out of here. And I didn't sleep very well last night. I could smell the smoke and feel the flames burning me again, just like I was back in that room. And I could hear that man again."

"That's to be expected," Cortez said. "I'd be surprised if you were okay after what happened yesterday. If you want someone to talk to, I can stick around for a while. My shift is up now, and I don't have anything better to do this afternoon."

"You can't," Pizarro said. "Detective Diaz and I need to question Miss Torres about yesterday's events. Not only that but since she's a witness in an active investigation it would not be appropriate for you to spend time with her in an unofficial capacity."

"I'm not involved with the investigation, Francisco, so there's no problem with me spending time with Miss Torres if I wish to. As for you needing to question her, I can wait outside until you're done. I'm sure Officer Murrieta will be grateful for some company."

Without giving Pizarro a chance to protest, or to make any kind of comment at all, Cortez stepped out of the room to find himself a seat for his wait.

A disgruntled look on his face, Pizarro stared at the door, which had swung shut behind Cortez. He had an urge to follow Cortez to argue the point with him, but Diaz's impatient shuffling reminded him of why he was there.

"Do you have any objections if we record our conversation with you, Miss Torres?"

"I suppose not. Do I need a lawyer here while you ask your questions?" Sofia asked nervously, her stomach filled with butterflies as she watched Detective Diaz take out a small tape recorder.

"No. We don't suspect you of any involvement in yesterday's events, we just want to get your statement about what happened, so there's no need for a lawyer," Pizarro said reassuringly.

"Okay."

Pizarro glanced at his partner to check that he was ready with the tape recorder, and then he got started, "Why don't we begin with you telling us what happened yesterday, in your own words. We'll ask whatever questions that come to mind after we're heard what you have to say."

Sofia spoke slowly as her mind drifted back to the events of the previous day. "I was in the master bedroom, cleaning, when I heard the gunshots. I wasn't too concerned, the guards are, were, always doing target practice or shooting at birds. The shots came from the front of the estate, though, not the back, and that made me curious because it wasn't normal. I went to the window to see what the guards were up to and saw a car out the front of the house. Next to it was three men. I saw two bodies on the ground as well, a couple of the guards. A short distance away was a van. It was still when I first saw it, but then it moved off, heading around the side of the estate. As it did there were more gunshots, lots of them."

Sofia continued. "I was scared. We all know someone might want to hurt Mr Abrantes, that's why he had the guards, but we never actually expected anything to happen. I made for the door — I didn't know where I was going, I just knew I had to get out of there — but when I heard someone coming up the stairs I panicked and hid in the wardrobe. It was Mr Abrantes. I heard him come into the bedroom. He was asking someone how the attackers got through the gates. He was angry and scared. When I realised it was my uncle with Mr Abrantes, I was going to leave the wardrobe, but the gunshots were getting closer, so I stayed where I was and covered myself with clothes..."

"Are you alright, Miss Torres?" Pizarro asked when Sofia fell silent. "Miss Torres?"

It was a few moments before Sofia registered that her name was being called.

"Are you alright?" Pizarro asked when he saw that Sofia was aware of her surroundings again.

"Sorry, I just realised, if I'd left the wardrobe when I heard my uncle, I'd have been killed as well."

"You did the right thing by hiding. Given the situation, it was the best, and probably the only, thing you could have done. By hiding, you kept yourself alive, and it might turn out that you're able to give us information that enables us to catch the people responsible for this tragedy."

"Did anyone else survive?" Sofia thought sadly about the death of her uncle — she couldn't imagine how he could have survived the carnage in the bedroom, but she hoped he had — and the deaths of the others who had worked at the estate. She hadn't liked everyone she worked with, but she didn't think any of them deserved to have been killed.

Pizarro shook his head. "No. An older man was found in an outbuilding. He was alive, but unconscious after a heart attack. Unfortunately, he suffered a second heart attack during the night and died. You're the only person in a position to help us with the investigation."

He gave Sofia a few moments to absorb his news and then said, "Do you feel up to continuing? Can you tell us what happened after Mr Abrantes and your uncle entered the bedroom?"

"Mr Abrantes and my uncle, he was head of security at the estate and got me the job there, talked about what they could do, and what could have happened. They were arguing. Mr Abrantes said one of my uncle's men must have helped them..."

"Helped who?" Pizarro asked, forgetting that he had said he would not ask any questions until Sofia was finished.

"I don't know, they didn't say."

"Okay, go on."

"The gunfire got closer, and then an explosion came from outside the room, and I hit my head on something in the wardrobe. Right after the explosion I heard some people run into the room, followed by a lot of shooting. I don't know who was shooting who, but I guess it was my uncle, Mr Abrantes, and whoever else was in the room being shot, because it wasn't long after that that He came into the room."

"He? Who is He?"

"I don't know, I didn't see him. At least not when he was in the room. I might have seen him by the car, but I don't know. I did hear him, though. He spoke English when he was talking to Mr Abrantes, I understood that, but he spoke French to whoever was with him, and I didn't understand that. He told Mr Abrantes that he had already warned him about something. I think he said something about invading his territory. I didn't understand that. And then Mr Abrantes said something I couldn't hear, but I did hear him call the man a monster after he said that everyone was dead. The man said something about business and stories, that Mr Abrantes should have listened to the stories. If he had, his family would still be alive."

As she spoke, Sofia recalled more of the conversation she had overheard.

"The man told Mr Abrantes that he should have killed him in France, but he had believed him about not wanting trouble. He said Mr Abrantes had lied to him, and that meant he had to make an example of him. After that he said something to his men. It was in French, so I don't know what he said. Then he told Mr Abrantes that this is what happens to people who lie to him. At least that's what I think he said. I don't know what happened after that, but it sounded like Mr Abrantes tried to scream."

Sofia fell silent then as she reached for the glass of water on the table at the side of the bed with a shaking hand. Once she had moistened her throat, she spoke again, "He said something in French and a few moments later I smelled smoke and the wardrobe started to get hot."

As she thought about the start of the fire an image of the body tied to the bed, which she had seen dimly through the smoke that filled the room, flashed into her mind and she had to force herself not to be sick.

"Are you alright?" Pizarro asked when he saw Sofia go pale and reached for the glass of water again. "Would you like my partner to get a nurse?"

He had spoken to the doctor about Sofia Torres' condition before coming to see her, so he knew her lungs had been injured by the smoke she had inhaled. She had oxygen on hand to help her breathe and he wondered if that was what she needed, or if she needed something more.

He became more concerned when Sofia began coughing and choking and had to hurriedly set the glass down. When she went red in the face, he hurriedly signalled to Diaz to fetch a nurse, who arrived almost immediately.

"I'm alright," Sofia gasped, pushing the nurse's hand away as she tried to place the oxygen mask over her face. "I tried to swallow some water too quickly and it went down wrong," she said as her chest heaved.

"Would you like to take a break?" Pizarro hoped the answer was no, he wanted to get the interview finished and had only asked out of politeness. There was a lot of pressure on him, thanks to the news reports on the massacre, and he knew that if he didn't show some progress soon there was a good chance that he would be replaced by someone more senior and more experienced. That would spell the end of his hopes for promotion, at least for the time being.

"No. I'd rather get this over with now," Sofia said. "The more I have to think about it, the worse it's going to be. Where did I get up to?" The coughing fit had made her forget.

"You could smell the smoke and the wardrobe started to get hot," Diaz supplied from his position in the corner of the room.

"Thank you." It was a few moments before Sofia took up her story again as she gave herself time to recall what had happened. "I think I heard the Frenchman leave, him and the men with him, after the fire started. I wasn't sure, though, and I didn't want to leave where I was safe. I stayed in the wardrobe until the heat and the smoke got too much. I don't know how long I was in there for, I just know the whole room was on fire when I crawled out."

With halting words, and frequent pauses to moisten her throat, she related everything that had happened from the moment she left the safety of the wardrobe. Everything she could remember at least. She didn't stop until she reached the point where she had collapsed at the side of the road as she tried to get away from the approaching car.

"I guess you already know what happened after that."

"Yes," Pizarro said with a nod. "Mr Perez, the gentleman in the car, called for an ambulance and the police. When he arrived, Sergeant Cortez spoke to you, though I'm not sure if you recall that. You told him about the fire and the dead people, and while you were taken to the hospital, he went looking for the house that was on fire. Why don't we take a break now," he said, reluctantly forced to do so by the need for a call of nature. "Detective Diaz and I will get ourselves a drink, and when we get back, we can try and fill in the details of what you saw and heard. As long as you feel up to it that is."

• • • •

"ARE YOU FINISHED ALREADY?" Cortez asked when Pizarro left the room. "I thought you'd be more thorough, given what's at stake for you."

"No, we're not finished." Pizarro was surprised to see that Cortez was still there. He had expected him to be long gone. "Enrique and I are getting something to drink while Miss Torres has a short break."

"In that case I'll pop in and sit with her till you get back. I imagine she'll appreciate some conversation that doesn't involve what happened yesterday."

Pizarro could think of no reason for keeping Cortez from talking to Sofia Torres, though he would have liked to, and he could only watch with annoyance as Cortez entered the room. Irritated, he turned away after a moment and followed Diaz down the corridor in search of a vending machine.

6

"Do you really think you should be sitting like that?" Pizarro asked of Cortez as Diaz returned to the position he had previously occupied in the corner of the room and took out the tape recorder once more. "Quite apart from it being inappropriate for you to have your feet up on the bed, Miss Torres has been in a fire and her legs are badly burnt."

"Strangely enough, I am aware of that, Francisco, seeing as how I saw her before she was brought here. My feet aren't touching Sofia's legs, though, so she isn't being affected, and I don't think the bed gives much of a damn where my feet are." Cortez was amused by the annoyance that flashed across Pizarro's face. "Do you mind that I have my feet on the bed, Sofia?"

"What's going on?" Pizarro asked before Sofia could respond to the question. "You're acting very strangely."

"I take it you want to continue your interview," Cortez said, removing his feet from the bed so he could stand. "It's been a pleasure talking to you, Sofia. I'll come back tomorrow if you like."

"Yes please," Sofia said with a small smile. "I know it's rude of me to ask since I don't know you very well, but would you mind bringing me some magazines when you come back, or maybe some books. I don't mind what, I just want something to take my mind off the boredom."

"I'll see what I can come up with. I don't have many books at home, I've never been much of a reader, but I'll bring you something. I know just how boring hospitals can be, though I imagine by the time Francisco's finished with you, you'll have found a whole new level of boredom to deal with." Cortez grinned as he delivered the verbal jab. He took his leave then and departed before Pizarro could think of a response.

"Was Sergeant Cortez bothering you?" Pizarro asked as he settled himself on the chair left vacant by Cortez's departure. "I can make sure he doesn't come back if he was," he said, ignoring the fact that Sofia had seemed perfectly content to be talking to his former partner.

"Why don't you like him?" Sofia asked. The animosity between the two men had been clear even in the brief time she had seen them together. "He seemed perfectly nice to me. Nicer than some people I've known. And no, I don't want you to stop him coming back. My family is gone, and I've got few friends, so it's nice that there's someone who wants to come and see me."

Pizarro couldn't help wondering if Cortez had an ulterior motive for being friendly with Sofia Torres. He knew well enough that Cortez was not inclined towards friendliness on most occasions, and especially not towards people he didn't already know or want something from, which made his behaviour unusual.

He chose not to voice his suspicions. Instead, he said, "I have personal reasons for disliking him. Are you ready to answer some questions for us now?" he asked, resolving to find out what Cortez was up to when he had a chance.

"I suppose I'd better get it all out of the way," Sofia said, unhappily resigned to the necessity of it.

"We'll do our best to finish this off as quickly and as painlessly as possible," Pizarro said. "We'll start at the beginning, if that's alright." He waited until Sofia nodded and then continued, "You stated that upon hearing gunfire you went to the window to see what was going on, and that you saw two vehicles, a van and a car. Can you describe them?"

"The van was just an ordinary van," Sofia said. "The sort you see making deliveries all the time. I don't know what sort it was. I was too surprised by what was going on to pay much attention to it."

"Are you sure you don't know what make the van was? It could be important. Every little thing you remember is important," Pizarro said when Sofia shook her head. "Would it help if we show you some pictures of vans? You might be able to recognise the make and model if you see a picture of it."

"If you think it'll help, I'll look at the pictures, but I don't think it'll make much difference."

"We'll compile a selection of pictures for you. What size van was it, small, medium, or large?"

"It was about the size of the ambulance that brought me here. Does that help?"

"Yes, it gives us a size range to work with. Once we have the pictures, someone will bring them over so you can look through them." Pizarro had no intention of handling such a menial job himself. He would get someone junior to take care of it. "What colour was the van?"

"It was a dirty white."

"Do you mean it was white and hadn't been cleaned in a while, or that it was an off-white?" Diaz asked.

"White, but it hadn't been cleaned in a while. Not a long while, just long enough to tell that it needed cleaning."

"I don't suppose, by some miracle, you saw the number plate of the van?" Pizarro was disappointed, but not surprised, when Sofia shook her head. "What about the car? What can you remember about it?"

"It was blue, a BMW, I think. It didn't look brand new, but neither did it look old. That's all I can tell you about it, I'm afraid. And I didn't see the number plate."

"Well, it's not much, Pizarro admitted, "but it is something. How about the men you said you saw by the car? Can you describe them?"

"One of them was mostly hidden behind the car, so I couldn't see much of him. The other two though, one of them was middle-aged from what I could see, maybe in his fifties, and I think he was the one in charge. The young guy, he was in his mid-thirties I'd say, was carrying a gun, a big one."

"What else can you tell us about them?"

"The young guy was, I don't know how tall. I was looking down so it's hard to be sure, but the car came up to about his elbow. On the old guy, the car was between his elbow and his shoulder. Can you work out how tall they were from that?"

"It's possible. There should be someone at the station who can work it out. Anything else?"

"From what I could see of him, the older guy was pretty ordinary. Like I said, I'm not sure about his height, but he wasn't tall, and he seemed about medium build. His hair was black, but I think he was starting to go grey. I've no idea what colour his eyes were, he was too far away for me to see." Sofia stopped speaking then as she tried to recall more of what she had seen. "He was wearing a blue suit. The other guy, the one with the gun, he had blond hair, very blond. I remember it because it was the sort of blond you see in American films, like the women in California have."

"I think I get the picture. What clothes was he wearing, can you remember?"

"A grey suit. I don't think he was used to it, though, he didn't seem very comfortable."

"What do you mean? As you said, you were a distance away, how could you tell he wasn't comfortable with the clothes he was wearing?"

"I saw him fidget with the collar of his shirt and the jacket he was wearing, like they didn't fit him properly."

"That is a remarkably acute observation given the events of yesterday. Unfortunately, it doesn't help us much. Did you notice anything else?"

"No, that was about it. I wasn't at the window for long before I went to go downstairs."

"And when you heard someone coming up the stairs, you hid, right."

"Yes." Sofia nodded. "I hid in the wardrobe."

"Okay, let's go through everything you can remember about what was said when the guy you heard entered the room."

"Like I told you, he spoke English when he was talking to Mr Abrantes, and in French, which I didn't understand, the rest of the time. I'm sure he was the older guy from by the car, though; I don't know what it was, but his voice just sounded like that of a man in his fifties, rather than someone younger," Sofia said in response to the questioning look from Pizarro. "The main thing I heard him say was that Mr Abrantes should have listened to him, and that he had told him what would happen if he invaded his territory. It was so strange. He sounded like he was talking to a friend, not someone he was going to kill."

"Some people are like that. They can kill without the slightest show of emotion. Psychopaths," Pizarro said. "What was said next?"

"Mr Abrantes wanted to know what had been done to the rest of his family, and he was told they were dead. The guy didn't seem to care in the slightest. I couldn't hear what Mr Abrantes said clearly after that, but it sounded like he was calling the guy names, and I definitely heard him say something about stories. The guy said something about stories as well. I think he said Mr Abrantes' family would still be alive if he had listened to the stories. He also said he should have killed Mr Abrantes in France. He believed him about not wanting a war, but he lied to him, and that meant he had to make an example of him."

Sofia paused then to moisten her throat before continuing, "The only other thing I understood was the man saying that this was what happens to people who lied to him. What he meant by that I have no idea. I might have been able to see through the keyhole in the wardrobe door, but I was too afraid to move in case I made a noise."

"You did the right thing," Pizarro reassured her. "I don't think anyone can blame you for not wanting to draw attention to yourself. Can you tell me anything about the voice you heard, the one you think belongs to the older man you saw?"

"No. It was just an ordinary voice."

"Think hard, Miss Torres. Was it loud, quiet, rough, smooth? Did he have an unusual accent, something distinctive you would be able to recognise if you heard it again?"

"It was just an ordinary voice," Sofia said, distressed that she was unable to help more. "If I heard it again, I might recognise it, but I couldn't say for sure."

"Okay. Can you remember anything else about what happened yesterday?"

Sofia spent several minutes thinking hard and then shook her head. "No, that's everything I can remember, and it's more than I wish I did."

"I understand, but are you sure that's everything? How about when you were leaving? Do you remember seeing or hearing anything on your way out of the house?"

"All I saw was the bodies in the kitchen. The people I used to know. People I spent time with. People I cared about. My uncle. They all died yesterday." Sofia was beginning to get frustrated by the seemingly endless series of questions and it showed in her voice. "Don't you care about the people who died? Don't you care about anything other than if I heard or saw something that will help you?"

"Of course I care. I care a great deal about the people who died," Pizarro said with as much sincerity as he could muster. He did care that numerous people had died, it was just that he cared more for the fact that their murders made for a good career opportunity for him. "But given the circumstances, there is only one thing I can do to help them, and that is to find the people responsible and make sure they go to jail. And I can only do that with your help."

"Well, I've given you everything I can. I don't know anything else."

Pizarro sighed. "In that case we'll be off. Thank you for your help, and for your patience. I'll make sure you're kept informed of how the investigation is going. If you think of anything that might help us, no matter how small or insignificant you think it might be, don't hesitate to contact either me or my partner. Even the smallest thing could help us crack the case." Taking a business card from his pocket he set it on the table at the side of the bed.

7

Pizarro knocked loudly when he reached the door of his superior's office and waited. It was nearly six in the evening, and he hoped the meeting he had been summoned to wouldn't go on too long. He was accustomed to being finished for the day and on his way home by then.

"Come in."

"Good evening, sir," Pizarro said as he entered the office, careful to show none of the annoyance he was feeling at being kept late.

"Have a seat," DCI Meteiros told his subordinate. "How did the interview with Miss Torres go?" he asked once Pizarro was settled.

"It might prove useful," Pizarro said carefully. "I think we need to find out if Sergeant Cortez's source has more information on the territories that Tomas Abrantes was attempting to expand into." He didn't like the thought of relying on his former partner's dubious connections, but if it was the only way to make progress with his investigation then he was prepared to accept the necessity, reluctantly. "Miss Torres overheard the person in charge of the men responsible for the massacre and it seems he both spoke in French and declared that he should have killed Mr Abrantes in France. Based on that I think we need to focus our attention on Mr Abrantes' recent activities in France. Unfortunately, I don't know the best way to go about that."

"If you're sure the investigation is going to lead to France then the best way for us to proceed is to take everything we've got to Interpol. They should be able to help us get whatever help we're likely to need from the French police," Meteiros said. "First though, why don't you tell me what you learned from Miss Torres."

· · · · ·

"DO YOU THINK SHE'LL be able to identify the two men she saw if we come up with possible suspects?" Meteiros asked after Pizarro had finished recounting what he had been told at the hospital.

"I believe the chances are reasonable, but the descriptions she gave are vague and could match a lot of people. An identification from her might not be sufficient on its own to secure a conviction, we'll need something more."

"Well then, you'll have to do everything you can to get additional evidence. Have you heard anything from the forensics team yet?"

"Diaz told me there are preliminary reports on my desk, but I haven't had a chance to read them yet. I plan on taking them home with me. Hopefully, the full reports will be available in the next couple of days. Not that I imagine there will be any surprises in them."

"Try to think positive, Francisco. What's the situation with the guard from the Abrantes' estate Cortez found murdered in his apartment? Have you got anything there?"

"Not yet. I'm still waiting for forensics there as well. Unfortunately, they've told me that it looks to have been a fairly clean kill, not much sign of the killer leaving anything for them to find. The neighbours didn't see or hear anything either. We'll keep on it. The killer's bound to have left something for forensics to find. Forensics did find a knife in Tevez's pocket that they say matches the type used to kill the guard in the gatehouse at the Abrantes' estate; it looks likely that Tevez was paid off to let the attackers into the estate and was then killed so he couldn't reveal anything."

"Not very helpful to us, but it might be enough to satisfy the press for a while," Meteiros said. "I want copies of everything you currently have on my desk first thing. I'll be keeping an eye on the investigation, so make sure you do everything you possibly can. If I'm not satisfied with your progress, I'll replace you with someone more senior." He knew how eager Pizarro was for promotion and figured the threat of being replaced would encourage him to do his absolute best. "What's your next course of action?"

"Diaz is typing up the interview with Miss Torres, and Franco is putting together images of vans that match the general description of the vehicle she saw. With luck she'll be able to identify the exact make and model, so we can put together a search. I've also got a search going for anyone in our system who matches the descriptions Miss Torres was able to give us. The list is likely to be long, given how basic the descriptions are, but it's a starting place."

"If Cortez's source is correct and the attackers are not from Spain, and Miss Torres is right about the person behind the attack speaking French, then searching our databases will be a waste of time."

"I realise that, sir. I don't want to rule out the possibility that Cortez's source is wrong, though, or that he was deliberately misled. It might still be Roberto Abrantes who arranged for his brother's murder. We know there's no love lost between them. He could have had the man who did the job speaking English and French to throw off any potential witnesses."

"Do you really think that's likely?" Meteiros asked sceptically.

"No, not really. Whoever organised this massacre intended that everyone at the estate should die, so there shouldn't have been anyone around to reveal what was said, let alone what language it was said in. French is almost certainly their first language, and English was used as a common language to be sure Abrantes understood them. Every avenue must be explored, though."

"True. Well, it sounds like you have everything in hand, for the time being at least. I'll look forward to receiving your report in the morning. Good evening," Meteiros dismissed Pizarro abruptly.

"Good evening, sir." Relieved to have the meeting over, and to still be in charge of the investigation, Pizarro got to his feet and left the office.

8

As had happened the previous evening, there was a knock on his apartment door just as Cortez settled down with his dinner and a glass of wine. Cursing, he got to his feet to answer the door.

"Is this going to be a regular thing, Diego?" he asked when he saw who was at the door. "If it is, I'll get you a key. That way I won't have to keep disturbing my dinner to answer the door."

"That's okay, Miguel, I don't think that will be necessary," Vega said as he stepped into the apartment. "I don't intend visiting you any more frequently than necessary."

"I'm glad to hear that. If anyone sees you coming here regularly it might result in some awkward questions, and I'd rather not have to try and explain what you're doing visiting me. So, what brings you here this time?"

"Mr Abrantes has sent me with a thank you for the information you passed on today," Vega handed over an envelope. It was not as thick as the one he had given Cortez the previous evening, but it was the same in all other respects. "And some instructions."

"What does he want me to do?" Cortez dropped the envelope onto the table at the side of him without checking the contents. Whatever Roberto Abrantes had decided his information was worth, it was good enough for him, especially since arguing would not get him any more money.

"He would like you to continue to report any developments in the investigation. Anything you learn will help him to find and deal with whoever ordered his brother's murder."

"That can't be all of his instructions. He already knows I'll report anything Francisco discovers. What else does he want me to do?"

"It has occurred to Mr Abrantes that once it is known there is a witness, the person responsible for his brother's death will want to eliminate her. Common sense dictates that he can't leave a potential witness alive," Vega said. "He would like you to ensure that nothing happens to her. He doesn't expect the situation to result in a need for her to testify at a trial, but he would like her to be available should the need arise."

"An officer is on duty outside her hospital room at all times. And I'm sure Francisco will arrange for more protection if he thinks it's needed."

"I'm not sure Mr Abrantes will be satisfied by that. His instructions are clear, he wants you to do everything you can to ensure that Miss Torres stays alive. It's entirely possible that whoever is responsible for the attack on Tomas' estate will employ a similar level of violence to eliminate her. A single officer is unlikely to be of much use against an attack like yesterday's. You are to persuade Pizarro and Meteiros that Miss Torres should be given adequate protection. Their reasons for keeping her alive are just as compelling as Mr Abrantes', so you shouldn't have too much difficulty. Mr Abrantes would also like you to volunteer to take charge of the security operation."

"I'll do my best, but I can't guarantee anything. I might be able to persuade them to increase the security around Sofia, but it's doubtful they'll want me in charge of it. Mr Abrantes will have to remember that I'm no longer held in high regard by my fellow officers."

"At the least, I imagine you will be able to persuade them to let you be a part of the security team. It's unlikely they will refuse you that, though you're probably right that they wouldn't want to put you in charge," Vega conceded. "Just make sure everything possible is done to keep Miss Torres alive. Mr Abrantes will be satisfied with that. He is understanding enough to accept when someone has done their absolute best, no matter what the result."

"Is he also understanding enough to realise that soldiers who go into combat zones are paid extra for hazardous duty?" Cortez asked.

"I'm sure you will be compensated adequately should an attack take place. If you get injured, you might even be able to retire on what you get."

"I'm not sure being able to retire will make up for being injured, but I'll bear it in mind. Is there anything else?"

Vega shook his head.

9

Paris

· · · ·

WHEN HE REACHED THE office of the Deputy Director of Interpol (France), Ben Bright announced himself and then took a seat to wait. He had no idea why he had been summoned but he didn't feel concerned. He was sure he would find out what was going on soon enough.

The possibility that seemed most likely was that he was being reassigned. He was often used as a roving trouble-shooter and sent to deal with situations the local Interpol officers couldn't handle, or which required someone with experience or knowledge they didn't have. He had been working in the Paris office for almost a year, something of a record for him, so it was past time for him to be reassigned.

Bright had to wait for almost a quarter of an hour before the intercom on the secretary's desk buzzed with the order for him to be sent through.

"Special Agent Bright," Deputy Director Lejour greeted him. "Have a seat. Would you like something to drink?"

"Thank you, sir, coffee, please." Bright relaxed a little more. If he was being offered a drink it was certain that he had nothing to worry about.

Lejour requested drinks from his secretary and then returned his attention to Bright. "I imagine you're wondering why I sent for you."

"Yes, sir."

"There's a situation in Spain."

"What sort of situation?" Bright suspected he already knew but thought it best to ask, he didn't want to assume and make an idiot of himself.

"Have you heard about the massacre that took place in Barcelona two days ago?"

"Of course, sir, not a pleasant incident." Like most Interpol agents, Bright had seen plenty of bad things, so it was hard for him to be shocked. "Have the local police got any leads?"

"It's being kept quiet, but they have a witness. Not a very good one by all accounts, but better than not having one. They have also received information, backed up by their witness, that suggests the person who ordered the massacre, and possibly led it, comes from here in France. Because of that they have requested our help. This is the information that's available so far." Lejour held out the file he had been reading when Bright came in.

· · · ·

HIS COFFEE HAD GONE cold by the time Bright finished with the file he had been given. There wasn't much in it, and it hadn't taken him long to get through it the first time. His second reading was more thorough, however, to be sure he hadn't missed anything.

"From the looks of this, the Barcelona police don't have much," he remarked. Placing the file on the desk in front of him, he picked up his coffee. He was used to getting so engrossed in his work that his coffee went cold, so it didn't bother him.

"There's a wealth of physical evidence that's still being processed," Lejour said. "There's every chance they'll find something once the results are in."

"Perhaps." Bright couldn't bring himself to agree with Lejour, though he knew well enough that cases were often cracked by one small, seemingly insignificant thing. "But if the attack was ordered by someone here in France, they're likely to have a hard time connecting anything their forensics people find to them. Any connection that is made is likely to come through our databases."

"That brings us to the reason for this meeting," Lejour said. "This investigation is going to require careful cooperation between us and the Barcelona police, and possibly the police here in France as well, if the information in the file is correct."

"I take it you're assigning me to the investigation, sir."

"Correct. I should tell you that there is a suspect in the frame, which is one of the reasons you have been selected for this, because you have knowledge of the suspect."

"There was nothing in the file about a suspect." Bright wondered if he had missed something, but he didn't see how he could have.

"It wasn't included because there's no evidence currently, and Agent Battista didn't want to do anything to tip the suspect off. After being asked for help by the Barcelona police, Battista and her team made a check of recent arrivals at Barcelona International Airport to see if any recognisable names came up. One did — Philippe Noir. He arrived the morning of the attack and flew out again that evening."

"The report certainly fits with what we know of Noir and how he likes to deal with people who upset him," Bright said. "He wouldn't think twice about killing women and children to get at someone who's a problem for him."

"He'd kill his own mother if she was a threat to his organisation," Lejour said. "The fact that he was there isn't conclusive proof, however. He's clever and will almost certainly have arranged it so he had a legitimate reason for being in Barcelona at the time of the attack just in case he comes under suspicion. I've discussed the situation with my Spanish counterpart and we both agree that the investigation needs someone who is familiar with Noir and his organisation. You are. We want you out there by this time tomorrow. Okay?"

"Yes, sir." Bright's thoughts immediately turned to preparation for a stay in Spain. He kept a bag packed with his passport, a change of clothes, a washbag, and other essentials in case he was given an urgent assignment and had to leave in a hurry. Now, though, he considered what else he might need for what could be an extended stay in Spain.

10

Barcelona

. . . .

"YOU CAN HAVE NOIR ARRESTED now," Pizarro announced the moment he walked into the office Bright was using. "Sofia Torres has positively identified him from the pictures you supplied."

He was pleased, and he made no attempt to hide it. He understood the necessity of having Interpol involved in his investigation, given the cross-border nature of it, but he didn't like it. It made him happy that it was his witness, and not the work of the Interpol team, that had resulted in the positive identification of Philippe Noir.

"I can't have him arrested based on one identification." Bright concealed the irritation he felt at the detective's assumption that it was okay for him to simply walk into the office, without even knocking. "I can request that the French police detain him for questioning in connection with the murder of Mr Abrantes, his family, and his staff. If we're lucky, they'll agree to the request, but you'll need a lot more evidence than a single identification if you expect to have Noir extradited, let alone secure a conviction against him."

"What do you mean 'if we're lucky'?" Pizarro asked sharply. "Do you think the French police will ignore the request?"

"No, I doubt they'll do that. I'm sure they'll give it their fullest consideration. I just don't think they'll feel that a single identification is sufficient to justify bringing Noir in for questioning, and it certainly won't be enough to get him extradited. Noir is rich and powerful, and he employs an expensive and capable lawyer,"

Bright said. "The odds are that given the circumstances, they won't want to risk doing anything that might upset Noir."

"Why not?" Pizarro was disappointed to hear that the identification he had managed to get didn't seem to be worth anything in the eyes of Interpol. "Why should they care about upsetting someone who is responsible for massacring dozens of people?"

"Because, as I said, Philippe Noir is rich, with powerful connections in all walks of life. The French police have been investigating him for two decades, and Interpol have been investigating him for over a decade, since he became the number one supplier of illegal narcotics in France. He has sued the police multiple times for harassment and won. The few times they have managed to get enough evidence or witnesses to charge him with something, his lawyer finds some way of getting it thrown out. Either that or the evidence and the witnesses disappear."

"You make it sound like it's impossible for us to get a conviction against him."

"That wasn't my intention. I'm not saying it will be impossible, just very difficult. If you get the chance to question Noir, you can't expect to trick him into confessing or letting something slip that will help your case. He and his lawyer know every trick in the book."

Bright could see that Pizarro was disappointed, but he thought it best to burst his bubble now, rather than leave him in the dark to be mauled by Noir's lawyer.

"You're going to need plenty of evidence if you want to get a conviction, and you're going to have to make sure that whatever evidence you do get is in no danger of being tampered with or made to disappear. You especially need to make sure that no harm comes to Sofia Torres, since without her you have nothing to connect Noir to the massacre, unless your forensics people can come up with something."

"We have an officer outside her room and another at the nurse's station," Pizarro said. "They should be able to cope with any threat. We also have a response team on alert for a possible attack at the hospital. I've been assured that they can respond within minutes."

"That all sounds good, but the people who attacked Tomas Abrantes' estate massacred everyone there, and they were up against guards with semi-automatic weapons. I doubt a couple of officers with handguns will stop them if they find out about Sofia Torres and decide to remove her."

The new voice made Pizarro spin towards the door behind him, where a woman with a look of sharp intelligence on her face stood.

"If it was Noir who was responsible for the massacre and he finds out about your witness, which he almost certainly will, if he hasn't already, then you won't be able to stop him killing her. Not if your best effort to protect her involves two officers and a response team that can't possibly get to the hospital before at least two dozen people are dead."

"Detective Sergeant Pizarro, this is Special Agent Marie Hapsburg, she's my number two on this operation," Bright introduced the new arrival. "Agent Hapsburg has extensive experience in dealing with organised crime, and she has been involved with the investigation into Philippe Noir since the beginning. Since she knows just about everything there is to know about Noir and the current Interpol and French investigations into him, I thought she might be able to help, so I've borrowed her for a while."

"I certainly hope I can help," Marie Hapsburg said as she stepped further into the office. "In fact, that's why I'm here now. About a month ago, Philippe Noir met with someone at a country club."

"Is that relevant to this?" Pizarro asked. He was sure that a man like Philippe Noir met with a lot of people in a lot of places.

"I believe so, yes. The man Noir met with was Tomas Abrantes. Before you say anything," Marie held up a hand to forestall Pizarro, "the reason you haven't been told about this before now is because it's only just been discovered. I have no idea how, but at the time the meeting was photographed the agents responsible failed to identify the second man as Tomas Abrantes."

"How is that possible?"

"I have no idea. I can only give you the information I have. I got it sent over by the team I've been working with in France." Marie placed the file she had brought with her on the desk and slid it over to Bright. "On the twentieth of last month, Noir and his bodyguard were followed from his home to the Pleasant Days Country Club outside of Paris. When he got there, he was shown to a table outside the restaurant. His bodyguard sat with him, while the area was patrolled by men with submachine guns. We figured he was up to something because it isn't often he brings out that level of firepower.

"It was a while before his guest arrived. I use the term 'guest' loosely since the gentleman was escorted to the table by four men with submachine guns. We know the man who led the group is called Marc Delcroix, and he handles a lot of special work for Noir. He's suspected of several murders: rivals of Noir who didn't have the sense to step aside, officers and agents who attempted to infiltrate Noir's organisation, and witnesses who were prepared to testify against Noir, but he's good at not getting caught. Anyway, to get back to the subject at hand," Marie said, seeing that Pizarro wasn't interested in what she was saying. "Noir's guest was there for some time, though what was discussed we have no idea, and was then escorted out by the same men who had brought him. The security at the meeting meant we weren't able to get close enough to record any of what was said but the man who we now know was Abrantes did not look happy when he left, in fact, he looked pretty scared. Why Tomas

Abrantes wasn't identified previously from the surveillance footage of the meeting, I don't know. Abrantes is in our database, so we should have been able to come up with his name."

"That's strange," Bright said. "We don't normally have a problem like that. If someone's in a database somewhere we're able to find them. How did you finally make the identification?"

"When I saw the pictures of Tomas Abrantes yesterday, I thought he looked familiar. After reading Sofia Torres' statement and her mention of a meeting in France between Abrantes and his attacker, whom we believe to be Noir, I recalled the meeting at the country club, so I sent pictures of Abrantes to Paris to be checked. The reply came back a short while ago. It was definitely Tomas Abrantes that Noir met with."

"That should help to convince the French authorities to let me question Noir," Pizarro said, a pleased look on his face.

"That was my thinking," Marie agreed. "I've requested copies of some of the audio recordings we have of Noir. If Miss Torres can identify Noir's voice from a recording, then it will improve your chances of getting help from the French authorities still further. It will also improve your chances of securing a conviction against him."

"That's good news." Pizarro's smile grew. "When do you expect to receive the recordings?"

"That's where we encounter a problem," Marie admitted. "Noir is very careful about not being overheard, let alone recorded. He's almost paranoid about it. We haven't been able to get many recordings of him, and I'm not sure we have any of him speaking English. The team is checking what recordings we have for instances."

"Does that matter?"

"It might," Bright said. "A person's voice can sound different when they speak a different language. Miss Torres might be able to recognise Noir's voice even if he is speaking French, rather than

English, but I wouldn't like to guarantee it, and I certainly wouldn't want to bet everything on that possibility. Still, the fact that Noir met Abrantes recently, and it fits with what Miss Torres overheard, will help a great deal. I'll coordinate with your superiors regarding a request to the French authorities to have Noir brought in for questioning. They'll most likely take time to consider it, but that's alright since it will give us time to strengthen our case."

"I didn't think you were going to visit me today," Sofia said when Cortez entered her hospital room.

"I had work to do," Cortez said as he dropped casually onto the chair by the bed.

"I thought you'd been put in charge of protecting me. Doesn't that mean you should be here all the time, making sure I'm alright and someone isn't trying to kill me?"

"That's what the officer outside your room is for, and the officer down the corridor at the nurse's station. I'm in charge of them. I don't actually have to be here." It still amazed Cortez that he had been put in charge of Sofia's protection, he had never expected that to happen.

"So, why are you here?"

"To check on you, make sure you're safe, and check on the officers looking after you. How's your day been?"

"Boring. I watched some TV and read the magazines you brought me. I must have been through them all at least half a dozen times now."

"Didn't anything interesting happen?"

Sofia shook her head. "Not unless you consider a couple of Interpol agents turning up with some pictures for me to look at interesting. Did they tell you I made an identification? Apparently, the guy I saw at Mr Abrantes' estate is called Philippe Noir and he's from France. They said he's a very nasty person and they've been after him for years."

"I don't imagine they felt it necessary to give me that information," Cortez said as he reached into the bag he had brought and took out a plastic tub and some cutlery. He set them on the table in front of Sofia and reached back into the bag for a pair of plastic plates, onto which he set the two slices of lemon cake he removed from the tub. "Perhaps they'll decide to tell me if they discover a definite threat against you."

"I don't understand why your wife left you when you can make cakes like this," Sofia said after finishing her first mouthful. The circumstances that had resulted in her hospitalisation were terrible, but she couldn't help thinking that the cakes and desserts Cortez brought her helped to make up for it in some small way. "Doesn't she appreciate how difficult it is to find a guy who can bake like this? Everything you've brought me has been delicious."

"Unfortunately, it takes more than good desserts to make a marriage successful. You need to be a good husband, and I wasn't that."

"Have you ever thought about opening a bakery? You like baking, and with desserts like this you'd probably do pretty well. You might even make more than you do as a cop."

"It's a nice idea but I bake to relax. If I was doing it as a job, I'm not sure I'd still enjoy it. Besides, I'd make a lousy businessman, and I couldn't deal with a partner. Anyway, I don't have that many years left before I can retire, and I'm looking forward to that. What about you? What do you plan on doing when this is all over?"

"I don't even want to think about that until it is over. The doctor said I'm going to start therapy soon, physical and psychological." Sofia didn't look happy about that, but whether she was unhappy about the prospect of the physical therapy or the psychological was unclear. "What happens now I've made an identification?" she asked to change the subject.

"To be honest, I'm not really sure. I imagine Francisco and Interpol will do what they can to make a case against this Philippe Noir and extradite him here so he can be prosecuted. If they do their job right, he and the rest of his organisation will get long sentences. After that, you'll be able to go back to your life, or maybe on to something new, if that's what you want."

"You make it sound so simple."

"Probably because I'm a simple person," Cortez said with a laugh. "I don't have experience with this kind of investigation, so it's impossible for me to be certain what's going to happen. There isn't much point in worrying about it, though. You've done your part in identifying the man you saw. The rest is up to Francisco and Interpol."

"And you get to babysit me until it's all over."

"I guess that's one way of looking at it," Cortez said as he slid his plate onto the table and got to his feet. "I'll be back in a moment."

When Cortez returned with drinks for the two of them, he found Sofia looking worried. "What's the matter?"

"Do you think many people know that I've identified this Philippe Noir?" Sofia asked in a voice that was tinged with fear.

Cortez shrugged. "A few at least, why?"

"I was thinking. The more people that know I've identified him, the more likely it is that he'll find out, and when he does, he'll send someone to kill me, won't he?"

"I wouldn't worry about it. You have two armed officers between here and the lift, and more nearby; there's plenty of officers around to protect you, and that doesn't include hospital security. I doubt this Noir will try and have you killed here, though. There are CCTV cameras all over the place, as well as plenty of people. It'd be crazy for anyone to try and get you while there are so many potential witnesses around."

"But what about when I leave here? There won't be plenty of people around then, and the doctor said I can go home next week some time. There's no reason for me to stay now my lungs are recovering. I just have to stay off my feet while my legs heal, and come back for therapy."

Cortez was both surprised and concerned to hear that Sofia would be going home so soon. While he was reasonably sure that no attack would take place while she was in hospital, he wasn't so confident that she would be safe after she left. He had been a police officer for long enough to know that for the right price any piece of information could be found, which meant that sooner or later Noir would learn of Sofia Torres' existence, and where she was, at which point her life would be at risk.

As he thought about it, Cortez realised that an uncomfortably large number of people knew there was a witness to the massacre at the Abrantes Estate. He could think of at least a dozen people who knew of Sofia, and who would soon know that she had identified Philippe Noir, including Diego Vega and Roberto Abrantes. Of those people, the only ones he trusted not to sell the information to Noir were Vega and Roberto Abrantes, which was a thought he found more than a little troubling.

"I don't know what arrangements have been made for when you leave here. I don't think anyone was expecting you to be ready to leave quite this soon." Cortez tried not to let his concern show. "I'll speak to Francisco first thing and make sure everything's been organised and you'll be properly protected."

"As long as you're protecting me, I'm sure I'll be safe."

Cortez wished he had her confidence.

PARIS

. . . .

PHILIPPE NOIR LOOKED up in surprise when the door to his office burst open unexpectedly. He relaxed when he saw that it was his cousin, Jean-Paul Renault, whom he employed to handle his security, who had entered so abruptly, but he remained annoyed at the interruption. All that kept him from venting his feelings was the look on his cousin's face, which told him something was up.

"What is it?" he asked in as even a voice as he could manage.

"The police in Barcelona have a witness."

"Are you sure?"

Jean-Paul nodded. "I got it from my usual source, and he's never wrong when it comes to this kind of information."

Noir had never met his cousin's source, but he knew who he was and, more importantly, what he did for a living. Because of that he trusted the information that was provided.

"What was he able to tell you about the witness?" Sitting back, Noir waited to hear what his cousin's source had been able to find out, so he could decide what to do. The news that there was a witness to the murder of Tomas Abrantes and his family was unwelcome, but he didn't panic. It wasn't the first time there had been a witness to one of his crimes, and none of those who had been found by the police in the past had caused him any problems.

"Not much," Jean-Paul admitted. "All he knows right now is that there's a witness, and they can identify you."

"How's that possible? Everyone at the estate was killed."

"I don't know, and until we know more about the witness, we won't know. I've instructed my source to find out everything he can, so we can determine how much of a threat they are, and what we should do about them. He's to report back as quickly as possible."

"Good. Did he have anything else for you?"

"Yes. Interpol and the Barcelona Police are putting together a request for the police here to take you into custody so you can be questioned."

Noir wasn't impressed. "If all they have is one witness and no evidence to back them up, they don't have much of a case."

"I assume you want the witness killed."

"Of course. If they can identify me, they need to die."

"I'll begin working on a plan just as soon as I have enough information to come up with something." Jean-Paul had anticipated what his cousin would want done about the witness, but he knew his cousin didn't like people to take the initiative, which was why he had checked. "I think this should be done discreetly, though, no blazing guns."

Noir studied his cousin for several long moments before asking, "Why? I've always had great success with that strategy." He was a firm believer in the terror inspired by a bloodbath. He had discovered early in his career that people were terrified by displays of violence. A few examples had been enough to persuade most people not to interfere with or obstruct his plans, which had made things a lot easier for him as he built his empire.

"No, you've been lucky," Jean-Paul said, hoping Noir was in a good mood. Cousin or not, if he was in a bad mood, Noir was likely to lash out in response to being disagreed with. "You've left people alive after several of your bloodbaths. We kill them when we find them, and they're almost always too scared to talk to the police, but that doesn't change the fact that your method is as likely to make a situation worse as it is to solve it. It's time you took a more sensible approach to business. You're sensible when it comes to banking, now you need to be sensible when it comes to everything else. You've proved to the world that you'll go after anyone who's a threat to you, and you don't care who gets in your way, now it's time for you to be sensible and discreet. Unless you want everything to blow up in your face.

"You know Marc's capable of dealing with problems without letting an entire neighbourhood know what he's doing, and without leaving witnesses, so why not have him do so."

"And you're saying that's better than killing everyone who gets in my way?" Noir asked in a dangerous voice.

"Yes. It served a purpose when you were starting out and needed to build a reputation, but you have a lot more to lose now." Jean-Paul subconsciously held his breath as he waited for an explosion that didn't come.

Instead of erupting, Noir pushed his chair back and got to his feet so he could step out onto the balcony behind his desk. He remained there for more than a minute, gazing out over his estate.

"So, your advice is to send Marc back to Barcelona to discreetly kill this witness," he said when he returned to his desk.

Jean-Paul nodded, relieved that his advice was being taken calmly.

"Fine," Noir said after another period of thought. "But this is on your head. Where's Marc now?"

"I'm not sure, but I can track him down and have him here in a few hours."

Noir shook his head. "Don't bring him here, that's a waste of time, send him straight to Barcelona. He's to find out anything he can about the witness, to go with whatever you can get from your source, and then take care of them. I want the witness dead before he or she can cause me any problems."

13

B ARCELONA

• • • •

BEFORE HE LOCKED HIS car, Marc checked he had everything: a pair of syringes in the inside pocket of the white doctor's coat he wore, a pistol tucked into the waistband at the back of his trousers in case something went wrong and he couldn't use the syringes and, as a last resort, a knife he could get to in just a few seconds. Satisfied, he made for the hospital's emergency room entrance.

It didn't take him long to reach the doors, which slid open at his approach, and he crossed the emergency department without anyone paying attention to him. It was just as his observations of the past three days had suggested it would be. The staff were too busy with their work to notice someone who appeared to be another member of staff, and the people waiting to be seen were only interested in whatever had brought them there and how long it would be until it was their turn to be treated.

When he reached the lifts, Marc stepped into the first to arrive and rode it up to the third floor. Thanks to the information Jean-Paul had been able to pass on from his source, and what he had gathered from his own reconnaissance, he was able to locate the room where the witness he was there to kill could be found without difficulty. The only problem he encountered was the absence of the officer who was supposed to be on duty at the nurse's station.

When he realised there was no officer where he had been told there should be one, he slowed his pace to give himself time to think. He was tempted to abandon, or at least postpone, the job he had been given but he quickly discarded that idea since it would invoke

Noir's wrath. Having been the instrument of that wrath when other people had upset Noir, he had no desire to have it turned on him.

His decision made, he continued down the corridor towards Sofia Torres' room and the officer seated outside it, making every effort to appear to be just another doctor on his way from one part of the hospital to another. It quickly became clear that he had succeeded in appearing normal for after a cursory glance the officer looked away, dismissing him as a threat.

The moment the officer's attention left him, Marc slipped a hand into his pocket to take out one of his syringes, which he concealed in the palm of his hand, his thumb on the plunger. He had practiced in his hotel room until he was able to bring out the syringe and use it in one smooth motion, though he realised the real thing wouldn't be the same as practicing on a pillow propped up on a chair.

He was half a step beyond Sofia Torres' guard when he made his move. Pivoting on one foot, he brought out the syringe and jabbed it into the side of the officer's neck. At the same time, he pushed down on the plunger.

He wasn't quick enough to prevent the officer reacting to the attack, but he was able to get his free hand to the officer's before he could get his pistol out. He held the hand and the pistol in place while he waited for the poison to take effect. Unfortunately, he didn't have a third hand with which to cover the officer's mouth and smother the half shout he was able to utter before the poison did its job.

Marc cursed as he pulled the syringe from the officer's neck and looked around. He was relieved to see no sign of anyone responding to the cry, but he was still annoyed that he hadn't anticipated the possibility of it.

• • • •

CORTEZ WOKE WITH A start, his back sore and his neck stiff. It took him a moment to realise that he had fallen asleep in the chair in Sofia's hospital room, which explained the aches and pains, though not why he had woken so suddenly or so completely. It usually took him a short while to come to his senses.

A sudden shaft of light drew his attention to the door and he hurriedly, if a little awkwardly, got to his feet. When he saw that the figure silhouetted in the doorway was holding something his instincts took over.

"Drop it!" he yelled, reaching for his gun. As he did so he wondered what had happened to the two officers who were supposed to have prevented anyone who wasn't a member of the hospital staff getting into the room.

Marc saw the movement before the order to 'drop it' came and he reacted instantly by lashing out with a foot. He assumed the figure by the bed was the second officer, though why he was in the room instead of at the nurse's station he didn't know. As the gun went flying from the officer's grasp, he adjusted his grip on the second syringe and stabbed it forward like it was a knife.

Cortez evaded the weapon, his eyes on the intruder as he watched for the next attack. When it came, he dodged out of the way, straight into the chair on which he had been sleeping. He stumbled but recovered in time to avoid the third attack.

"Miguel!"

Cortez ignored the cry, but the intruder couldn't help turning towards the bed. It provided Cortez with an opening, and he took it. Lunging for the man, he secured his wrist in a vice-like grip and pushed the weapon away, at the same time he drove his fist into the man's stomach, doubling him up.

Cortez forced the hitman to drop his weapon, squeezing the wrist and hand until he had no choice but to let go of what he held. When the weapon hit the floor, Cortez swept it away with his foot.

He went cold when it passed through the shaft of light from the still partly open door and he saw that it was a syringe, not a knife, which could be far more dangerous, depending on what it held.

He may have been temporarily disarmed but Marc was not about to be beaten so easily. He drove forward from his doubled-up position to ram his head into Cortez's stomach, shoving him back so he tumbled over the chair. As his opponent fell, Marc let go of him and whipped a hand under the back of his jacket for his knife. He could have gone for his gun, but he was too close for it to be a good choice of weapon, and he didn't want to draw attention with the noise of a gunshot.

He stabbed with the knife as his opponent struggled to recover from his awkward position and felt a grim satisfaction as the blade sliced through the skin at the officer's side. He followed that up by slashing with the blade, aiming to rip open the officer's stomach and put a quick end to the fight so he could finish the job he was there to do.

Cortez let out a sharp exclamation of pain as the knife drew blood, but it wasn't the first time he had been injured, nor was it the worst injury he had received. With an effort, he ignored the pain and kept moving, putting the chair between himself and his attacker to give him time to manoeuvre. At the same time, he called out to Sofia.

· · · ·

SOFIA WAS ALREADY LIMPING down the corridor searching for help when she heard Cortez call out to her. She didn't know why he had done so when she knew he had seen her leave the room, but she was sure he had a good reason. Whatever the reason for the call, it spurred her on and she did her best to speed up.

She couldn't move well because of her injuries, but she shuffled down the passage as quickly as she could, away from the fight, and away from the officer who had fallen to the floor, dead, when she shook his shoulder.

She wanted to call out for the second officer who was supposed to be there to protect her, to scream for help from anyone. She held back, though. The man who had entered her room to kill her had been dressed as a doctor, and that made her worry there might be other disguised assassins in the hospital.

She didn't want to draw the attention of anyone she didn't recognise in case it turned out that someone she thought would help her was there to kill her.

• • • •

IGNORING THE SHOUT, which he was sure was meant to distract him, Marc shoved the chair with his foot to knock his opponent off-balance. He then lunged forward to slash with his knife, leaving a deep gash that bled freely in Cortez's stomach.

Cortez fell back away from the knife, painfully aware that he hadn't been quick enough. He tumbled to the floor and banged his head on the wall behind him, though he retained enough presence of mind to kick out, sending the chair skidding across the floor and forcing his attacker to jump out of the way.

He used the time and space the move gave him to scramble across the floor and snatch up his gun. He squeezed the trigger the moment he had the weapon pointed in the general direction of the hitman, firing off three shots in quick succession. In the semi-darkness he couldn't be sure of his aim, but seeing the man fall he assumed he had got him with at least one of his shots.

He ignored the pain from his injuries and pushed himself to his feet so he could move slowly to where his attacker lay. He kept his gun pointed at the man the whole time, his finger on the trigger, ready to react should he try anything. He did nothing, however, except writhe in pain.

Cortez kicked the knife away from the man when he reached him and slowly, painfully, bent. He pressed the muzzle of his gun to the man's head to keep him still as he ran his hands over his body in search of other weapons.

"Sergeant!" The officer from the nurse's station burst into the room, his pistol at the ready, as Cortez was throwing away the gun he had found on the hitman. "What happened?"

"What does it look like? Where the hell were you?" Cortez demanded, angry beyond belief that a hitman had made it all the way into the room. If he hadn't fallen asleep watching a film with Sofia, nothing would have stopped the man achieving his goal. "And where the hell is Garcia?"

"Dead," Officer Quintaro said. "Garcia's dead, and I was in the toilet." He knew it was a lousy reason for not being at his post, and he felt suitably embarrassed.

"Where's Sofia?" Cortez's voice was as tight as the finger he still had on the trigger of his gun.

"She's at the nurse's station, she's safe," Quintaro said, hoping to reassure Cortez.

"Well get your ass back there and make sure she stays that way," Cortez said sharply. "And while you're at it, get a doctor down here and radio for backup. I want more officers here right now. Before you go, put some cuffs on this guy." He eased back so Quintaro could secure the prisoner, while keeping his gun trained on the man to keep him from doing anything stupid.

14

Pizarro almost fell out of his chair when the door of the office he was using crashed open to slam noisily into the wall. Recovering from his shock, he looked up to see Cortez in the doorway, anger written in every line of his face.

The look on Cortez's face changed from one of anger to one of pain as he moved slowly into the office, but he didn't once take his eyes from his former partner. His eyes bored into Pizarro as he approached.

"Sergeant," Pizarro said, doing his best not to give away how disturbed he was by Cortez's sudden arrival.

"Is that all you've got to say?" Cortez demanded. "You son-of-a-bitch!" He made to lunge across the desk but was brought up short as pain lanced through his stomach and side. He was sure he had pulled at least one of his stitches.

"Calm down. What's the problem?" Pizarro asked. He was so taken aback by the anger in Cortez's voice that he pushed his chair away from the desk, not certain that the expanse of cheap office furniture would prove to be adequate protection should Cortez lunge for him again.

"You bastard! I told you two officers wasn't enough to protect Sofia." Pain again stabbed in his stomach, forcing Cortez to take several deep breaths to calm himself before he ripped out all his stitches.

Putting aside his fear, Pizarro straightened in his chair and did his best to appear more authoritative. "If you don't calm down, I'll have you escorted out."

"Screw you, Francisco! Because you couldn't stand to take advice from me, an officer died last night, and you nearly lost the only witness you have in the biggest investigation of your career."

"As I understand what happened, Officer Garcia died as a result of his own stupidity." Pizarro kept his voice as calm as he could. "If he had been doing his job right, he would never have been killed. He let that guy get close enough to stab a syringe into his neck and inject him with poison. No-one's to blame for his death but him. Now, I am in charge of this investigation, and that includes the protection of my witness, regardless of what you may have been led to believe about your role, and I don't appreciate you questioning the way I do my job."

"You have no idea how things work, do you." Cortez couldn't believe that Pizarro was so ignorant of things that should be obvious to him. "You think because your father-in-law is the Adjutant-General that you can screw up like this and not face any consequences?"

With an eye on Cortez in case he made to lunge across the desk at him again, Pizarro picked up his phone. "I want two officers to escort Sergeant Cortez out," he told the officer who answered.

Cortez was not about to let things go that easily, however. "I told you two officers wasn't enough to ensure Sofia's safety. I told you that, but you chose to ignore me because you don't like me, and you think you know better than me. You arrogant bastard! There's no way two officers could have protected her, especially in a hospital with so many people walking around at all hours. It was impossible for them to be sure who was who, and whether they should be there."

"He let the man get close enough to stick a syringe in his neck. That should be enough to tell you he wasn't doing his job properly. If it's anyone's fault that Miss Torres was almost killed, it's his. He's the one that screwed up, not me. If you want someone to blame, blame him, but he's dead, so you'll be wasting your time."

"If you had any idea how things work in the real world, you'd know that one person can sneak up on another, especially if they're in disguise or employ a distraction. It happens all the time, no matter how observant someone is. It might not reflect well on Garcia that he let someone get close enough to stick him with a syringe, but you're the one responsible, as you've made very clear. If you had assigned more officers to protect Sofia, it wouldn't have been possible for someone to get that close to Garcia."

"I made a decision based on the information that was available to me at the time," Pizarro said defensively. "Despite the level of violence used in the attack on the Abrantes' Estate, I had no reason for thinking that Noir would attempt to have Miss Torres killed."

Cortez bit back the angry comment that rose to his lips and said instead, "Now you do have a reason for believing that Noir wants Sofia dead, so you'd better make damned sure you do a better job of protecting her from now on. And in case you haven't figured it out yet, she's going to need to be moved from the hospital. She can't stay there since Noir knows about her and keeping her there will only put other people's lives at risk."

"I've already told you not to try and tell me how to do my job. I'll make a decision regarding Miss Torres' protection once I've had an opportunity to fully assess the situation, and I will arrange whatever I feel is appropriate."

"You'll arrange enough protection to ensure she's safe no matter what you feel is appropriate," Cortez said firmly. "If you don't, I'll take the matter to Meteiros. I doubt he'll want to take a chance on the only witness to the worst crime this city's seen in decades being killed. Not only would it damage, maybe even destroy, the case you're building, it would likely destroy both his career and yours."

The two officers Pizarro had requested arrived then and Cortez, realising he had made his point and there was nothing to be gained by continuing, left the office. The look on his face enough to make the officers stand aside and let him leave without being escorted.

The moment Cortez was gone, Pizarro turned to the other man in the office, whose presence had been completely ignored until then.

"I'm sorry about that, Sergeant Cortez has always been prone to displays of anger. It's one of the reasons for his demotion from detective."

"You might give some thought to what he said," Bright suggested. He had seen much worse displays of anger in his time and so was unimpressed by Cortez's outburst. "Two officers was never going to be enough to prevent an attack on your witness. If Cortez hadn't fallen asleep in the room with Miss Torres, or there had been more than one hitman and they had gone in with guns blazing, like Noir's men did at the estate, Miss Torres wouldn't have stood a chance."

"I can hardly be blamed if the officers on duty failed to do their job correctly, can I?" Pizarro said defensively, unwilling to admit that he was even partly responsible for Officer Garcia's death.

"True," Bright admitted. "But by separating the two officers, you made them vulnerable, and the moment one of them needed the toilet, or was otherwise occupied, as happened last night, you were down to just one officer protecting Miss Torres. I think the trouble, if you'll forgive me for saying so, is that you have no experience in security matters." Having read Pizarro's personnel file, Bright knew he had little to no experience in most areas. "I can assure you, as Sergeant Cortez said, it's not difficult for one person to get past two separated guards, especially in a building as large and as busy as a hospital. It didn't help that none of the officers you had available are trained as protection officers, so they didn't know what to look out for. That wasn't your fault, however," he said diplomatically. "You could only work with what you had available."

"What am I supposed to do now?" Pizarro didn't like asking for help, he didn't like doing anything that made him seem incapable of doing his job, but he consoled himself with the thought that Interpol was a larger agency, with experience in areas he couldn't be expected to know about. "I can't leave Miss Torres at the hospital, not now

Noir knows she's there. He's likely to send someone else to kill her when he learns she's still alive. He might even send more than one person, which means more protection will be needed, and, as you said, I don't have any officers with the right kind of training."

"You're right, you can't keep her at the hospital, as much for the protection of others as for her own protection. I suspect Noir's next attempt to eliminate her will involve his usual excessive violence, so keeping her at the hospital would put a lot of innocent people at risk. I almost wish he'd hire a professional to do the job right. We'd almost certainly lose the witness, but at least we wouldn't have to worry about innocent people dying."

Pizarro was shocked. "Surely you're not suggesting that you wish Miss Torres was dead."

"No, of course not. I'm just saying that if Noir is going to send someone, I'd rather he send a professional than another amateur. A professional, regardless of whether he or she succeeds or fails, would get in and out, and the only people at risk of getting hurt would be Miss Torres and those protecting her. Professionals don't hurt people they don't have to, it causes them too many problems. An amateur on the other hand is liable to injure or kill a lot of people, without necessarily even getting close to Miss Torres.

"Can you imagine the carnage last night if Noir's man had gone in with the same attitude as those that attacked the Abrantes' estate? At the first sign of trouble, he'd have started blasting away, and he'd have kept on until he either got away or was killed." Bright shook his head. "I don't like to think how many people would have died."

"Do you have any advice on how I can keep my witness alive long enough to identify Noir in court?"

Bright was silent for a few moments as he considered the situation. Finally, he said, "I might be able to do a little better than advice. I think I can get you some agents trained in protection duties to help keep Miss Torres safe." He was sure he could since his superiors were as interested in securing a conviction against Philippe Noir as the Barcelona Police were, and they had made it clear they would give him almost anything he needed to manage it. "If we make up a protection team of Interpol agents and officers from your force, Miss Torres should be safe. Given that this investigation is yours, officially, I think it would be sensible to have one of your officers in charge of the security operation, with a senior security officer from Interpol to advise. If I might suggest Sergeant Cortez for the job."

Pizarro tried and failed to conceal his dislike for the suggestion as he said, "I don't believe it would be possible for Sergeant Cortez to take charge of the security operation, he's injured."

"Fair enough, but I think you should at least continue to include him in the operation. In my experience, one of the biggest problems when it comes to protecting witnesses is convincing them to go along with the restrictions that need to be imposed on them. It tends to be easier if there's someone on the protection detail the witness likes and trusts. They're usually more willing to go along with what is being asked of them if that's the case. I believe Sergeant Cortez could be useful in that capacity, if no other, and his injuries shouldn't affect his ability to persuade Miss Torres to do what is necessary. If anything, they might help since they will remind her of why she needs to be protected."

"I'll give what you say some thought and discuss it with my superior. I'll pass on your suggestion of a joint protection team as well. I'm sure he'll at least agree to that," Pizarro said, thinking that with Interpol involved in the protection of Sofia Torres, they would have to take at least some of the blame if anything went wrong, which would take the heat off him.

"Good. I'll start the ball rolling on my end. I suggest you move Miss Torres out of the hospital today. You might have to keep her in a temporary location for a day or two, until something more long-term can be arranged, but that's better than keeping her at the hospital.

I would also suggest that you arrange a press release stating that Miss Torres has been moved from the hospital. That should stop Noir sending anymore hitmen there and potentially killing innocent people while they try to find her." Bright got to his feet then but turned back when he reached the door. "There is one positive you can take from this attack."

"What's that?" Pizarro couldn't imagine what part of the attack could be perceived as a positive, aside from the fact that Sofia Torres had survived it.

"The hitman is a known associate of Noir. It'll be a lot easier to get the French authorities to grant our request now. In a week, perhaps even in as little as three days, Noir will be taken into custody, and we'll be able to go to Paris to question him."

"I hope you're right. It will make things even easier for us if we can get a confession out of this Marc Delcroix, especially if he agrees to testify against Noir. If he does that, the case is pretty much sewn up. It will just be a matter of getting Noir extradited, which shouldn't be too difficult."

"That's probably hoping for a little too much. I'd guess Delcroix is more afraid of his boss than of anything we can do, or threaten to do, to him. Let me know when Delcroix wakes up and you're ready to question him, I'll sit in with you."

15

Pᴀʀɪꜱ

• • • •

BRIGHT SAT AT THE BACK of the large room with Marie Hapsburg, listening to Captain Fouret as he briefed his officers on the planned operation.

They were both surprised that the request from the Spanish police to have Philippe Noir brought in for questioning had been approved so quickly. It had only been two days since Marc Delcroix was arrested following his failed attempt on Sofia Torres' life, and already the necessary paperwork and procedures had been completed in both Spain and France.

They had expected more problems, with either the French authorities dragging their heels in the hope they wouldn't have to face the consequences of upsetting Philippe Noir, or Noir getting wind of the request and taking steps to block it.

"What do you think the chances are that this operation will turn into a bloodbath?" Marie asked quietly out the side of her mouth, trying not to draw attention to herself.

Bright shrugged. "I'd like to think Noir's smart enough not to go down that route. Killing a bunch of cops on property he owns would guarantee he ends up either dead or behind bars for the rest of his life."

He would have preferred it if a request had been submitted to Noir for him to come in voluntarily for questioning, rather than armed police going to arrest him, but he could understand the reasoning behind the decision. Such a request would have given Noir an opportunity to disappear, until either his lawyer dealt with the problem or the case in Spain collapsed, most likely due to the death of Sofia Torres.

"That's true, but smart as he is when it comes to his legit businesses, he isn't as smart when it comes to the illegal stuff. His idea of problem-solving there tends to be of the kill or smash variety," Marie said. "It isn't just Noir we have to worry about, though." If it had been possible, she would have lowered her voice still further, not that the officers in the room were paying any attention to her. "A lot of these officers have lost friends and colleagues to Noir, officers who tried to infiltrate his organisation and were killed, officers who died trying to protect witnesses. They aren't likely to forget that, and there's a chance someone here will decided to take matters into their own hands, if they get the opportunity."

"I've already considered that," Bright said. He was sure the thought of simply shooting Noir had occurred to at least a few of the officers in the room, but he hoped they would all remain professional. "I don't think there's much we can do about it, though. If we bring the subject up, they're likely to be offended, and they could get awkward about things. It might also put the idea in their heads if it isn't there already. The only thing we can do is make sure that one of us, preferably both, is in the room when Noir is arrested. If they're thinking about doing anything, they won't dare do it while we're there to witness it, and I doubt they'll do anything once Noir is in custody. It'd cause too many problems given his connections."

· · · ·

NOIR LOOKED UP QUESTIONINGLY when Jean-Paul walked in.

"I've just received word from my source. The police are on their way and should be here soon. Are you sure this is the best course of action?"

"Yes," it was Olivier Boucher, Noir's lawyer, sitting across the desk from his employer, who answered Jean-Paul's question. "This is by far the best course of action for Philippe to take. If he leaves the country or goes into hiding, like you think he should, it will only cause more problems in the long run."

"Since I'm going to let the police take me in," the notion of simply giving himself up to the police when they arrived did not sit well with Noir, and it was only with the greatest of reluctance that he was going along with Olivier's plan, "it would be best if you make yourself scarce, at least for today," he told Jean-Paul. "I doubt I'll be in any danger, and if you're here, the police might be overzealous and arrest you as well, even if they don't have a warrant for you. I'd rather Olivier didn't have to waste his time getting you out. I need you to look after things while I'm in custody, which I hope won't be for too long." He looked pointedly at Olivier as he said that.

"Is there anywhere in particular you want me to go?"

"Not really. You should only need to be out of sight today. If the information your source gave you is correct, the police only have a warrant to arrest me. There should be no problem with you returning either here or to the townhouse tomorrow. Get hold of your contact while I'm away, I want everything he can get on that bloody witness: where she's being kept, what sort of protection she has, the best way to get to her, and anything else that might be useful. Once you have the information, pass it on to Yves, he should have found somewhere in Barcelona to plan his operation by now."

"He has. He contacted me last night. He has a pair of hotel rooms for him and the men he took with him."

"Good. Make sure he understands that the witness must be removed as quickly as possible. As long as she's around, the Spanish police will keep pressuring the locals here. I want her dead inside of a week. Get the same information for Marc. I want to know where he is and what's being done to protect him. I want to know everything he's told the Barcelona Police as well."

"You think he's talked?" Jean-Paul asked. "He's been very loyal over the years. I doubt he'll tell them anything, no matter what pressure they put on him."

"I don't know, but I'm not about to take any chances. I'm not risking jail on your belief that Marc can be trusted to keep his mouth shut. I want him dead," Noir said firmly, giving his cousin a long hard look. "If he had done the job he was sent there to do, we wouldn't have a problem now, and we wouldn't be having this conversation. He knows the consequences of failing me."

Reluctantly, Jean-Paul agreed. Everyone who worked for his cousin knew what they could expect if they failed him. As far as Noir was concerned, accepting failure encouraged it, so he made an example of everyone who failed him to discourage others from doing so.

"I'll make sure Yves is aware of what he's to do about Marc. It's likely that he'll be well guarded, so I'll organise more men in case Yves needs them."

"Good. You'd better get going now before the police turn up." Noir turned his attention to his computer then, where he was clearing up some work for his legitimate businesses that his manager's couldn't take care of for him.

· · · ·

A SATISFIED SMILE ON his face, Captain Fouret strode across the room to stare down at the man on the other side of the desk.

"Philippe Noir, I am arresting you on suspicion of murder and conspiracy to commit murder." As he read the man before him his rights, he held out the arrest warrant, which Noir ignored. "Do you have any questions?" he asked when he was done. He was still holding out the warrant, which was finally taken from him by Olivier Boucher.

Noir continued to ignore Fouret and instead looked questioningly up at Boucher, who had moved to stand at his shoulder when the police entered the room.

"The warrant seems to be in order. I'm afraid you'll have to go with them," Olivier said apologetically, as if neither he nor Noir had been aware of what was to happen before then.

The sound of footsteps from outside the office made Fouret turn towards the door.

"The house is clear, sir," the officer who entered reported. "There's no-one else here."

Fouret nodded. "Can I take it you're not going to resist, Mr Noir?" he asked, turning back to the desk. He was prepared to take Noir into custody in handcuffs if he had to, he wanted to in fact, but given how rich and influential the man was, he didn't think it a good idea, especially when Noir was cooperating and putting up no resistance.

"I will be more than happy to go with you, Captain," Noir said pleasantly. "I just hope you won't have to detain me for long, I do have a business to run, several in fact."

"If you'll accompany me, sir," Fouret said. He felt cheated by the way the arrest had gone. He had arrived with enough officers to arrest a dozen heavily armed people, when he could have made the arrest with just himself and two uniformed constables. "I'm afraid your lawyer will have to make his own way to the station."

"Noir was warned we were coming," Marie said quietly to Bright as the two of them followed Fouret and his officers from the house.

"What makes you say that?" The thought had already occurred to Bright, but he was curious to know if she had something more definite to go on than he did.

"The absence of Jean-Paul for one. I suspect Noir sent him away to avoid any unnecessary trouble. Then there's the absence of not only the staff but the security guards as well. We know from surveillance that there's normally at least half a dozen guards patrolling the grounds and two dozen people working here, either in the house or around the vineyard. None of them are here today. There's also the fact that Noir's lawyer was with him, and neither of them showed much surprise when we burst in."

"Do you think it was one of Fouret's officers or one of your team who warned him?" Bright asked. He didn't like suggesting that an Interpol agent might be corrupt, but he knew it was a possibility that couldn't be ignored.

"I'd like to say it's definitely someone from Fouret's team," Marie said. "But Noir's had enough warnings over the years to make me suspect everyone. It's entirely likely that he's got multiple people on his payroll, both in the French police and in Interpol. Unfortunately, I've never been able to find any proof of who is keeping Noir informed of the investigations into him and his business. If I had any evidence, I'd have done something about it by now."

16

Barcelona

. . . .

DIEGO VEGA KNOCKED loudly and then stepped back to wait.

"What d'you want?" The woman who answered the door kept it on the chain and opened it just wide enough to ask the question.

"I'm looking for your husband, Mrs Nunez," Vega said.

"He's not here," Rosie Nunez replied. "He's out doing business."

"I'm aware of that," Vega said. "But nobody seems to know where I can find him, and he isn't answering the number I have for him. Nor has he replied to the message I left on his answerphone."

"What d'you want with Pablo?" Rosie Nunez asked suspiciously. "You a cop?"

"No, my name is Diego Vega, and I need to speak to your husband urgently. He may have done business with someone I need to locate."

The change that came over Rosie Nunez when she heard his name was immediate and dramatic. "Please, come in, Mr Vega," she said in a much more polite tone as she slipped off the chain and opened the door. "I'll call Pablo for you and tell him you need to talk to him."

"I have already called your husband, several times," Vega said as he stepped into the apartment. "He hasn't answered."

"That was probably his business phone," Rosie Nunez said. "He tends to ignore calls on it if it's someone he doesn't want to talk to, or he doesn't recognise the number. He's very cautious."

"That would probably be it. I've never had occasion to contact your husband before, so he wouldn't have a reason to know my number," Vega said, keen not to give Rosie Nunez cause to worry and warn her husband away.

• • • •

"HERE HE IS." ROSIE Nunez sighed in relief when she heard the apartment door open. "What took you so long?" she demanded the moment her husband reached the living room.

"I was finishing up a deal," Pablo Nunez told his wife irritably. "Since I'm the only one of us that works, I can't afford to break off a deal halfway through. You understand the need to finish one deal before you move on to the next, don't you, Mr Vega," he said.

"It is good business sense," Vega said. "Is there somewhere private we can talk?" he asked.

"Into the kitchen," Pablo ordered his wife. "You can get to work on dinner while we talk business in here. Close the door behind you, and don't come out 'til I call you."

Vega expected Rosie Nunez to object to being ordered about in such a peremptory fashion after how she had spoken to her husband when he arrived. She didn't, though. Meekly, she got to her feet and made her way into the kitchen.

"Right, how can I help you, Mr Vega?" Pablo asked once they were alone. "Dare I hope you want to change your weapons supplier?"

"I'm after information, not weapons," Vega said. "I need to know if you have sold weapons to anyone new in the last few days. I'm especially interested in whether you have dealt with any foreigners."

"No," Pablo said without hesitation. "I never deal with people I don't know, not unless they're recommended by someone I do know. I haven't dealt with anyone new in the last three months."

Vega studied Pablo Nunez for a moment, gauging whether he was telling the truth. "Have you heard about any foreigners, most likely French, trying to buy weapons?" he asked finally. He knew it was possible that Noir's hit team, which was who he was trying to find, might have brought weapons with them, but he had to explore all possibilities in his search.

"No." Pablo shook his head reluctantly. He wished he could help Diego Vega. Helping Roberto Abrantes' number one man would put him in good with the most powerful criminal organisation in the city, which was bound to be good for his business. "What's this all about?" he asked, hoping the question wouldn't cause offence.

"There is a small group of foreigners, most likely French, who are either in the city already or will be here soon. They wish to cause trouble, and Mr Abrantes would prefer that they weren't given the opportunity," Vega explained. "If you hear anything, please call me, Mr Abrantes is offering a reward to anyone who helps locate the people he is looking for."

"I'll talk to my contacts and make sure they've got their ears to the ground. If they hear anything, or I do, I'll let you know," Pablo promised. He was sure Diego Vega had access to more sources than he did, but it was always possible that his own sources might discover something useful. If they did, he was sure it would be good for him. "Have you talked to Fernando Senna?" he asked.

"Yes. I spoke to him this morning." The moment he had been given the job of finding Noir's hit squad, Vega had called the man who supplied Roberto Abrantes' organisation with weapons. It was a call that had accomplished nothing, except to remove Fernando Senna as a potential source of weapons for Noir's men. "I guess I'll have to look elsewhere for the information I'm after." He had people scouring the city, but he still had to do some of the work himself, which he wasn't happy about. It was too much like doing police work.

"What about Ruiz Battista?" Pablo asked. "Have you checked with him? I've heard he'll sell weapons to anyone. Doesn't care who they are or what they have planned, so long as they have the money to pay him."

"Ruiz Battista?" Vega asked. He had never heard of the man, which he found strange, since he would have expected to hear about someone new selling weapons in the city, as he heard about everything major that happened. How a new arms dealer had managed to set up shop without him being aware of it was something he intended looking into when he had a chance. "I've never heard of him."

"I'm not surprised. He only started up about a month ago."

"Do you know where I can find him?"

"I'll write the address down for you." Pablo got to his feet so he could find a pen and a piece of paper. "He does business from a liquor store, so I've been told. You might want to take a couple of guys with you. Apparently, he's a rough character with an attitude problem, and he keeps a couple of thugs around for protection."

"I'll bear that in mind." Diego took the slip of paper with the address and stuffed it in his pocket.

• • • •

"THIS IS THE PLACE, sir."

Vega thanked his driver and got out.

It was immediately clear that Ruiz Battista was someone comfortable amongst the lowest of the low. Half the shops in the street were either out of business or had boarded up windows, and of those that were still in business, only one of them was still open at that time of the evening. That one being in the shop he was there to visit.

The only people he could see was a gang of teenagers loitering outside the liquor store. They were desperately trying to look tough, but far from intimidating him they only succeeded in amusing him with their posturing and tough-talking.

When he reached the door of the shop he turned to face the gang, who were eyeing his Mercedes like a pack of hyenas closing in on a wounded antelope. "I wouldn't even think about it," he said in a conversational tone, offering a brief glimpse of the gun he carried in case the two men behind him weren't enough to convince the gang not to touch his car.

Vega looked around as he entered the liquor store. There was only one customer, a lady who looked years older than he suspected she really was, and he waited for her to pay for the bottle of cheap wine she had selected and leave before he made his way to the counter.

"I'm looking for Ruiz Battista," he said once he was alone with the cashier, and his two bodyguards.

"What d'you want with him?" the cashier asked suspiciously.

"I have business to discuss with him," Vega said, ignoring the way the cashier scrutinised him, presumably for some indication that he might be a cop.

"Does he know you?"

"He probably knows my name, it's Diego Vega." The mention of his name brought an immediate look of recognition and respect, which he was pleased to see.

"Please wait here, I'll be right back." Almost falling off his stool in his haste, the cashier got up and made for the back of the shop, where he disappeared through a door.

He returned a couple of minutes later. "Follow me please. Your men will have to wait here," he said apologetically when they entered a storeroom filled with shelf upon shelf of cheap alcohol, where two men stood guard in front of a door.

Vega looked from his men to the two who were clearly there to protect Battista's business and decided that he had the advantage, physically speaking at least. His men were bigger, both in height and in muscle, and he felt confident that if it came to a fight, things would go his way.

In a whisper, he instructed his men in what he expected of them. He had a feeling that his meeting with Battista was not going to go well, and he wanted to be sure his men knew what to do if there was any sign of trouble.

His instructions given, Diego followed the cashier past Battista's thugs and through the door. Beyond was another door, which he guessed led outside, and two flights of stairs, one leading up and the other down. He was surprised when he was led up the stairs to the floor above the shop, rather than down to the basement.

Uncertain what to expect, and unsure if Battista had more men with him, Diego kept his hand on the mobile phone in his pocket. At the first sign of trouble he was ready to send an alarm signal to his men.

"I'm told you're an important man in this city, Mr Vega," Ruiz Battista said once Vega had taken the empty seat in the office. "What can I do for you?"

"I'm after some information," Vega told him.

"I deal in weapons, not information. If you want information, I suggest you try Google." Battista ignored the cashier from the moment he entered the room to the moment he left, focusing instead on the man he had been warned about.

Vega settled himself more comfortably on the chair, which wasn't easy for it was a cheap, plastic thing. "I assume you aren't fully aware of who I am, Mr Battista, and that is why you don't feel inclined to help me."

"I know enough. You're supposed to be important and someone I should pay attention to. I don't give a damn who you are or who you work for, though. Unless you want to buy weapons from me, we've got nothing to discuss."

The response didn't surprise Vega, he had taken the man's measure and figured he wasn't likely to be cooperative. He had to persist, though, since that was what Roberto Abrantes would expect of him.

"My employer is looking for information, and it is in your best interests to cooperate." He rubbed his finger over the send button on his phone as he spoke. "Mr Abrantes, whom I represent, is looking for a Frenchman, or a group of Frenchmen. They may be in the city already, or they may be arriving soon, we aren't sure. What we are sure of is that they are coming here to cause trouble, and they will almost certainly be in need of weapons. I have spoken to the other two weapons dealers in the city, and they have assured me that they have not sold weapons to anyone from France recently, nor will they. That just leaves you. Mr Abrantes would like to know anything you can tell me about anyone from France you may have sold weapons to in the past week. If you haven't sold weapons to anyone from France, he would like an assurance from you that you won't, should any such person approach you."

"Roberto Abrantes can go screw himself," Battista said harshly, leaning forward abruptly, his hands on the desk in front of him. "I don't give a damn who he is, nobody tells me how to run my business. I'll sell weapons to whoever the hell I want, whether they're French, Spanish, or bloody Martian. If they've got the money, I've got the weapons, and I sure as hell won't tell anyone who's been buying from me."

"It would be a mistake not to help Mr Abrantes with this matter," Vega said, continuing to speak calmly, though he tightened his grip on the phone in his pocket. "Mr Abrantes runs this city, and he can make life very difficult for you if he chooses to. He can even end your business if he wants to."

"Ricky, Ding, get the hell up here, right now!" Battista yelled. "You get the hell out of here, you prick. Nobody threatens my business, especially in my own shop."

Vega could hear feet thundering up the stairs towards him as he hurriedly sent an alert to his men, though he was certain they would have already realised there was trouble. His certainty was rewarded when he heard three shots in quick succession and saw a look of concern cross Battista's face.

Battista yanked open the top drawer of his desk. Vega was quicker, though, and had his gun pointed at Battista before he could reach his own weapon.

"I think you might want to reconsider your decision not to cooperate," Diego said as his men burst into the room, their weapons at the ready and their eyes darting to every corner, searching for trouble.

"Screw you!" Battista swore defiantly. "If you think this is the way to get my help, you're tapped in the head. I don't give a damn about your boss, or what those French guys are here to do, I didn't ask, it's none of my business. I just sell weapons and keep my mouth shut. That's what keeps people coming back."

"So you know something about them," Vega said, certain the slip meant he had found someone with the information he was after. "I suggest you tell me what you know about the men you dealt with, everything you know. I want names, descriptions, plans, what they bought, where they're staying."

"Screw you!"

"I guess you really don't want to do this the easy way," Vega said with a regretful sigh. "Take him down to the basement," he told his men. He figured that any noise made in the process of getting the information he was after would be better contained down there. "Where's the cashier?"

"He ran off the moment he realised there was going to be trouble," Esteban said as he and Julio grabbed Ruiz Battista, who struggled in vain to free himself from their grip.

"How helpful of you to have soundproofed this place," Vega remarked to Battista as he looked around the cellar below the shop.

Not only had the room been soundproofed, it had been reinforced, making it resemble a small arsenal with the variety of weapons on display around the walls.

"It will stop us having to worry about disturbing anyone. Now, would you care to change your mind about cooperating?" he asked as his men secured their prisoner to a chair and made preparations.

For answer, Battista spat in Vega's face and snapped, "Screw you!"

Vega's sigh was almost theatrical. "I hate stupid behaviour. You will tell me what you know, Mr Battista, it's just a question of how much pain you have to endure before you do."

. . . .

IT TOOK AN HOUR FOR Vega and his men to extract all the information Ruiz Battista had, most of which time was spent with Battista refusing to cooperate, and by the end of that time he had been reduced to a blubbering, bleeding wreck.

"Are you absolutely certain that is everything you know?" Vega asked one final time as he got to his feet to look down on the moaning and quivering figure tied to the chair before him.

He had seen enough violence over the years that the sight of Battista's injuries didn't bother him. His only thought was that if the man had cooperated he would not have suffered so badly.

"Yes," Battista mumbled through the pain.

"In that case we are finished here. I guess I should do the humane thing and put you out of your misery."

Taking out his gun, Vega placed the muzzle against Battista's head and pulled the trigger. The body jerked and twitched for a moment before becoming still.

17

Cortez, technically on sick leave because of the injuries he had received during the attack at the hospital, was playing cards at the table in the Interpol safehouse when his phone rang. A glance at the screen revealed that it was Vega calling.

"No cheating," he warned Sofia with a smile as he put his cards down and stood. "It's me," he answered the phone once he found a measure of privacy.

"I've got some information for you," Vega said, skipping the pleasantries, just as Cortez had. "Noir has definitely sent some guys to kill your witness."

"What've you got?"

"Come on down here and I'll tell you."

Cortez didn't waste any time trying to get Vega to give him the information over the phone. He knew Vega didn't like talking on the phone about sensitive matters if he could avoid it.

"Where are you? Okay, I can be there in about twenty-five minutes," he said once he had been given the location of the meeting.

With the call finished, Cortez returned to the living room. "I'm afraid we're going to have to end the game for now," he told Sofia. "I have to go out."

"Why?" Sofia asked as she gathered up the cards.

"I need to meet one of my sources. He may have some information about the men sent to kill you." The moment he said that Cortez realised that he should have thought before speaking.

"They're not coming here, are they?" Sofia asked fearfully, looking around as though she expected armed men to burst through the door right then. "You said they'd never know where I am if anyone was sent to kill me, that's why I wasn't allowed to go home. You said staying here instead of at home would keep them from finding me."

"Calm down. It's okay. Right now, I have no information to suggest that Noir's men have the slightest clue where you are," Cortez said reassuringly. "And no reason to think they'll find you. Only a few people know you're here, and they aren't likely to give you away since that would put them in the line of fire."

"If you say so." Sofia's voice betrayed her doubts as she got to her feet to put the cards away. "Hurry back. I feel safer when you're here."

"I won't be away any longer than necessary," Cortez promised. He knew it wasn't logical for Sofia to feel safe simply because he was there when there were seven police officers and Interpol agents in and around the house to protect her, but he also knew feelings were rarely logical.

Leaving the living room, Cortez went in search of Agent Trotsky, so he could apprise her of the situation. Since she was in charge of the protection detail for that shift, she needed to know he was going out. She was also going to need to know at least some of whatever Vega had discovered when he got back in case changes had to be made to the protection arrangements.

· · · ·

"IS THERE A REASON FOR meeting here?" Cortez asked as he climbed into the back of Vega's Mercedes, which was parked on an ordinary street made up of office buildings and medium standard hotels.

"Of course. The men Noir has sent to kill your witness are staying in that hotel." Vega pointed across the road to a building opposite. "I don't know what room they are in, but I do know there are four of them."

"Are you certain?" Cortez studied the front of the hotel, which he suspected had been chosen because it was about as average as a hotel could be. It was the sort used by businessmen on a budget, or families, he decided. The staff were likely too busy to worry about any one group of guests without good cause.

At a better hotel, the staff would be more observant and more inclined to report anything untoward, while the cheaper hotels would be the first places checked by the police if they were looking for people from out of town.

Vega nodded. "Yes, I spoke to the gentleman who sold Noir's men their weapons. He was very certain that this is where they are staying. His men delivered their weapons here. The guy in charge is going by the name Yves and he has three men with him. They're all armed with submachine guns and pistols, nothing special, but they did buy a fair amount of ammunition. They also bought half a dozen flashbangs and a couple of grenades."

"Is that everything?" Cortez asked as he scribbled down what he had been told so he could pass the information on when he got back to the safehouse.

"Yes. My informant became very cooperative towards the end of our conversation, and he assured me that that is all the weapons he sold them. He was also able to give me a brief description of Yves: he is medium height and build, with dark hair and grey eyes, and he has a strong French accent." Vega noted the look Cortez gave him in the rear-view mirror. "I know it isn't a very good description but it's all I was able to get. My informant only met the man once."

"You're right, it isn't very good, but it's better than I expected when I told you Noir probably had people in the city." Finished with his scribbling, Cortez put his pad and pen away. "I take it I don't want to know how you got this information."

"What you don't know can't damage your career," Vega told him.

"Okay." Cortez was more than happy to remain ignorant. As Vega had said, what he didn't know couldn't hurt him. "I'm surprised you haven't already gone in there and dealt with them. I wouldn't have expected you to let them stay alive for this long when you know where they are."

"I was going to send some men in to take care of things, but Mr Abrantes insisted that I discuss the situation with you before taking any action. So, what do you think?"

"I don't think it's a good idea for your men to get into a gunfight with Noir's men," Cortez said after giving the situation a few moments' thought. "I don't imagine Roberto will care too much about the risk to his men, but I'm sure he wouldn't like the attention, there's enough on him already after what happened to his brother, or the investigation that would follow."

"That's true," Vega said. "Are you going to fetch some of your fellow officers and arrest them?"

"Without revealing your involvement or making up a lot of lies that probably won't hold up to close inspection, a judge wouldn't sign off on a search warrant, let alone an arrest warrant, so that option's out. Can you have a couple of your guys watch the hotel?"

The expression on Vega's face suggested that it wouldn't be a good idea for his men to refuse the job.

"Good. I want Yves and his men followed when they leave the hotel. They probably won't do a lot of moving around the city, especially not together, so if they do all head out at the same time, the chances are it means they've found out where Sofia is being kept and are on their way there. You'll be able to warn me, and we'll be ready for them when they get there."

"It sounds like a good idea in principle," Vega said, "but I can think of a couple of problems. You won't know who to look out for, and since my men won't know when they are close to your location, you won't have a clue how close Noir's men are until they open fire on you."

"That will make things difficult," Cortez said. "I'm sure one of your guys can get pictures of Noir's men, though. You can send them to me, and then Sofia's protective detail will know who they should be looking out for. Even if your men can't do that, they can contact me when they're following Yves' group. A running update of their location as they follow will tell me when they're close to the house."

"Why don't you get some officers to follow them? Surely that would be better than having my men do it," Vega said. It was not that he was bothered about having his men follow Yves' group, he had been told to do whatever was necessary to handle the situation, and to cooperate with Cortez in doing so, but he knew the police were better equipped to do the job.

"It would only be better in some respects. They might do a better job of tailing this hit group, assuming I could get Francisco to organise a surveillance team, but they wouldn't be prepared to make Noir's men disappear if an opportunity presents itself, whereas your men would."

Murder was not something Cortez condoned under normal circumstances, though he had been forced to turn a blind eye to it on a few occasions, but if it was the only way to keep Sofia safe, he was prepared to accept the necessity, especially if the people being murdered were themselves murderers.

"That's true," Vega agreed. "I'll make the necessary arrangements, and keep you posted. I hope you get everything resolved soon, my men have other work to do, work that earns money."

"You're not the only one who'd like things to go back to how they're supposed to be." Cortez couldn't help thinking about how hard it was at times to balance the two jobs he was paid to do: maintain law and order and protect Roberto Abrantes' business interests, which were often in opposition to one another. "It's difficult enough keeping things under control without dealing with massacres and gangs of international assassins. We just have to make the best of things. Is there anything else you need from me, or can I go back to the safehouse?"

"You can go."

18

"You drive, Claude, you two in the back," Yves directed his men when they reached their car, which was parked at the rear of the hotel. He didn't need to give any other instructions just then, the five days they had spent together in the hotel had given them plenty of time to familiarise themselves with the simple plan he had come up with.

Oblivious to the car that pulled away from the curb to follow them once they started down the street, Yves and his men headed towards their destination.

"They're on the move, Mr Vega," Seve reported from the passenger seat as his partner concentrated on following the car containing the hit squad sent by Philippe Noir.

"Keep on their tail, but don't get too close," Vega instructed. He hoped everything was going to be okay. If it wasn't, he knew Roberto Abrantes would hold him responsible. "You'll be contacted shortly by someone else. Tell him where you are and keep him updated with your location. If he gives you any instructions, I want you to follow them as if I'm the one giving them to you. Is that understood?"

"Yes, sir. Anything he says, we do." The phone in Seve's hand went dead then and he tossed it onto the dashboard while he waited for the new person to contact him. "We're getting new instructions from someone else," he answered his partner's questioning look.

• • • •

"YES?" CORTEZ ANSWERED his phone.

"Noir's men are on their way," Vega told him. "If they know where you are, they'll most likely be with you in half an hour, perhaps less. I hope you're ready for them."

"Me too. Get Trotsky," Cortez told the nearest Interpol agent. "Where are they now?" he asked of Vega, returning his attention to the phone.

"You'll have to find out from my men," Vega said. "I've told them to expect your call. They don't know who you are, but they know to keep you up to date on the location of Noir's men, and to do whatever you tell them to."

"I'm surprised you trust me enough to give me that sort of control over your men," Cortez remarked.

"Don't make me regret it. I don't think either of us would like that," Vega said, a warning note in his voice. "I'm putting these men under your control for the sole purpose of ensuring that Sofia Torres stays alive, so try not to get them arrested. That would be awkward for everyone concerned."

"Don't worry, I've no intention of putting them anywhere near trouble. I'll let you know how everything turns out when it's all over." Cortez ended the call then and looked around the room. "You should go upstairs to the back bedroom, Sofia," he told her. He knew she was going to worry, perhaps even panic, but that couldn't be helped.

Sofia, surprised by Cortez's tone, was going to question him but the expression on his face told her it wouldn't be a good idea. With a nod, she obediently left the room so she could make her way upstairs to the bedroom at the back of the house, where she had been sleeping during her stay there.

"Are Noir's hitmen on their way?" Agent Trotsky asked the moment she arrived.

Cortez shrugged. "Hard to say right now. They've left the hotel they've been staying in and are heading somewhere. Chances are they're coming here, though that raises an ugly question: how do they know where we are? I don't think any of us likes the implications of them knowing where to find us."

"You're bloody right about that. If I find out someone's told them where to find us, I'm gonna kill them."

"I'll help," Cortez said, dialling the number Vega had given him. "Give me a minute and we'll know if they're heading in this direction. Fingers crossed they're going somewhere else entirely."

It was ten minutes before Cortez was sure they were in trouble.

Regular updates from Vega's men made it clear the group Noir had sent to Barcelona was heading in his general direction, but it was a while before he was sure they knew where the safehouse was.

"Okay, it's obvious they know where they're going, you can back off now," he told Vega's men. "Head back to the hotel. I don't expect any of them to get away, but if they do, that's where they'll go. I want you waiting for them. If they get there, I want you to follow them when they leave again." He ended the call then. "They're definitely coming here," he reported to Trotsky.

"Shit! How far away are they?"

"A couple of minutes, perhaps a little more. It depends on whether they know exactly where we are. They might need a short while to figure out which house they're looking for."

"Okay, gentlemen, let's get ourselves ready," Trotsky said briskly. "Madeira, Santos, you two stay down here. Gomez, Addams, you two take the front bedroom and keep a lookout from there. Miguel, you go up to the bedroom with Miss Torres. You'll be our last line of defence, and I sincerely hope it doesn't come to that."

· · · ·

"OKAY, CLAUDE, STOP here," Yves said. "We'll give the two of you fifteen minutes to get in position and then we'll make our move," he told the two in the back of the car, who immediately got out and made their way across the road and up the drive of the first house they reached.

Yves left Claude to keep track of the passing minutes while he took out a pair of binoculars so he could examine the street ahead and the house their target was being kept in. The streetlamps were widely separated, leaving large areas of dark, which made it hard for him to make out much, but there was only one thing he was interested in.

"Have you got them?" Claude asked when Yves lowered the binoculars.

Yves nodded. "They're just past the house, on this side of the road." Although there were numerous cars parked along the street, only one of them was occupied. "I can't see any movement at the front of the house, but I didn't expect to. How long have we got?"

Claude checked his watch. "A little over five minutes."

"We'd better get going then. Remember to keep low. I'll take care of the car."

When the last of the fifteen minutes he had given Henri and Julian were up, Yves took a grenade from his pocket and stepped from the shelter of the car he had been hiding against. His toss was gentle, just enough to allow the grenade to bounce twice before rolling under the car holding the Interpol agents.

The moment he released the grenade he turned and ran. He had only experienced a grenade once before, but that was enough for him to know that he wanted plenty of distance between himself and the explosion. Only when he had put more than fifty feet between himself and the Interpol car did he stop so he could duck between two parked cars, hoping they would protect him. He had barely done so when the grenade exploded.

Slowly, he counted to five, and then he got to his feet. His eyes darted all around as he dashed across the road, and he saw that the car with the two agents in had been flipped over and torn apart. There was no way the agents could have survived the blast, so he paid the vehicle no more attention.

"They know we're here now," Claude remarked when Yves reached him.

· · · ·

"WHAT'S GOING ON?" SOFIA asked fearfully when the sound of the explosion reached her and Cortez in the back bedroom of the house.

"Nothing good," Cortez said. He was sure the explosion had been caused by one of the grenades Noir's men had bought, but what it had been used on, he didn't know. The only thing he was certain of was that the grenade hadn't exploded in the house. It had sounded too far away for that. "Stay here, I'll be right back."

He crossed to the door and pulled it open. With four quick strides he reached the door of the master bedroom at the front of the house. He was about to throw open the door when it occurred to him that it was not a good idea to barge into a room that contained armed men expecting trouble. Knocking, he announced himself before entering.

"What's happening?" he asked of Gomez and Addams.

"We're screwed, that's what's happening," Gomez said as he smashed the window in front of him with the butt of his submachine gun so he could fire at the movement he had spotted. He was copied a moment later by Addams, who fired at the same figure.

After firing another burst at a second figure he had seen, Gomez turned his attention back to Cortez to say, "They've blown up the car with Oliveira and Ribera."

"Shit!" Cortez swore. "That's bad. We're not screwed yet, though, Raul, so keep your mind on the job. If you see someone moving out there, shoot them. I'm sure Trotsky has backup on the way, and we're only up against four men."

"Yeah, well, those four men have already killed a quarter of our number, and we haven't got any of them." Gomez fired a prolonged burst that emptied his magazine but failed to accomplish anything other than to encourage his target to keep his head down.

"Just stay alive and keep them out. Once backup arrives, they'll be caught between us and them and won't stand a chance." Cortez turned away and made for the door, keeping low to avoid any stray bullets that found their way into the bedroom.

· · · ·

HENRI AND JULIAN HAD barely made it to the back garden of the safehouse when the grenade exploded at the front of the house. Hearing the explosion, they crouched in the shadows and waited for the second grenade, which was to be their signal to move in.

The moment the signal came, they straightened up and hurried to the kitchen door. Julian took out a flashbang as they went, pulling the pin so he could throw the device while Henri kicked the door in.

Once the device went off, they burst through the broken door, their weapons at the ready. As expected, the kitchen was empty, all attention in the house having been drawn to the front and the street outside by the explosions. Despite that, they remained cautious as they crossed the kitchen and made their way down the passage beyond.

The door to the living room was burned and blackened and hanging from one of its hinges, revealing what room the second grenade had exploded in. There was gunfire coming from the room, however, indicating the grenade had not killed everyone in there.

Julian took out another of the flashbangs he carried and tossed it into the room. When he and Henri entered the room after the flashbang had gone off, they saw that it had been ripped apart by the grenade. The bay window was shattered, the furniture had been overturned and was burnt and scorched, and the walls were blackened.

Crouched behind the smouldering sofa, bleeding and injured, was a woman. Her left arm hung useless at her side, but she still held a submachine gun in her right hand, and she swung it from side to side as she squinted and strained her eyes in search of a target to fire at.

It was clear that her hearing had been affected as well as her vision for she neither heard nor saw Henri as he approached. A quick burst from his weapon finished her off, and once he was sure there were no more threats in the room, he left.

. . . .

WITH HIS WEAPON HELD loose and at the ready, Cortez listened to the sounds from the rest of the house and concluded that things were not going well.

The explosion from the rear of the house, though not as strong as the other two had been, told him that Noir's men had split up so they could attack the house from both the front and the back simultaneously. It was a good tactic, and one that should have been thought of and countered.

Looking out the window carefully, he searched the rear garden, but could see no sign of anyone there. He guessed that the attackers out there had already entered the house, since all the defenders were at the front and there was no opposition at the back.

A burst of gunfire from the living room, different in pitch to what he had heard previously, made Cortez leave the bedroom so he could try to make sense of what was going on. No sooner had he done so than he spotted two men at the foot of the stairs, neither of whom were part of the security team.

Before they could react to his presence, Cortez swung his submachine gun around and fired a long burst. He kept his finger on the trigger as he moved the weapon from side to side, spraying bullets down the stairs, to encompass both men.

He didn't take his finger off the trigger until he had emptied his magazine and both men were on the floor. When they stopped moving, he ejected the spent magazine and quickly shoved a new one into place.

Stepping across the passage, he pushed open the door to the master bedroom and moved inside at a crouch. Cautiously, he crept across the room to the window. When he got there, he saw that Gomez was dead, killed by a bullet that had struck him just above his right eye.

"Have they got a sharpshooter out there?" he asked of Addams, who was okay, other than having a few cuts on his face and arms.

"No, they got bloody lucky," Addams said angrily. "The bullet took a deflection. Just how screwed are we?"

"I'm not sure what's going on downstairs, but I got two of them just now. They were at the foot of the stairs, so I'm guessing things aren't good for Trotsky and the others. What are things like out there?"

Addams shrugged before firing another burst through the window at the movement that caught his eye. "Hard to say. I'm pretty certain I've got one of them, but there's at least one more out there."

"He should be the only one left then, and if the information I got is correct, he doesn't have any grenades left, so all you have to do is keep him pinned down. Don't worry about trying to kill him, just keep him where he is. The backup," Cortez was relieved to hear sirens getting steadily closer, signalling the approach of the much-desired backup, "can take care of him when they get here. I'm going downstairs to see if I can find out what's happened there. Keep yourself safe." Patting Addams on the shoulder, he crept from the room.

Before he headed downstairs, he returned to Sofia.

"What's happening?" she asked fearfully. The gunfire reminded her of all the people who had died at the estate, and it scared her.

Cortez ignored the question and said reassuringly. "Help's on its way, they'll be here soon. I need to go downstairs to find out how Trotsky and the other two are doing, so I want you in the front bedroom, where Addams can protect you." Taking her hand, he gently pulled her off the bed and led her out of the room. When they reached the door of the master bedroom he stopped her and said, "Get on your hands and knees." She looked at him questioningly, but he didn't explain. "Crawl into the room and hide behind the bed, you'll be safe there."

Without another word, Cortez turned and headed back along the passage to the stairs. He stepped over the bodies when he reached the ground floor but slipped when his foot landed in the blood that had pooled under them. It was only by grabbing the banister that he kept himself from falling on top of the bodies and covering himself in their blood.

After righting himself and discovering that the slip had caused him to pull out the last of his stiches, which he wasn't happy about, Cortez crossed the passage to the living room.

He found Trotsky's body behind the sofa, which had been overturned and lay on its back, and saw that she hadn't been killed by the grenade that had wrecked the room but had been shot in the head at close range. He assumed she had been killed by one of the men he had gunned down at the foot of the stairs.

Since he could do nothing for Trotsky, Cortez put her from his thoughts. He was far more concerned with the possibility that one of the two Interpol agents who had been with her might still be alive.

He found Agent Madeira by the window, dead from shrapnel wounds to his back and side. Santos on the other hand seemed to be virtually untouched, despite being unmoving, and Cortez was surprised to find that he still had a pulse.

19

"Claude?" Yves called out to his partner when he heard the approaching sirens.

When Claude didn't answer him, Yves cautiously made his way along the wall at the edge of the garden. The wall was only three feet high, and he soon discovered that he wasn't being cautious enough as a burst of gunfire chipped stone from the top of the wall by his head.

Ducking quickly, he scrambled for the dubious safety of a car, which he crawled around to the far side, where he discovered Claude. His partner was on the ground, bleeding, and it didn't take a medical degree for Yves to see that he wouldn't be able to escape without help.

As best he could, Yves ignored the increasing volume of the sirens and considered the situation. He didn't know if Henri and Julian had accomplished their mission, he didn't even know if they were still alive, and he had no way of contacting them to find out, so he could only assume they had failed. He regretted the decision to leave behind anything that could be used to identify them now, including their mobile phones.

With backup for the protection detail on its way, there was no time for him to get into the house and finish the job, not if he wanted to get away as well. Attempting to finish the job would almost certainly see him either caught or killed, neither of which possibility appealed to him, especially since if he were caught Noir was likely to have him killed to keep him quiet.

When the sound of the sirens doubled in volume, Yves looked around in concern and saw a police car rounding the corner a hundred and fifty yards away. That made up his mind for him.

"I'm sorry," he apologised to his friend as he raised his weapon.

He could see in his eyes that Claude understood the decision he had made, and what was about to happen, and accepted it. That understanding didn't make him feel any better about what he knew he had to do. With a shaking hand he aimed his gun at Claude's head and squeezed the trigger, firing a three-round burst to be sure the job was done. He stared down on his friend for a second, saying a silent goodbye, and then he straightened.

Two long bursts emptied his gun and dealt with the approaching police car. The first burst shattered the windscreen and killed the driver, making the car veer violently and causing his second burst to miss the officer in the passenger seat. He forgot about the officer he had failed to kill as he reloaded and turned his attention to the car following on the heels of the first.

He missed the driver as the car swerved, so he fired again, holding his finger on the trigger for longer as he aimed at the radiator to stop the car dead. When his weapon clicked on an empty chamber again, he reached for another magazine. He had used his last one, however, and he dropped the submachine gun so it swung from its strap. In its place he took out his pistol.

A burst of gunfire from somewhere in the house shattered the window of the car next to him, sending a fresh wave of adrenaline through him. It gave him the impetus to pick up his pace until he was running flat out down the road.

He didn't stop until he reached the car he had arrived in. He yanked the driver's door open, threw himself behind the wheel, and scrambled to start the engine, glad that the keys had been left in the ignition.

Once in gear he shoved his foot down on the accelerator and spun the wheel sharply. The car shot away from the kerb, and he swung it in a tight U-turn to head up the road away from the house he and his men had attacked.

He took the first turn he came to, and it was only by the narrowest of margins that he avoided driving headfirst into an oncoming police car. He scraped past it and took the next turn with no idea if he was going in the right direction to get back to the hotel he and his friends had been using.

It didn't matter just then if he was going the right way. He was more concerned with putting as much distance between him and the safehouse as he could, and in escaping the police, whose sirens seemed uncomfortably close as he took turn after turn to try and lose them. It sounded as though they were always just around the last corner, and that kept him going.

After yet another random turn, Yves saw a young woman getting out of a car. He slammed on the brakes, bringing his car to a skidding halt a short distance from her, and threw open the door at his side.

The woman was frozen to the spot, paralysed by nearly being run down, but at the sight of the gun in the hand of the man rushing towards her she screamed.

"Tais-toi!" Yves struck the woman with his gun, slashing her cheek open with the muzzle. Her scream ended abruptly, and she stared at him in silent shock. "Monte dans la voiture," he ordered, waving his gun in her face.

When she continued to stare at him, now in incomprehension, Yves pressed the muzzle of his gun against her bloody cheek and said slowly and deliberately in English, "Get in the car or I'll kill you." He hoped she understood him that time because he couldn't speak Spanish and she clearly hadn't understood his French.

"Please, don't hurt me," the young woman pleaded in halting English.

"Then get in the bloody car!" Yves pressed the gun more firmly against her cheek to get the message across and she quickly unlocked the car door. "Get in and move over to the other side," he said when she had the door open. He then slid in beside her.

He held his breath when a police car, its siren silent but its lights flashing, raced past the end of the road. When the car didn't reappear, he slowly let out his breath and snatched the keys from his hostage's grasp so he could start the engine.

Yves kept to the speed limit as he pulled away from the kerb and started down the road, but after a few minutes of driving aimlessly at what felt like a crawl he found himself becoming impatient. He wanted to increase his speed, but he knew that if he began racing through the streets again, he would end up with the police after him once more. He also realised that without knowing where he was going, it didn't matter how fast he drove. Reluctantly, he forced himself to slow down every time he found his speed creeping up.

He considered asking his hostage, who stared fearfully at the gun in his lap the whole time, if she knew where the hotel was but he dismissed the idea the moment it entered his mind. Even if he could make her understand what he wanted, there was every chance she either would not know where the hotel was, wouldn't be able to make him understand how to get there, or, more likely, would direct him to the nearest police station instead.

Since he couldn't ask for directions, all he could do was keep driving and hope he found himself somewhere he recognised.

• • • •

ALMOST TWO HOURS AFTER leaving the safehouse, Yves finally found the hotel where he and his friends had been staying. It felt like he had gone up and down every street in the city during his search, though he was sure that wasn't true.

Parking the car down the street from the hotel, he took the keys from the ignition and turned to look at his hostage. He wasn't sure how to get her from the car to his hotel room without anyone seeing his gun, but he realised he had to think of something. He couldn't let her go, and he couldn't shoot her right there in the street. Doing either was certain to have the police there in no time.

Finally, he got out of the car and hurried round to the passenger side before his hostage could do anything. He looked around quickly and then took his gun from his pocket to remind the woman that he had it, and that she should do what he wanted.

"Don't do anything unless I tell you," he said in slow English.

He shoved the gun back into his pocket before moving off, and with one hand on the weapon in case his hostage tried anything, he took her by the arm and almost dragged her up the road to the hotel.

20

"**S**orry to call you so late, sir," Seve apologised when his call was finally answered, "but we've got a problem here."

"What sort of problem?" Diego asked, an unpleasant, cold feeling in the pit of his stomach. "And where are you?" He reached for the watch on his bedside table to find out what the time was and was dismayed to see that it was almost three in the morning.

"We're back at the hotel. One of Noir's gunmen just turned up and we need to know what to do."

"What did my friend tell you to do?" Diego asked. He pushed the covers back and got up to leave the room to avoid disturbing his wife.

"He told us to keep an eye on the hotel in case any of the group got away and came back here. If they did, he told us to watch and then follow them if they leave again. One of them, I think he's the guy in charge, has just returned and we need to know what to do."

"You do what you were told to do, wait and see if he leaves again, and if he does, you follow him."

"What about your instructions to kill the men if we get a chance? Do you still want us to do that?"

"Yes," Vega said after a moment's thought. "If you can kill him without making a lot of noise or drawing attention to yourself, do so. If not, just watch him and wait for instructions from my friend."

"What about the woman he had with him? Do you want us to kill her as well?" Seve asked.

"What woman? Where did she come from?"

"No idea. When he left the hotel, it was him and the three guys. Now, it's just him and a woman, and he came back in a different car to the one he left in."

"Describe her." Vega hoped he was wrong, and he wasn't looking at a catastrophe.

"Youngish, early twenties, slim, with long dark hair. She was too far away for me to see more. Oh, I don't think she wanted to be with him. It looked like he was dragging her up the road towards the hotel."

The description matched what he knew of Sofia Torres and Vega's fear of a disaster increased. "Wait where you are, I'll get back to you in a minute," he said, fighting to keep calm. Ending the call, he dialled Cortez's number to find out what was going on.

"Damn!" he swore loudly in the silence of his kitchen when he failed to get hold of Cortez after five minutes of trying. His inability to get hold of Cortez meant it was up to him to decide how to deal with the situation, and he dialled Seve's number to give him his new instructions.

"Change of plan," he said the moment Seve answered.

"Yes, sir."

"Kill the guy and get the girl out," Vega said. He uttered a silent prayer that he had made the right choice. As important as he was to Roberto Abrantes, he knew the wrong choice would put his life at risk.

"That could be a problem. We don't know where in the hotel the man is, we only know he's in there. Finding out and taking care of him could be noisy and attract attention." Seve didn't have a problem with killing the guy, he had killed before and would do so again if it were asked of him by Vega or Roberto Abrantes. Having been to jail, though, he didn't want to go back if he could avoid it.

"None of that matters now, all that does is getting that woman away from him. I don't care how noisy or messy you have to be, just get her to safety," Vega instructed in a firm voice. "Mr Abrantes will clear up any trouble you get into, you have my word."

"Yes, sir." Seve reached under his jacket to loosen the gun he was carrying in its holster. "What do you want us to do with the woman, bring her to you?" He didn't have a clue who the woman was or why she was so important, but that didn't matter to him, all that did was that he knew what to do with her.

"No. When you've got her, take her to the nearest police station and drop her off. Call me when you're finished," Vega said in a tone that forestalled any questions before ending the call. He debated going back to bed but decided against it. Whether things went well or not he was going to be disturbed again, so he figured he might as well wait for the inevitable call.

"Okay, Cris, we've got to go in and kill that guy," Seve told his partner. "The boss says he wants the guy dead, and he doesn't care how we do it. The woman's not to be hurt, though. Once we've got her safely away, we're to drop her off at the nearest cop shop."

Cristiano was a man of few words, but he did look questioningly at his partner when he heard what they were to do with the woman.

"Bugger knows," Seve said in answer. "We'd better get on with it, though."

Together they got out of the car and walked up the road to the hotel.

"Good evening, sirs, how can I help you?" the night clerk asked when Seve and Cristiano stopped in front of the reception counter.

"We're after some information," Seve told the clerk. "A short while ago one of your guests came in with a young woman. We'd like to know what room he's in."

"I'm sorry, sir, I can't give out guest information, it's against hotel policy."

"I think you might want to reconsider that policy," Seve said, taking out his gun. He figured that intimidating the clerk was the quickest and easiest way to get the information he was after. "What room is he in?"

The clerk swallowed nervously, his eyes going from the gun to the face of the man holding it. He didn't doubt for one second that he would be shot if he didn't cooperate, so he quickly turned to the computer. He hit the wrong keys several times in his haste, but he finally found the information he had been asked for.

"He's in room fifty-four," he said in a quavering voice.

"I wouldn't tell anyone we were here," Seve advised before turning away from the counter.

While the frightened clerk wondered what was about to happen in the hotel, Seve and Cristiano crossed the lobby to the lifts so they could ascend to the fifth floor.

"Security tapes," Cristiano said as they were waiting for a lift to arrive, the first words he had spoken in hours.

It took Seve a few seconds to figure out what his partner meant, and when he did, he nodded. "Good thinking. Why don't you go and get them. And while you're at it, take care of him. Make sure he can't talk to anyone. Do it quietly if you can, there's no point making more noise than necessary. I'll wait for you upstairs."

Cristiano nodded and turned away from the lift as Seve stepped into it. When he reached the counter he found that the clerk had disappeared into the back room.

"Security tapes, where are they?" he asked in his unusually deep voice, surprising the clerk, who jumped violently, spilling the whiskey he had poured to calm himself.

"In-in the manager's office," the clerk said after a moment, pointing with a trembling hand to the door at the back, his eyes on the large, to him, blade of the knife in the hand of the man before him.

Watching the clerk in case he decided to try something foolish, Cristiano walked over to the door of the manager's office, which he discovered was locked. "Open it," he instructed.

"I can't. The manager has the key, and he won't be in 'til morning."

Cristiano was sure the clerk was telling the truth, he was too scared to lie, so he lifted his booted foot and slammed it into the door. Two kicks was all it took to make the door fly open and hit something behind it with a loud crash.

"Where're the tapes?" he asked after looking around the office and failing to see what he was after.

"In there." The clerk pointed to the door to one side of the office. "It's locked as well," he said, though he didn't think another locked door would stop the man.

A single kick was all it took for Cristiano to get the second door open. The room on the other side of it was no bigger than a broom cupboard, with a quad of monitors and another quad of DVD-recorders on a table. He ejected the disks from each recorder and returned to the front office, where the clerk was looking around nervously, as if searching for some means of escape, though he made no move towards the open door.

"Is this all of them?"

"I-I think so, I don't really know how the security system works."

Cristiano walked towards the door as if to leave the room, but the moment he was past the clerk he dropped the disks and spun back to him. He stabbed the clerk in the chest, puncturing the heart and ending the man's life instantly. When he pulled the knife free, the young man slumped to the floor, where he lay in a heap. Cristiano bent to wipe the knife clean on the clerk's clothes and then he gathered up the disks he had dropped.

• • • •

WHEN THE LIFT REACHED the fifth floor, Seve got out and went looking for room four, which wasn't hard to find. He was tempted to burst into the room and kill the guy on his own. He didn't imagine it would be difficult since surprise was on his side, but he dismissed the idea almost immediately. If all he had had to do was kill the man, he wouldn't have hesitated, but knowing that he had to rescue the woman made him cautious.

Instead of kicking in the door, he took up a position a short distance from the room to wait for Cristiano to catch up to him, so they could enter the room together.

Barely a minute after he arrived, the door swung open, startling Seve. He recovered quickly and was pulling the trigger on his gun when the woman he had been told to rescue was pushed into the corridor, blocking his shot. He jerked the gun away and the bullet smacked into the wall further down the passage, making the woman scream.

"Let the woman go," he ordered as he stepped sideways in the narrow passage to try and get a clear shot at his target.

Yves still hadn't fully calmed down from the tensely alert state he had been in since leaving the hotel earlier that night. Because of that he reacted without hesitation to the shot and the order. Shoving his hostage in the direction of the gunman, he dropped the suitcase he was carrying and thrust his hand into his pocket for his gun. Drawing the weapon, he fired three times in quick succession, hitting the man in the chest as he stumbled backwards away from the woman and knocking him off his feet.

Cautiously, Yves approached the mystery gunman, His first thought was that he was a police officer, but he wasn't dressed like one, and a cop wouldn't have shot first without identifying himself, which made him wonder who he was and why he was there. He was tempted to search the man's pockets for some means of identifying him, but decided against it when it occurred to him that the gunman might not be alone, and there might be other gunmen in the hotel.

When the gunman twitched as he was retrieving his suitcase, Yves put a bullet in his head to be sure he was dead, and then he shot his hostage as well. He had no further use for her, and he wasn't about to leave her behind to talk to the police, not that there was much she could have told them about him.

Yves ignored the lift when he reached it and entered the stairwell next to it instead. The lift would have got him to the lobby quicker, but since he couldn't be certain there wasn't someone waiting to kill him, he thought it best to be cautious.

Slowly, and as quietly as he could, he opened the stairwell door when he reached the ground floor, his gun at the ready. He couldn't see much of the lobby, but there was no sign of anyone, so he cautiously opened the door wider. When he was satisfied the lobby was empty, he picked up his case and left the stairwell.

With rapid strides, and eyes that darted everywhere, he exited the hotel.

· · · ·

CRISTIANO FOUND SEVE the moment he exited the lift, his body was less than twenty feet from the lift doors, as was the body of the woman they had been told to get out alive. He looked around for whoever had killed his friend but saw no sign of anyone; the fact that Seve's body was not far from their target's room told him all he needed to know, though.

Since it was obvious his friend was dead, he didn't waste time checking for a pulse. Instead, he cautiously crossed to the open door of room fifty-four. Ready for anything, he entered and quickly determined that his quarry was gone, and the room was empty, of people at least. Personal items remained, but they were of no interest to him.

Once he had made certain the man he was supposed to kill wasn't hiding somewhere, he left. He wanted to get as far from there as he could before the police, or anyone else, arrived.

On his way back to the lift he took out his phone. "There's a problem, sir," he reported when Vega answered.

21

Pain lanced through Cortez's brain as he opened his eyes.

"He's coming around, sir."

The loud voice was unfamiliar, and Cortez looked around quickly to find the owner. In doing so he discovered that moving his head wasn't a good idea, it made the pain worse.

He did his best to ignore the stabbing sensation above his right eye as he searched for the person who had spoken, only relaxing when he saw it was a uniformed officer who was standing a short distance away. Hearing footsteps, he attempted to push himself into a sitting position.

"You might want to take it slow, sergeant."

The new voice was one Cortez recognised. Special Agent Ben Bright was making his way across the living room of the safehouse, and with slower moves than before to mitigate the pain, Cortez shifted about so he could see him without turning his head.

"What the hell happened to me?" he asked. "The last thing I remember is checking on Trotsky, Santos, and Madeira."

"It looks like you caught a stray bullet," Bright said as he settled himself on the upturned and scorched sofa as if it was the most natural thing in the world. "You got lucky. The bullet only creased the side of your head. The paramedics said that aside from a monster headache, you'll be fine, though you'll probably have a scar to show where you didn't duck quickly enough."

"If I'd known someone was aiming a shot in my direction, I might have tried to duck," Cortez said with a groan. "Does anyone have anything I can take for this headache?"

"You should be thankful a headache is all you have to worry about. If you had done your job right, none of us would have to worry about this mess."

Cortez groaned again at the harshly voiced comment. "Oh God! Does he have to be here? I don't think I can cope with the headache and listening to him bitch about how everything is my fault," he said, looking over at Pizarro, whose expression revealed his distaste for the mess that filled the room. "If you're going to try and lay all of this on me, Francisco, I think I'd prefer it if you found whoever shot me and get them to come back and finish the job."

"This is no time for bad humour," Pizarro told him. "This is a very serious situation. Four Interpol agents and one officer from our station are dead because you screwed up. There will have to be an inquiry into what happened here tonight, and I think it very unlikely that you will still be an officer at the end of it. You are suspended."

"Go screw yourself," Cortez said in as calm a voice as he could manage to avoid worsening his headache.

Slowly, to avoid exacerbating the pain lancing through his brain, he got to his feet and moved to take a seat in one of the armchairs, after he had righted it. "You don't have the authority to suspend me. Doesn't anyone have anything for this headache?" he asked, looking around the room. Aside from Bright and Pizarro, the only people there were two armed officers, neither of whom appeared able to help him. "I guess I'll have to endure it then," he said when nothing resembling a painkiller appeared. "Where's Sofia? Is she alright?"

"Miss Torres is fine," Bright said. "She was escorted to the station by Officer Gomez and a couple of officers. I believe she's spending the night in a cell for her safety. We'll have to decide tomorrow how best to protect her after this attack."

"I'm relieved to hear she's alright."

"We're all glad she's alright," Pizarro said insincerely. "Of greater concern right now is the monumental screwup that took place here. Do you want to tell me how the hell five people died? You assured me that you had the situation well in hand."

"You're an idiot," Cortez said, resisting the urge to shout at Francisco only with an effort. "If you had half a brain rattling around in that empty skull of yours, you'd remember that I wasn't put in charge of this security operation. I was only here because the two of you felt that Sofia would find it easier to put up with any trouble she had to go through if I was here."

"That does not excuse you. You assured me that everything was in hand. This does not look like everything was in hand." Pizarro waved a hand around the destroyed living room. "This looks like a room from a bloody warzone."

"Considering you ignored the information I gave you, that's hardly a surprise, is it. You decided you couldn't do anything when I told you where Noir's hitmen were staying because the information came from a criminal, and when I asked you to position the backup closer so they could react quicker, you ignored me." Cortez had to fight to keep his voice level and not let out his anger.

He wasn't just angry over how bad things had turned out, he was angry because he knew Francisco would do his best to make sure he was the one who took the blame for what had happened.

"I even called you when I was told Noir's men had left the hotel they were staying at, and again when I was certain they were coming here. You didn't bother to have the response team move in, you just arranged for some patrol cars to head in this direction. What the hell did you think they were going to accomplish?"

"I arranged for them so they could help you. I didn't want things to turn into an all-out gunfight, and I hoped they might be able to arrest your attackers." Pizarro made no attempt to hide his disappointment that that hadn't happened.

Bright, realising that nothing was going to be accomplished if the antagonism between the two men continued, stepped in. "You can discuss all of this later. For now, I think it would be more productive if Sergeant Cortez tells us what happened, from the start." He turned to Cortez. "Would you like something to drink, or shall we jump straight into it."

"Something to drink would definitely help, my throat is very dry," Cortez said, pleased to see one of the two uniformed officers immediately leave the destroyed living room.

The requested drink arrived in short order, and he took several long sips from the glass he was handed before he spoke again.

"I got a call from my source, telling me that Noir's men had left the hotel they were staying in. After letting Agent Trotsky know what was happening, I contacted Francisco to tell him, so he could make the necessary arrangements." His tone revealed what he thought of the arrangements Francisco had made. "While Trotsky organised her men, I got updated reports on the location of Noir's men from my source. When I was sure they were heading in this direction, I contacted Francisco again. After that I waited with the others. It was a longer wait than I anticipated, and I was beginning to think they weren't coming here when the car Trotsky's two agents were in blew up. I'd guess Noir's men used one of the grenades I was told they'd bought on it. Things were chaotic for a while after that, with a fair amount of gunfire from both sides."

Cortez paused to sip some more water and then he continued, "I stayed in the back bedroom with Sofia until the second grenade went off. The explosion came from downstairs at the front of the house and was followed by another at the back of the house. I couldn't see anyone in the back garden when I looked out the window, so I figured whoever had been out there was already in the house. I left the bedroom to try and find out what was going on and spotted two guys at the foot of the stairs. Fortunately, I saw them first and emptied a full magazine into them. I wanted to make sure they were both dead before I headed into the front bedroom to check on the officers there and see what was happening."

"You didn't kill both the men you shot," Bright said.

"What?" Cortez looked at Bright in surprise. "I put enough bullets in them to kill a whole bunch of guys."

"Clearly you aren't as good a shot as you think you are," Pizarro said nastily.

"Considering the injuries I saw, it's a miracle that either man is still alive," Bright said. "I'd expect anyone to be dead after being shot that many times. Only one of them is dead, though. The other is at the hospital having emergency surgery. Given his chances of survival, I think you can say you did kill both men, the second just hasn't died yet."

"I'm so glad to hear that, for a moment there I was worried my reputation was in trouble," Cortez said, not troubling to hide his sarcasm. "To be honest, I was more interested in making sure they couldn't shoot me; dead was the best way to ensure that, but it's probably better if one of them survived."

"That's true. We might be able to get some information from this hitman, should he recover. He might know something that will help us improve the case against Noir. What happened after you shot the two men at the foot of the stairs."

"I went into the front bedroom, where Gomez and Addams were. Addams was dead, apparently hit by a lucky shot, and Gomez was doing his best to deal with the man at the front of the house. He reported that he had only seen two men and was fairly certain he had killed one of them, but the other was still moving around. I left Gomez and went back to get Sofia. I didn't want to leave her alone while I came down here to check on things, so I got her into the master bedroom where Gomez could look after her. When I got down here, I found Trotsky dead, she'd been shot in the head. Santos was dead as well, while Madeira was alive but unconscious."

"He was in the same condition when we got here," Bright said. "I take it not much happened after that, since you were found only a short distance from Madeira."

"Aside from me standing up, no," Cortez said with a shake of his head that he immediately regretted. "I'd barely got to my feet when I felt a sharp pain in my head, and everything went black. I guess that's when I got hit." He chose not to dwell on how lucky he had been that the bullet had only grazed his skull and not caused more damage. "What happened after I got knocked out? I get the impression from the look on Francisco's face that things didn't go great."

"I would have thought that everything that happened before you got knocked out would be more than ample reason for DS Pizarro to look unhappy."

"Maybe, but since I know Francisco well, I know he's only unhappy when something happens that could affect his career. He figures that everything that's happened here, he can blame me or someone else for, so he doesn't need to worry about it, yet he still looks worried. Something must have happened somewhere else, something he can't blame me for, something he might have to take the blame for. So, what happened?"

"One of the gunmen got away," Bright said when it became clear that Pizarro was not going to respond to the question. "We're still a long way from understanding everything that happened tonight. Hopefully, we'll have a better idea when we've put together all the available information. All we know for certain right now is that one of the gunmen killed the driver of a patrol car responding to the emergency call and disabled a second patrol car before escaping. He must have had a car nearby because a few minutes later he almost collided with another patrol car. After that he disappeared."

"And you don't have the slightest clue where he's gone," Cortez said.

"The car the killer was driving was found, abandoned, a few streets from the near collision," Pizarro spoke up. "We're trying to determine if he's still in the area, or if he left it in a stolen car, or perhaps on foot. It's a slow process. The officers involved have to be extremely cautious since we know he's armed and dangerous."

"As I said, you don't have the slightest clue where he is. Have you bothered to send anyone to the hotel where he was staying to see if he's gone back there?"

Bright saw that Pizarro was about to respond angrily to that question and quickly intervened. "I think it would be a good idea if we leave this for now. I don't know about the two of you, but I'm tired, and I'm sure you could do with some rest," he said to Cortez. "You must have a killer headache."

· · · ·

EXHAUSTED, CORTEZ ENTERED his apartment as it was approaching dawn.

He wanted to sleep, both to rest and to rid himself of the remains of his headache, but he knew he couldn't surrender to that need yet. He needed to call Vega, from whom he had received numerous missed calls and messages.

With leaden steps, he made his way into the kitchen, where he poured himself a large glass of wine, which he felt he had more than earned after what had happened that night. Alongside the wine, he prepared himself a snack to quiet his complaining stomach. Only then did he take out his phone.

"Where the hell have you been?" Vega's voice exploded from the phone.

"Calm down." Cortez yanked the phone from his ear with a wince as the loud voice lanced through his brain. "I'm not up to having you yell at me right now. I've had a very bad night."

"And it's not going to get any better. Mr Abrantes was furious when I told him your sole witness was killed last night."

"What are you talking about? I was with Sofia no more than three quarters of an hour ago and she was perfectly fine, aside from being shaken up. Where did you hear she's dead?" He didn't imagine that anything could have happened to Sofia since he had seen her, and if anything had he was sure he would have been called.

"It sounds like I have been misinformed," Vega said, relaxing a little. "I'm relieved to hear that." Waking his employer in the middle of the night to deliver such bad news had not gone down well. He was glad that he was going to be able to report better news now, especially since he was not the one responsible for the original bad news.

"I'm sure you are. I don't imagine Roberto was any happier with you and your men than he was with me when you told him Sofia was dead. So, how did you come to think she had been killed?" Cortez guessed that Vega's inability to get in touch with him had something to do with the mistaken conclusion, but he would have expected him to get confirmation of his suspicions before waking his boss.

"The men you sent back to the hotel reported that one of the men they had tailed had returned there. He had a young woman with him, and her description matched what I know of Sofia Torres. Since my men couldn't contact you, and you hadn't contacted them, they called me for instructions. I told them to go in, take care of the guy, and get the woman out safely. Unfortunately, things didn't go well, which is why I thought Sofia Torres was dead."

"That would explain it," Cortez said. "Rest assured, Sofia is alive and well, if a little freaked out by everything. So, how bad is the situation at the hotel, I've heard nothing about it."

"I'm surprised. From what I was told there's three bodies: the hotel clerk, one of my men, and the woman."

"Sounds bad." Callous as it might seem, Cortez wasn't concerned that one of Vega's men was dead, he was a criminal who had taken chances with his life, so his death was no great loss. He was sorry to hear about the deaths of the hotel clerk and the young woman mistaken for Sofia Torres, though. Where the woman had come from, he had no idea, and it was only the certainty that Vega didn't know either that stopped him asking about her. "Francisco's going to be embarrassed when he learns that the killer who got away went straight back to the hotel I told him about," Cortez said, not even trying to hide the pleasure he felt at that thought.

"I imagine he will. I wouldn't be surprised if he finds himself being taken off the case once Meteiros hears everything that's happened."

"We can only hope. They might put someone sensible in charge instead. Anyway, I'll leave you to give Roberto the good news, I need to eat and get some sleep, I'm bloody knackered." Ending the call, Cortez took his food and wine into the bedroom, so he could eat and drink while he got himself ready for a long sleep.

22

Paris

....

IT WAS A LITTLE AFTER midday when Yves made it home to his apartment on the outskirts of Paris. He had made it to the airport in Barcelona in good time after leaving the hotel, but once there he had been forced to wait for an available seat on a flight to Paris. The wait had caused him some concern, especially when the news began reporting the attack on the safehouse and the escape of one of the attackers.

He was relieved when he heard nothing to suggest the police had the slightest clue who they were looking for, but disappointed by the discovery that Sofia Torres was still alive. He had failed, and that meant Noir was going to be disappointed with him. Since there was generally only one punishment for someone who disappointed Noir, he thought briefly of catching a flight to somewhere other than Paris. He didn't have a destination in mind, he was only thinking of taking the first available flight, regardless of where it took him.

He dismissed the thought almost immediately. Running from Noir's wrath was only going to cause him more trouble. Without money, family, friends, or other connections, he would struggle in a new place. Even without that difficulty he knew Noir had the resources to find him wherever he went.

Arriving home, Yves switched on his television and turned it to a twenty-four-hours news channel. With half his attention on the TV in case the attack in Spain, or his name, should be mentioned, he took out his phone to call Jean-Paul. When he got no answer, he left a brief message and then stripped off so he could get into bed.

....

HOW LONG THE PHONE had been ringing for, Yves didn't know, but the sound eventually seeped into his brain and woke him. Blindly, he groped for the phone on the bedside cabinet.

"Hello," he croaked, feeling as though he had only just fallen asleep. He came fully awake the moment he heard the voice on the other end of the call.

"I was beginning to think you weren't going to answer," Jean-Paul said. "I was about to hang up and send one of the boys 'round to make sure you're alright. Your message had me concerned you were in trouble."

"I was asleep and didn't hear the phone," Yves said, rubbing sleep from his eyes. He doubted Jean-Paul had truly been concerned about him, he thought it far more likely he had been concerned about possible trouble for his cousin. "I was up all night and didn't get to sleep until I left that message for you."

Jean-Paul grunted. "Meet me at the Louis XIV Park in an hour."

Yves was so tired it was several moments before he realised the phone had gone dead. Once he did, he dropped it onto the cabinet and sank back onto the pillow with his eyes closed. He remained like that for a minute before reluctantly throwing back the covers so he could get up. The clock on the bedside cabinet revealed that he had managed to get only an hour's sleep before being disturbed, which explained why he still felt exhausted.

With a groan, he got to his feet and made for the bathroom, where he turned on the shower and stepped under the freezing cold downpour. As he had hoped, the shock went some way towards reviving him.

After enduring the torrent for as long as he could, which was barely sixty seconds, he stepped out and vigorously towelled himself off. Feeling a little more awake, he brushed his teeth and then returned to the bedroom to get dressed.

Fifteen minutes after getting up, Yves left his apartment.

. . . .

"AFTERNOON," YVES GREETED Jean-Paul when he joined him at the side of the lake near the centre of the park.

"Yves." Jean-Paul's return greeting was frosty. "You're early." His tone suggested he was surprised Yves had turned up at all.

"Traffic was light," Yves said. He glanced around, looking for anyone he might recognise. The fact that the meeting was in a public place raised his hopes that Jean-Paul was not going to kill him for his failure, but he wasn't so foolish as to think it wasn't still a possibility.

"Your message was brief, and left a lot of unanswered questions," Jean-Paul said, getting down to business. "Let's have a seat while you tell me what went wrong."

Yves followed Jean-Paul to a nearby picnic table and sat down across from him. Sensing the other man's impatience, he threw away the last mouthful of the croissant he had stopped to buy on the way there, which was immediately dived upon by a bird.

"First off, I'd like to point out that when I was given the job, I said four men wasn't enough to guarantee success. We were outnumbered two to one and did our best." He saw that Jean-Paul was not impressed by that statement and continued hurriedly, "When we got to the safehouse we split up. I sent Henri and Julian round to the back of the house, and while they got into position, Claude and I created a distraction to pull everyone to the front of the house."

"Sound planning," Jean-Paul reluctantly approved. "What did you do?"

"I blew up the car two of the Interpol agents were using with a grenade, and Claude threw a second grenade through the downstairs window where a lot of the shooting was coming from. I reckon there were three people in that room, and only one of them was left after the grenade went off."

"That's half the protection detail taken care of. You should have been in a good position to finish the job. What happened?"

"Unfortunately, Claude got hit as he was ducking down after throwing his grenade. I wasn't able to get to him straight away because there was still two people firing from an upstairs window and I had to keep my head down to avoid having it blown off. All I could do was keep firing at the front of the house to keep what was left of the protection detail focused on me."

"What happened with Henri and Julian?"

"They got into the house and took care of whoever was left in the living room, but someone must have got them after that because the shooting continued from the first floor. When I heard sirens approaching, I realised the job was a bust and I had to get out of there."

"Without killing the witness," Jean-Paul said accusingly. "You chose to save your own skin rather than finish the job you were given." He made it sound as though it was the worst decision Yves, or anyone, had ever made.

Yves nodded reluctantly. "Given the situation, I didn't think any other option made sense, especially since I was running out of ammo. As far as I was aware, there was at least two people still alive in the house, not including the witness. If I'd tried to get in there to kill her, I might as well have committed suicide, especially since I had no idea what sort of officers were being brought by the sirens. I made my way to where Claude was, but there was no way he could get away on his own, and I couldn't carry him. I knew Mr Noir wouldn't want me to leave him alive to be questioned, so I finished him off."

That piece of information elicited a nod of approval from Jean-Paul, though he immediately quashed any hopes Yves might have been harbouring. "How is it you managed to get away uninjured?"

Yves had worried about that, and had even thought about shooting himself, either in the arm or the leg, to make his situation look better. He had chickened out of doing so, though. He wasn't prepared to inflict pain on himself unnecessarily, especially when he might have caused himself more harm than he intended.

"No idea. I was lucky, I guess," Yves said, though he didn't feel lucky. "Plenty of bullets came close. I expected to be hit by every one of them. As for how I got away, I emptied what ammo I had into the first couple of cop cars that came along, and then I ran up the road to the car and made my escape from the area before switching cars and grabbing a hostage in case the cops caught up with me." In his haste to explain his uninjured escape from the attack, his voice sped up until his words were almost tripping over one another as they fought to get out. "Something wasn't right when I finally got back to the hotel. There was someone waiting for me, and he wasn't a cop."

"Explain."

"I made it back to the hotel with the woman I took as a hostage and went straight to the room to grab my stuff. When I left there was a guy there. I didn't even realise he was there until he fired at me. Whoever he was, he gave no warning, and he didn't try and arrest me, he just fired at me. If the woman hadn't got in the way and thrown his aim off, he'd probably have killed me. I shoved the woman at him and then shot them both. After that I got out of the hotel as quickly as I could and made for the airport to wait for a flight back here."

"Are you certain he wasn't a cop?"

"As certain as I can be," Yves said. "I didn't stop to check for ID, and I didn't want to wait around to find out if he was alone. He didn't identify himself, or warn me, before he tried to kill me, a cop would have done both. Whether he was a cop or not doesn't really matter, at least I don't think it does. What matters is that he knew to be at the hotel. Those cop cars turned up at the safehouse too quickly as well. They never should have got there that soon."

Jean-Paul immediately grasped what Yves was getting at. "Who knew you were going to Barcelona?"

"Aside from you and Mr Noir, only Henri, Claude, and Julian. I know they wouldn't have told anyone where they were going or what they were doing. They've worked for Mr Noir long enough not to do anything stupid. I don't think anyone else knew."

"What about your girlfriend? Did you tell her where to contact you if she needed you? How about any of the others, would they have done anything like that? Someone must have known where to find you," Jean-Paul said when Yves shook his head.

"The only person I can think of is the guy we got our weapons from. He had his men deliver them to us at the hotel, but he didn't know what room we were in. I didn't even let him know what floor we were on. All he knew was the hotel and my first name. His men had to go to the front desk and ask for me. I arranged that with the clerk. The guy was waiting for me right outside my room. There's no way that was a coincidence."

Jean-Paul was silent for a while, and when that silence had persisted for a couple of minutes, Yves felt compelled to speak, "What happens now?"

"For the time being, nothing," Jean-Paul said. "I need to check a few things out, and I need to talk to Mr Noir. As always, he'll make the final decision on what happens next. I'll let you know when a decision has been made." Getting to his feet, he left the picnic table, happy with the thought that Yves had no idea if he was going to be safe. He didn't want Yves to relax or to think that failing his cousin would be accepted without consequences.

23

Barcelona

. . . .

"SO, HOW DID THE HEARING go?" Sofia asked when Cortez walked into the living room of the house she had been moved to following the attack on the previous safehouse.

"About as well as I expected," Cortez said as he settled himself on the sofa with his mug of coffee. "How's your day been?"

"Aren't you going to tell me what happened?" Muting the volume on the television, Sofia turned to Cortez.

"You didn't answer my question," Cortez said. He didn't really want to go over what had happened that morning. The preliminary hearings into the attack on the safehouse, which had taken place over the past few days, were boring, annoying, and had accomplished nothing. If he had been able to avoid them, he would have, so the last thing he wanted was to talk about them. "How was your day, did you get up to much?"

"It was fine. Boring, like yesterday, and the day before, but that's good since it means no-one was trying to kill me. I watched TV, read, and did some puzzles, but time is still dragging. If things get any worse, Noir won't need to send someone to kill me, I'll die of boredom."

"I know this isn't easy for you, but the alternative to boredom isn't worth thinking about," Cortez said. "I'll be right back, I need to have a word with the inspector."

"You will tell me about your hearing when you get back, won't you," Sofia called after Cortez as he headed for the door.

"If you think it'll keep you from getting bored," Cortez said, though he doubted that.

• • • •

"I WAS TOLD YOU'RE STILL attached to the case," Jacinto Jovellanos, the inspector who had been placed in charge of Sofia's protective detail, commented when Cortez walked into the dining room, where he was playing cards with a couple of the officers under his command.

"I expected that someone would let you know what's going on," Cortez said, dropping into the empty chair at the table. "Has there been any trouble today?" He had heard nothing from Vega or any of his men since the attack on the previous safehouse, but he wasn't convinced they were safe from another attack.

"No, nothing much has happened today. A delivery van dropped off a new fridge at number three this morning, and number eight had a package delivered this afternoon, but that's it for people who don't belong here. I think we're safe," Jovellanos said, as he had each day they had been there. "I doubt Noir will find this place, let alone attack us here. Even if he does, he won't be successful. About all we have to worry about is boredom while we wait for Noir to be extradited and put on trial."

"I think you're being optimistic, as I've said before," Cortez said. "The evidence suggests that Noir has a source, either in the department or in Interpol. Someone who was able to give him the location of the last safehouse, and that means there's a good chance he'll find out about this place. Even if his source isn't able to find out about this house, we're in the middle of a small neighbourhood of people who have at least some idea of what is going on. We've been as discreet as we can, but two vehicles with officers and agents in a small cul-de-sac is a bit of a giveaway that a police operation of some kind is going on. The parents probably won't say anything, if only because they won't want to have to worry about their families being put in danger. There are five children of various ages here, though, and they also have some idea of what is going on. Any one of them could let slip something that gets back to Noir. It would be an accident, but that won't help us."

"We've been over this," Jovellanos said as he tossed several Euros into the pot. "And I'm not about to discuss it again."

"I didn't imagine you would." Cortez had got tired of trying to persuade both Jovellanos and their superiors that the cul-de-sac was not a good place for Sofia's safehouse. It had been made clear to him that his only role was to entertain Sofia and keep her out of the way of the security detail.

• • • •

"COME ON, TELL ME WHAT happened in the hearing," Sofia said the moment Cortez joined her on the sofa. "Are you in trouble?"

"Probably, but that doesn't matter right now," Cortez said with an indifferent shrug.

"So, what did they say?"

Cortez smiled. "They said my methods were unorthodox —I suppose that's better than saying they were potentially illegal — but that I was forced to employ them because of Francisco's unwillingness to either believe or act upon the information I got from my sources."

"So, what happens now? Is he going to be punished?" Sofia had been surprised by Pizarro's refusal to do anything, even when he was told where to find Noir's men.

"Probably not, not seriously anyway," Cortez said in a resigned tone. "He's been taken off the case, and it's likely that his next promotion will be delayed, but other than that, I doubt anything much will happen to him. He's too well-connected, thanks to his father-in-law. There's more chance they'll try and put the blame on me, but not until this situation's over. They won't do anything that might upset you, or otherwise interfere with the possibility of them securing a conviction against Noir."

"You mean they let you off, for now, because they don't want to upset me?" Sofia couldn't believe that senior police officers would do that.

"I doubt that was the only reason for their decision, but it was almost certainly a part of it. It's always possible they actually believe in the decision they came to. Until the official hearing happens, though, which is unlikely to take place before Noir's trial, there's no way to be sure what's really going to happen. I might get all the blame while Francisco gets off, or they might actually put the blame on Francisco, though I think that's unlikely. They might even decide that no-one deserves to be blamed." Cortez had been around for long enough to know that the final decision would be as influenced by politics as it would be by the facts.

"So, you could still end up in trouble?"

Cortez shrugged, as if to suggest that anything was possible, and then sought to divert Sofia by asking, "What's on TV?"

24

Paris

• • • •

WITH AN EFFORT, YVES concealed how nervous he was as he approached the bench where Jean-Paul was waiting for him. With each step, his eyes darted around him, searching his surroundings. He was worried that Noir had decided the failure in Spain was his fault and he was going to be punished for it.

The closer he got to the picnic table without seeing any sign of trouble, the safer Yves felt. There was still the possibility that Jean-Paul was going to kill him personally, but since there was nowhere nearby for anyone to hide, he could at least feel confident that he wasn't going to be ambushed.

"Morning," Yves greeted Jean-Paul while discreetly checking to be sure he could get to his gun without difficulty, should it prove necessary. He was sure it would be futile for him to put up a fight if the order had been given to kill him, but he had no intention of simply giving in and allowing himself to be killed.

"This is where the witness has been moved to," Jean-Paul said without preamble, sliding a folder across the table. "Mr Noir has given instructions that you are to have her dead by this time next week; her, Marc, and Julian. Their locations and the details of the security assigned to protect them are in there as well."

Yves was surprised to hear that Julian was alive and in the hands of the police. Since that was the case, he was even more surprised that he was not only being allowed to live but was being given another chance to complete the job, though the deadline for it dismayed him.

Even if he was able to put together a plan quickly, and it went perfectly, it would take a miracle for him to accomplish the task he had been given.

Reaching out, he pulled the folder towards him and opened it. A quick skim of the contents was enough to tell him that Jean-Paul's source, whoever he or she was, had incredibly good access to the investigation taking place in Spain. Only someone intimate with the investigation could have come up with the information in the folder.

"A week is nowhere near enough time to come up with a plan that has any chance of succeeding," he said after he had finished reading. "If this information is correct there's a dozen people protecting the witness. Without the time to plan properly it'll take a small army to be certain of killing her. It'll take longer still, and more men, to take care of Marc and Julien."

Unconsciously, he shook his head. He couldn't believe that even Philippe Noir, who was known for his impatience and impetuosity, could think that a week was enough time to complete the job he had been given.

"Mr Noir was very definite about the length of time you have to do the job," Jean-Paul said. "How many men will you need to get it done? You can have as many as you think necessary. Within reason."

Yves was trapped, and he knew it. There was no way out for him. If he refused to do the job he would be killed, and if he failed to kill Sofia Torres, Marc, and Julian, he would be killed. He couldn't even run for it. If he did that, he would have to spend the rest of his life looking over his shoulder, afraid that every shadow hid a hitman sent by Noir to punish him, and it would only be a matter of time before he was found.

"By now I imagine the protection detail are familiar with everyone who lives there and what they drive, not to mention their regular visitors. The moment anyone or anything they don't recognise enters the cul-de-sac they're going to be running a check,"

Yves said, certain that anything or anyone that seemed the slightest bit suspicious would be intercepted as quickly and as discreetly as possible. "Probably about the only thing that could get down there without arousing suspicious is..." His voice trailed off as the idea occurred to him.

"What?" Jean-Paul asked. It didn't make much difference to him, but he was curious to know what Yves had thought of since he hadn't been able to come up with a way to get close to the safehouse without being detected.

"A delivery van," Yves said after a few moments. "The cops will notice it and check it out, but if that check shows the van is genuine, they won't pay any attention to it. I'm not sure what would be the best course of action after that, but I suppose the start of a plan is better than no plan at all."

Jean-Paul nodded his agreement. "You're free to use whatever plan you wish, just don't fail again. How many men do you want?"

"A dozen," Yves said without hesitation. "I'm going to need at least as many as there is cops protecting that damn woman, and I'll probably lose half of them, if not more. If I'm lucky, I'll have enough men left to deal with Marc and Julian. We'll need to smuggle weapons in with us this time, or you'll have to get someone to do it for us."

"Why? You can just buy weapons when you get there like you did last time, can't you?"

"I don't think that's a good idea. If I'm right about someone knowing we were there before, and according to your source I am, then the most likely suspect is the guy I got the weapons off. I'd rather not take more risks than necessary. I'm sure you know some way of getting weapons into Barcelona in time to meet Mr Noir's deadline."

He wasn't prepared to admit it, or even suggest it with his body language, but he hoped Jean-Paul would not be able to get the weapons to him, at least not without providing him more time to plan and increase his chances of success.

"Not personally, but I'm sure someone in the organisation can manage it. I'll talk to a few people once we're finished here and let you know what arrangements can be made. I'll tell you who's available to go with you as well. I'm sure I won't have any difficulty getting a dozen volunteers by tonight."

"I'm sure you won't. It would probably be best if the men you pick travel to Barcelona either singly or in pairs to avoid attracting attention," Yves said. "I hope to be there by early evening, if I can sort everything I need to in time, so I should be able to organise somewhere for the men to stay. If I wait for them and the weapons to be organised it'll eat into the time I have for planning, and I don't have much time to spare." He got to his feet. "I'd best get going so I can get started."

"You'll want to take this with you." Jean-Paul held out the folder he had brought. "If I were you, I wouldn't waste any time."

"I don't intend to." Yves took the folder and walked away without another word, his mind racing as he considered the predicament he was faced with.

25

Barcelona

· · · ·

"DON'T FORGET THE PLAN," Yves admonished the man in the passenger seat before shutting the door on the van so he could walk down the road towards the cul-de-sac where Sofia Torres was being protected.

He knew the plan he had put together over the five days since being given the job was risky in the extreme. It was all he had been able to come up with in the time available to him, however, and none of the men sent to help him had come up with anything better.

As he walked the short distance to the cul-de-sac, he mentally reviewed his plan for what seemed like the thousandth time. Every detail was engraved on his mind, and he had gone over it often enough to ensure his men knew the plan intimately, but he couldn't help worrying that something would be forgotten, and it would be the difference between success and failure.

A minute after he turned off the main road, his phone rang. He tried not to think too consciously about the fact that he was almost certainly being watched as he reached into his jacket for his phone. Just as he tried not to think about the people watching him, he tried not to make it too obvious that he was watching the house where Sofia Torres was being protected.

· · · ·

"WHAT HAVE YOU GOT?" Jovellanos demanded as he bounded into the front bedroom, where two officers were keeping watch on the cul-de-sac. He was followed by Cortez.

"A white male, mid-to-late-thirties," one of the officers reported while his partner continued to watch the unidentified man who was moving slowly in the direction of the house. "We spotted the weapon when he reached into his jacket for his phone. We're searching for an I.D. now." He played back the appropriate section of the surveillance footage on the laptop next to him.

Jovellanos silently watched the fifteen-second clip twice with Cortez before he said or did anything. "Keep watching him closely," he said finally. "I'll send a couple of men to intercept him. There's a chance this guy's just a diversion, so we all need to remain alert." Taking out his radio, he called the officers in the surveillance van. "Keep an eye out. If this guy's been sent by Noir, he's not going to be alone. The rest of his men are bound to be somewhere nearby."

"Yes, sir," came the reply as the two officers in the van re-focused their attention on the entrance to the cul-de-sac.

• • • •

"OKAY, I'VE GOT TWO guys heading my way, both with submachine guns," Yves said into his phone as he watched the pair walk out the front door of the house. Showing, supposedly by accident, that he was carrying a weapon was a risk, but a calculated one. Silently, he prayed that he was right, and the officers would try to arrest him, rather than simply gunning him down. "You can come in now."

"Drop the phone and get your hands in the air!" one of the officers yelled as he and his partner cautiously approached the suspected gunman.

Relieved, Yves tried not to smile as the first part of his plan worked out just as he had hoped it would. He let out the breath he had been holding while he did as he had been instructed and lifted his hands above his head, while letting his phone drop to the ground.

• • • •

"WE HAVE A VAN APPROACHING, sir," came the report from the surveillance post as Jovellanos watched the events taking place just a couple of houses from where he was.

"What sort of van?" Jovellanos wanted to know.

"It's alright," the officer replied after a moment. "It's just a delivery van. We've seen it and the driver a few times in the past week or so. He's been checked out, he's clean."

"Keep watching," Jovellanos instructed. "The rest of Noir's men must be somewhere nearby. Don't let them catch us by surprise."

"Yes, sir."

• • • •

IN OBEDIENCE TO HIS orders, the delivery driver turned his van into the cul-de-sac and drove at a steady speed towards the end. His eyes darted nervously in every direction as he drove, but they kept coming back to the man crouched in the footwell of the passenger seat and the gun in his hand; he flinched every time the gun moved so much as a millimetre.

"Fire as soon as you get a shot," Pierre, the gunman, called out to the men hidden in the back of the van as he took out his phone to call the driver of the second van. "We're almost in position. Come in as soon as you hear the first shots," he instructed unnecessarily. Almost before he had finished speaking there came a burst of sustained gunfire.

Since there was no longer any need to conceal himself, Pierre got up from his hiding place, grabbed the steering wheel, and shot the driver. With the man dead he reached across him to open the door and shove his body out, he then slid behind the wheel.

"Brace yourselves," he called out as he accelerated.

• • • •

IN DISBELIEF, JOVELLANOS watched as the two officers he had sent to apprehend the armed figure were cut down by a hail of bullets from the van he had been certain was safe. To make matters worse, he saw the driver of the van shoved out as it accelerated towards the house.

"All positions, we're under attack," he shouted urgently into his radio, not that the call was necessary since the sound of gunfire was loud enough to wake those officers who were asleep following their duty on the night shift. "I repeat, we are under attack. Team Two, continue to watch the rear. Everyone else, take up positions at the front of the house."

Leaving Jovellanos to give his orders and direct his men, Cortez hurried downstairs to the living room, where he found Sofia behind the sofa. He had a bad feeling about what was going to happen with the van if it wasn't stopped, and he was sure the living room was the last place in the house they wanted to be. Unceremoniously, he dragged Sofia out of the room, ignoring her demands to be told was what going on.

• • • •

YVES WAS GLAD HE HAD been ordered to lie face down on the pavement when his men opened fire on the officers approaching him. Even knowing his men were aiming at least three feet above his head he couldn't help flinching and praying, which he only stopped doing when the gunfire stopped and he heard the van pick up speed.

Cautiously, he lifted his head and looked around to be sure it was safe. When he saw that the two officers were on the ground and weren't moving, he pushed himself to his feet so he could get a better look at what was going on.

The delivery van, which they had intercepted earlier that morning along with its driver, was being hit by numerous bullets but wasn't slowing. He didn't have time to worry about the van, though, for the two officers who had been using a supposedly non-descript van as an observation post were running towards him.

Darting over to the bodies on the ground he grabbed up the submachine gun dropped by the nearest of them and turned towards the approaching officers so he could shoot them. He stopped with his finger on the trigger as the van containing the second half of his men raced into the cul-de-sac, it ran down the two officers without slowing before taking up a position in the middle of the street.

Yves forgot about the officers the moment he saw them hit by the van, if they weren't dead, they were at least no longer a threat to him, and instead made for the safehouse. Before he could get there a deafening crash announced that the delivery van had smashed its way into the living room, as his plan had called for it to do.

· · · ·

THE SHOCK OF SMASHING through the wall into the house stunned Pierre, and the men with him. They recovered more quickly than the officers in the living room, though, and they swarmed out of the van with their weapons at the ready.

Crouched at the side of the van, Pierre listened to the sound of gunfire as his men engaged the officers who had taken refuge behind the furniture in the living room. The officers returned fire for a short time, but it wasn't long before the gunfire died away, telling Pierre they had all been dealt with and the living room was free of opposition.

"Numbers," he called out to his men when the room had fallen silent.

"Two," came back the call, closely followed by, "Four." A moment later, in a voice that was clearly trying to control a measure of pain, came the last call, "Five."

The numbers told Pierre that Jules, Charles, and Marcel were still alive, though Marcel was injured, while Matthieu was either dead or otherwise unable to respond.

"Two and Five, you head for the kitchen, Four, come with me." Pierre gave his instructions crisply as he lifted his submachine gun and left the protection of the van. He felt confident after the early success of Yves' plan and had to force himself not to become overconfident.

While Jules and the injured Marcel headed for the kitchen, which he wasn't even sure had anyone in it, Pierre gestured for Charles to approach the dining room from the opposite side to him. In order to keep his partner safe, he fired a long burst through the partly open door while Charles moved closer. They then swapped roles, with Charles providing cover for Pierre as he approached the dining room.

There was a single burst of return fire from the dining room that was cut off abruptly, suggesting the gunman had been hit.

Once Charles had reloaded and was ready to cover him again, Pierre darted through the doorway to make sure the room was secure. He realised he had been tricked when he was forced to dive out of the way to avoid a burst of gunfire that missed him by the smallest of margins. If he hadn't spotted movement just before the shots were fired, enabling him to dodge out of the way, he would have been killed. Remaining on the floor, he shoved a chair out of the way to try and get a clear shot at the man who had nearly ended his life.

He was so intent on the officer in the dining room with him that he didn't see the other officer who appeared from the passage that led to the kitchen, and thanks to the covering fire being provided by Charles he didn't hear him. He had no idea the man was there until bullets tore into his side and back.

Charles heard the gunfire in the passage but assumed it was from Jules and the injured Marcel. It was only when he saw Pierre had been hit that he realised his mistake. Cautiously, he poked his head around the doorframe and then fired a quick burst to cut down the officer in the doorway when he spotted him.

After dealing with that officer, he rolled into the room to avoid the shots from the man Pierre had been after. As he rolled, Charles emptied the remainder of his magazine, aiming below the table. Two chairs were thrown backwards by the bullets, and he saw his target had been hit, though he was still alive and returning fire.

Charles cringed away from the expected impact and scrambled back towards the door. At the same time, he fumbled to insert a fresh magazine into his weapon. He had just succeeded in doing so when a bullet slammed into his shoulder. The impact threw him backwards and snapped his head up, allowing the next two bullets to hit him under the chin and explode out the top of his head.

• • • •

FROM HIS POSITION BEHIND the van, which had been turned sideways to provide as much protection as possible for his second team, Yves watched the front of the house. When the gunfire from the ground floor died out, he took out his mobile phone, which he had retrieved before taking cover behind the van.

Yves swore when he got no answer. He had no idea if Pierre was injured or dead, or if his phone was damaged, and that left him with no clue to what was going on in the house.

"I think we've got a problem," he called out to William, who was in charge of the second team at the other end of the van.

"What sort of problem?" William called back after firing a five-round burst at the movement he spotted near the corner of the left side bedroom window.

"I can't get hold of Pierre. You need to send some guys in to check out what's going on and deal with those officers on the first floor." Though he had no idea how the situation stood in the house, he knew that four of the officers assigned to protect Sofia Torres were dead. That meant there was still up to ten people left in the house, though, not including Sofia Torres, assuming the information from Jean-Paul's contact was accurate.

Against those ten men, Yves had seven, including himself, whom he was certain could fight. That meant the situation was against him. He had no choice but to proceed, however. So long as he had men in a fit state to continue, he had to do so.

"Take three men and get in there. Find out what's happened with Pierre and finish the job. I'll stay here with the other two and cover you."

• • • •

FROM THE MASTER BEDROOM of the neighbouring house, Cortez watched the four men race from the van to the safehouse. He could tell there was still people at the van, but he guessed there was only two or three, which was a lot better than six or seven.

"Stay here," he told Sofia as he left the bedroom and made his way out of the house, exiting through the kitchen door, whose window he had smashed so they could get in.

The effort of climbing the fence had been almost too much for him the first time he did it. The second time, he was sure it would have been easier to kick the fence down and walk over it. He was far too out of shape to be doing anything that even remotely approached that level of energetic behaviour.

Once he was over the fence, Cortez scanned the garden, his gun at the ready, in case any of the attackers were there. When he was sure the garden was clear, he made his way into the garage, where he saw that his car had survived the assault undamaged to that point. He was relieved to see that, not because he had any affection for the car, but because he needed it.

• • • •

THE LARGE HOLE IN THE front of the house provided William and his men with an easy way into the house, and the van that had made it gave them protection from the gunfire that came from the dining room.

While William and one of his men provided covering fire, filling the dining room doorway with gunfire, the other two moved forward to take up positions on either side of it. They then took up the role of keeping the officer's head down while William and the other man approached. Within a minute of them entering the house, the officer in the dining room had been dealt with.

26

Yves was caught by surprise when a car burst through the garage door at the side of the safehouse. It took him a moment to recover, and when he did, he brought up his gun to fire at the car, which he saw was being driven by Sergeant Cortez, the man Jean-Paul's source had identified as being closest to Sofia Torres.

The car swerved violently as the bullets struck the windscreen and Yves tracked the vehicle with his gun as it raced down the cul-de-sac. He fired until his gun was empty, his bullets leaving a series of small holes in the vehicle, though the damage did nothing to stop the car.

"Shit!" he swore when Cortez's car skidded out onto the main road before disappearing from sight. "Get in the van," he ordered the two men with him. "We're going after that son-of-a-bitch. You drive, Guy."

While Guy swung the van around, Yves dialled William's number. The sharp crack of gunfire was all he could hear for several moments after the call was answered, and he had to wait for it to abate before he could deliver his instructions.

"The witness is gone," he said, speaking quickly to avoid being drowned out by anymore gunfire. "She's making a break for it in a car with the sergeant. I'm going after her with Jacques and Guy. You and the others stay here and finish off everyone in the house, but don't let yourself get trapped. If backup turns up for those officers, get out of there, we've got other work to do so I don't want you getting killed."

"You can be sure of that. The moment we hear sirens, we're out of here," William said. "The only guys left are upstairs and charging the stairs would be suicide, but I've got a plan. Don't worry about us, just get after the witness and deal with her."

• • • •

SKIDDING AROUND THE corner, Cortez ignored the blood that ran down his face from the cuts caused by the shattered windscreen and kept one eye on the road ahead of him and the traffic he had to contend with, and the other on his rear-view mirror. He wasn't sure if he was going to be chased by any of those who had attacked the safehouse, but if they did come after him, he wanted to know about it straightaway.

When he saw the van race out of the cul-de-sac in pursuit of him, he pushed his foot down still further on the accelerator and swerved from one side of the road to the other, dodging in and out of traffic. A chorus of angry beeping and rude gestures rang out in response to his wild driving, but he paid them no mind, focusing instead on staying ahead of his pursuer and avoiding crashing into any of the other road users.

He had no sooner offered up a fervent prayer that those in the van would avoid shooting at him while they were in busy streets with lots of people around when his rear windscreen disappeared in a hail of bullets.

As he spun the wheel to take the next turn, Cortez wondered where all the other police in the city were. He had called in a report of his situation, and his location, but there was no sign of any backup or support of any kind.

• • • •

CROUCHED IN THE DOORWAY near the foot of the stairs, William considered his situation while his men fired at every movement they saw near the top of the stairs. There was no sign of them hitting anyone, but they kept firing in the hope they would get lucky.

"You two stay here and keep this up. Andre, you come with me." Without waiting for an acknowledgement of his instructions, he left the doorway and made his way into the kitchen.

"We're looking for something flammable," he told Andre, who was looking at him questioningly as he pulled open cupboards and checked bottles and tins.

Andre nodded in understanding. "I'll look in the garage."

William found nothing of use in the kitchen, but Andre did find a bottle of turpentine and a half-filled can of petrol in the garage. It wasn't much, but it was enough for what William had in mind.

One thing that worried William as he tore a tea-towel into strips to use as wicks for the crude Molotov cocktails he was making was the absence of sirens. He had expected to hear them long before then and the lack made him wonder what was going on.

"Okay, I think we're good to go," he said after he had prepared a third cocktail. "We'll go out into the garden and toss two of these into the back bedrooms. The third one goes up the stairs. Those bastards will be caught between fires on both sides and burn to death."

"Better than us trying to shoot our way up the stairs to get at them," Andre said, a mixture of relief for avoiding such a suicidal action and relish at the thought of police officers burning to death in his voice.

Before he was even out the back door, Andre had his lighter out. A quick glance at the bedroom window above made him realise it wasn't a good idea for him to try and throw a cocktail through it. There was too great a chance the bottle would simply bounce back and then he would be the one likely to burn to death.

Swapping the cocktail to his left hand, he lifted his gun and fired a quick, three-round burst to shatter the window. As an afterthought, he fired a second burst to shatter the window of the other bedroom, and with that done he dropped the weapon, so it hung from the shoulder strap, while he lit the wick on the bottle in his other hand.

He was drawing his arm back to launch the bottle when he saw movement in the nearest of the two bedrooms and a tongue of flame seemed to reach out towards him.

As if in slow motion, William, who was still by the back door, saw Andre drop the bottle he was holding as he was knocked to the ground by the torrent of bullets that thudded into his chest.

The contents of the bottle spilled out, igniting as it flowed over the wick, and set the grass ablaze. In seconds the flames had jumped to Andre's clothes, and from there they raced up and down his body.

William saw the flames licking at his friend's skin and hair, yet he neither moved nor made a sound. He wanted to go to his friend in case there was any hope of saving him but he was sure he would be gunned down if he did, as Andre had been.

Instead of going to Andre, he lit the wick on the first of his Molotov cocktails and stepped away from the door. Tense, and ready to dive for safety at the slightest movement from above, he edged out into the garden, being careful to avoid the flames that were spreading rapidly across the dry grass.

The moment he had an angle to do so, he lobbed the cocktail through the smashed window of the bedroom he was sure the gunfire that had killed Andre had come from. He then darted back into the relative safety of the house. He glanced back briefly at the body of his friend, which was being consumed by the flames, and then forgot about him and returned to Luke and Mathieu. There was nothing he could do for Andre, and trying would only put him at risk.

He knew from their questioning looks that Luke and Mathieu were wondering what had happened to Andre, but he was more concerned with finishing his job so they could get out of there than in answering them.

"Make sure that bastard keeps his head down," he instructed as he lit the wick on his remaining Molotov cocktail.

He waited until he was sure the officer at the top of the stairs was hiding behind whatever cover he had, and then William stepped out from the doorway so he could toss the cocktail he held. The flaming missile bounced once, right at the top of the stairs, and for one horrible moment he thought it was going to tumble back down towards him. He breathed a sigh of relief when it bounced forward instead of back.

• • • •

THE SOUND OF CURSING from the head of the stairs brought Jovellanos out from the front bedroom, where he was watching the cul-de-sac. He already knew the situation was becoming critical, with his men downstairs dead and no sign of the backup he had been promised, he didn't need more trouble.

No sooner had he reached the door than he saw that Rodriguez, the officer he had set to watch the stairs, was on fire and flames were spreading along the carpet and climbing the walls of the passage.

Jovellanos was frozen to the spot as he watched Rodriguez stumble along the passage, getting closer and closer. He tried to get out of the way, but his body didn't seem to want to respond to the commands his brain was giving it.

It was only when Rodriguez fell on him that he rediscovered the ability to move. He tried to back away but wasn't quick enough. Flames leapt from Rodriguez's clothes onto his own before he could get out of the way, and swearing he let Rodriguez fall to the floor as he hurriedly returned to the front bedroom, tearing off his burning clothes as he went. Quick as he was to strip off, he could still feel the flames burning his skin and hair.

"We've failed and we're in big trouble," Jovellanos told Montoya. "It looks like it's just you and me left," he said as calmly as he could while stamping on his shirt and jacket to put out the flames. "And we've got a fire up here, right outside the door. If that bloody backup doesn't arrive soon, we're going to burn to death before we have to worry about being shot by those bastards downstairs."

How things had come to this, he couldn't imagine. He had thought his preparations were good enough to ensure Sofia Torres was safe from any attempt by Philippe Noir's men, but he had been proved very wrong.

"We might be alright, sir, I think I can hear the backup now."

Jovellanos strained to hear what the younger man had.

• • • •

"I THINK IT'S TIME TO get out of here," William said over the sound of approaching sirens.

He doubted there had been time for the fires he had started to kill everyone upstairs, but there was nothing he could do about that, nor did it matter. Their target was no longer there according to Yves, so there was no point in them staying and risking their lives any further just to kill a few cops and Interpol agents.

Darting across the passage, in case by some miracle the officer at the head of the stairs was still alive and a threat, he entered the dining room, and from there he led his men into the living room. The engine was still running on the delivery van and he quickly climbed behind the wheel while his men got into the back.

Less than two minutes after first hearing the sirens that heralded the approach of more police, William had freed the van from the wreckage of the house's front wall, turned it around, and was heading out of the cul-de-sac.

He was aware the van was liable to draw the attention of everyone they passed because of how damaged it was. He wasn't concerned about that, however. They only had to go a couple of streets before they could ditch the van in favour of the car they had prepared in readiness for their escape.

• • • •

CORTEZ TURNED CORNER after corner as he tried, and failed, to shake off the van following him, which drew steadily closer. He even went past a police station in the hope that the van would back off — it didn't.

Briefly, he considered stopping at the station, but his instincts told him he would be cut down by the gunmen in the van if he tried to make a run for it from the car.

As he turned yet another corner, it felt like his fiftieth, the van slammed into the rear of his car. He almost spun out of control, but after a fight with the steering wheel he managed to keep the car going in a relatively straight line.

Cortez felt the van slam into him a second time and he gripped the wheel until his knuckles went white as he fought to control the car. Before he could straighten up again, the van hit him once more, and this time the impact wrenched the steering wheel from his grasp and sent the car spinning. The car stalled as it spun, but he had no time to fully appreciate his predicament before the van slammed into the side of the car.

Frantically, he tried to restart the engine as he felt the car begin to tip, and for about twenty yards he was pushed sideways down the road on the passenger side wheels before the car tipped over completely. It landed on its roof, where it continued to slide for a short distance as the other traffic on the road swerved to avoid it.

• • • •

YVES BROUGHT THE VAN to a skidding halt the moment the car tipped over and jumped out so he could hurry to it with Guy and Jacques. Sergeant Cortez was struggling to free himself from the wreck, but he ignored him and dropped to his knees to look for Sofia Torres. There had been no sign of her during the chase, but he was sure she had to be there. He was wrong, however.

"Ou-est-elle?" he demanded of Cortez, who had been dragged from the car by Guy and Jacques. "Where? Where is she?" he asked in English after realising he was speaking in French, which Cortez might not understand.

Cortez smiled. He knew he was going to die whether he told the man what he wanted to know or not, so there was nothing to gain by answering him. He wouldn't have done so even if he thought it would save his life. He had set out to protect Sofia by drawing at least some of her attackers away, and he was pleased to see that he had succeeded. He was determined to keep doing what he could to protect her, no matter what happened.

"Where's the girl?" Yves screamed, angered that he had been tricked in such an obvious way and by the mocking smile which was the only response he received.

"He's not going to talk," Guy said, trying to pull Yves away from the figure at his feet. "Forget about it. We've got to get out of here. The cops'll be here soon. The girl's probably back at the house. William will have dealt with her by now. We've got other things to do. If we don't leave now, we're going to end up dead or in jail."

"Fucking bastard!" Yves yelled angrily. Lifting his gun, he fired a three-round burst into Cortez's face, destroying the smile that tormented him. He then turned away from the body and the wrecked car to stalk back to the van.

He took a savage delight in running over Cortez's body as he raced away down the street.

27

"Is she alright?" Bright asked the moment he reached Meteiros.

"That's hard to say," Meteiros said without turning away from the house, where fire-fighters were attempting to put out the blaze started by Noir's gunmen. "From what Inspector Jovellanos told me before he was taken to hospital, Miss Torres was not upstairs with the men he had there. He said Sergeant Cortez was with her, but whether they were still downstairs or if Cortez got her out of the house after the shooting started, he doesn't know."

"So, there's a chance she could be alright."

Meteiros shrugged. "There's a chance, but I doubt it. If Cortez managed to get her out of the house and to safety, we'd surely have heard from him by now to tell us that. That suggests she was still in the house, and according to Jovellanos the attackers had control of the downstairs when they started the fire, which means she's almost certainly dead. I imagine her body will be found by the fire-fighters as they make their way through the house, and that will be the end of this case," he said regretfully.

No sooner had he said that than a car sped into the cul-de-sac. A dozen officers spun around to aim their weapons at the car as it braked sharply to a halt a short distance from Meteiros and Bright.

"I think you'd better tell your men to relax," Bright said when he saw how tense everyone was. He was sure it would only take a sneeze to startle one of them into firing, and the others would almost certainly follow suit. "He probably lives in one of these houses and is now wondering what the hell is going on and wishing he hadn't come home."

"He doesn't live anywhere near here," Meteiros said, his gaze intent as he watched the man who had got out of the car, his hands held out to show he was unarmed. "And it wouldn't be the best idea to have my men relax, not while he's around."

"Why? He doesn't look as if he's here to cause trouble, and even if he is, I doubt he'd be able to do much with a dozen armed men around him. Not unless he's a suicide bomber." Bright didn't imagine that was the case, the man didn't have the look of someone who was prepared to die.

"He's more dangerous than a suicide bomber," Meteiros said as he continued to watch the man cautiously, while wondering what he was doing there at the time. He doubted his arrival was a coincidence. "He's one of the most dangerous men in the city."

"I gather you know him." Bright followed Meteiros as he slowly approached the man, who seemed oblivious to the submachine guns aimed at him. Bright couldn't help but admire the man's cool. He was sure he wouldn't be half as relaxed if he had that many weapons trained on him.

"Not personally, but I know who he is. At this time, he's probably the second most powerful criminal in the city, if not the country. If he's here, we might have a bigger problem than we originally thought. I can't imagine why he's here if it isn't to make things worse for us. I just hope we don't have cause to be glad of all the guns we've got here.

"Good morning, Mr Vega," he greeted the man in a carefully controlled voice.

"DCI Meteiros," Vega returned the greeting. He was pleased to see the consternation on Meteiros' face at being recognised by him. "This saves me the effort of tracking you down. Am I right in thinking this is Special Agent Bright from Interpol?" he asked.

"I am," Bright said, surprised the man knew his name. "Is there a reason you were looking for us?" He couldn't think what such an apparently dangerous Spanish criminal could want with him, or why he would turn up at the scene of a gunfight between police and a group of French hitmen in search of him. The timing and the location couldn't be a coincidence, he was sure of that.

"Yes. Miguel Cortez asked me to," Vega said, as if there was nothing unusual in a police sergeant asking a criminal to find a DCI and an Interpol agent. "He said one or both of you would be here, and if you weren't I should track you both down and get the two of you together."

"Why did Sergeant Cortez tell you to do that?" Meteiros wanted to know. "For that matter, why did Sergeant Cortez contact you at all? He could have contacted us both himself. Where is he anyway?"

"I have no idea," Vega said. "When I spoke to him, he was being chased through the streets by a van containing several armed men. I believe he did attempt to contact you both but was unable to reach either of you. As for why Sergeant Cortez contacted me, I believe it was because he needed someone he could trust."

"Why would he feel he could trust you with whatever he needs the two of us for?"

Vega smiled. "I guess you could say we have matters of mutual interest at this time. At least, the two of you, along with Sergeant Cortez and my employer do."

"What is this matter of mutual interest?" Bright asked, though he thought he knew.

"Sofia Torres."

"I think you'd better talk quickly," Meteiros said sharply, resisting the urge to yell for his men to arrest Diego Vega. "I want to know everything you know about Sofia Torres."

"Why would Sofia Torres be a matter of interest between us?" Bright asked, trying to inject some calm into the situation.

"I doubt Mr Vega has any interest at all, but he works for Tomas Abrantes, who is the brother of Roberto Abrantes, so the question is, why is Tomas Abrantes interested in Miss Torres? I suggest you start talking, Mr Vega, or the situation could turn very unpleasant for you."

"He is interested in Sofia Torres because he is as keen as you to see his brother's killers brought to justice, if not more so."

"Okay." Meteiros was sure Vega wasn't telling the whole truth, if he was telling the truth at all, but he accepted it for the time being. "So why did Sergeant Cortez tell you to find us?"

"Because he wanted to make sure Sofia Torres is safe."

"Maybe he should have thought of that before he went driving off, because Miss Torres is dead," Meteiros said.

"Are you sure?" Vega asked.

"As sure as we can be," Bright said. "She was either killed by the men who attacked the house or by the fire. We won't know which until the fire's out."

"You're going to be disappointed, or more probably relieved, if you think you're going to find Miss Torres' body in that house," Vega said indicating the burning building.

"Why do you say that?"

"Because that's not where she is."

"How do you know?"

"How do you think I know. Sergeant Cortez told me where he hid her before he drove off to distract Philippe Noir's hitmen."

Meteiros started at the mention of Noir. "You seem to know a lot about this situation. I think we should take you in for questioning, see just how much you know."

"I wish I could say I'm surprised, but I'm not. In fact, my lawyer is waiting for my call to say you've taken me in," Vega said, making it clear he had planned ahead. "Before you do that, though, don't you think it would be sensible to let me take you to Miss Torres. I'm sure you're more interested in getting her somewhere safe than you are in talking to me."

"Fine, but no funny business." Meteiros signalled his men to keep their eyes and their guns on Diego Vega.

Vega looked around for a moment to find the location he had been given and then he set off towards the house where Cortez had left Sofia Torres.

"Are you suggesting that Miss Torres is here?" Bright asked when Vega knocked loudly on the front door of the house neighbouring the still burning safehouse.

"I'm not suggesting anything, Agent Bright," Vega said without turning away from the door. "This is where Miguel told me he put Miss Torres before he drove off to divert the attackers."

"And is she still alive?" Meteiros asked.

"I wouldn't have a clue. She was when Sergeant Cortez left her, according to him. Anything could have happened after that. Miss Torres," Vega called out loudly after banging on the door a second time, before taking a couple of steps back so he was visible from the windows of the house. "Miguel Cortez sent me to find you."

• • • •

CROUCHED IN THE MASTER bedroom, Sofia listened to the banging on the door and the man calling out to her. She made no attempt to go down and open the door, however.

She hadn't moved from the bedroom, where Cortez had told her to hide, since he left to draw off the men Noir had sent to kill her. Even when the backup for her protection detail and the firefighters had arrived, she hadn't left the bedroom.

She had crept to the window so she could look out on the cul-de-sac and see what was going on, but had been mindful of the instructions Cortez had given her and had simply watched the firefighters struggle to get the blaze next door under control while resolutely staying out of sight.

"Miguel said you would understand the phrase 'pastry wizard'," Vega called out. He didn't have a clue what the code phrase meant, but he imagined it had some significance to both Sofia Torres and Miguel Cortez, and that was why it had been chosen.

Sofia felt relief wash over her when she heard the phrase Miguel had told her to listen out for. She hadn't been told who would be coming to tell her it was safe, only that someone would, and she should trust no-one unless they knew the phrase he had given her. That was why she hadn't revealed herself when she saw Special Agent Bright arrive.

Leaving the window, she crawled to the door of the bedroom. She couldn't bring herself to get to her feet while she was still in sight of the window, just in case someone was still out there, waiting to shoot her.

Once she was out in the passage and couldn't be seen through the window, Sofia got to her feet and slowly descended the stairs to the front door. When she reached it, she hesitated. She had heard the code phrase she had been told to listen out for, but in the space of just a couple of weeks there had been multiple attempts on her life, and she found herself unwilling to open the door.

"What did you say?" she called through the door finally, one hand on the catch.

"Miguel Cortez told me to tell you that he is the pastry wizard," Vega said. He waited to see if there was going to be a response, and when there wasn't he spoke again, "I'm here to take you somewhere safe, or at least to make sure you are looked after by people who can keep you safe." He had his doubts about that since the two men he had been told to take her to had been responsible for her protection from the start, and under their care she had almost been killed on three occasions.

"Miguel sent you?" Sofia asked uncertainly once she had the door open.

"Yes," Vega said. When he couldn't get hold of either DCI Meteiros or Special Agent Bright, he asked me to come and get you out of this house. I was supposed to keep you safe until I could find these two, but they were already here when I arrived. They'll see to your safety now."

"Where's Miguel?" Sofia asked as she looked dubiously at Bright and Meteiros.

"I'm afraid I don't know," Vega said apologetically. "I only know that he was leading several of the men who were sent to kill you away from here when he contacted me. I don't know where he was when he called, or where he was going, only that he was doing his best to protect you."

Meteiros stepped in then. "I don't think we have the time to talk about this right now, Miss Torres, we need to get you somewhere safe."

"But what about Miguel?" Sofia asked insistently.

"I'll have officers looking for him just as soon as I can arrange them," Meteiros promised. "You have to come with us now, though, we need to get you to safety."

"I haven't been safe since I told you people what I saw and heard at Mr Abrantes' estate," Sofia said. "Three times they've tried to kill me. Three times. Despite you protecting me. I won't be safe until you put Noir behind bars. Assuming you're able to do that." Her anger and disbelief, caused in part by the stress of what she had been through, were obvious. "The only reason I'm alive right now is because of Miguel. If it wasn't for him, I'd have been killed several times, but you'll only get people looking for him when you can arrange it."

"I appreciate that you're unhappy and concerned about how things have gone, and you feel we haven't done a very good job of protecting you up to this point. You cannot change your situation now, though. Mr Noir knows about you, and he will continue to send people to try and kill you so long as you are a threat to him. If you don't come with us and accept our continued protection, they'll find it easy to do so, and when you're dead he'll walk free. You owe it to the officers who have died protecting you to do everything possible to stay alive and testify against Noir and put him behind bars."

Reluctantly, Sofia accepted that Meteiros was right. Whether she liked it or not, she had little choice but to accept the continued, dubious, protection of the Barcelona Police and Interpol.

28

P ARIS

• • • •

"YOUR COUSIN IS AN IDIOT. Does he think he's Al Capone, and this is nineteen-twenties Chicago?"

Jean-Paul ignored the tone of the question. "I couldn't begin to say what Philippe thinks of himself, but I am certain he is fully aware of what year and city he is living in."

"Really? I wouldn't be so sure of that. In the past month he has been responsible for the deaths of somewhere in the region of thirty people, either directly or indirectly. That's bad enough, but he actually seems to think he can avoid going to jail for them."

"You're paid to do what Philippe wants, just as I am, Rene. You're an intelligent man, you should know better than to question how he conducts his business. People who do that tend not to last long in this organisation."

"Blind obedience is more often a failing than a virtue," Rene Dubois, the corrupt Interpol agent who supplied Noir's organisation with information, remarked. "Blind obedience to your cousin's orders has resulted in more than..." He fell silent as the lift came to a stop and the doors slid open, and he was forced to remain silent when a middle-aged lady entered the lift and it descended to the ground floor.

As soon as the woman got out, Dubois pressed the button for the top floor. "More than thirty deaths if you include the massacre at Tomas Abrantes' estate. For all those deaths, Mr Noir has failed to eliminate the witness to his original massacre."

"You're wrong, the witness is dead," Jean-Paul told him.

Dubois shook his head. "The witness is alive." He realised the news would not be received well but he couldn't help that. He was paid to ensure Noir and his organisation received accurate information, not information Noir liked.

"Are you certain?"

The news was not good, but Jean-Paul couldn't help feeling a measure of relief at hearing it. It had been his intention to pass on the news of Sofia Torres' death to his cousin later that morning. It would have been embarrassing, not to mention hazardous to his health, to have to tell his cousin he had been wrong.

"Very certain. Miss Torres was alive and safe, and in a new location, as of seven this morning when I spoke to my contact, though I don't imagine she's very happy, given the sergeant she befriended was killed by your men yesterday," Dubois said. "Not only is the witness still alive, but every effort your cousin has made to have her killed has made the situation worse. Yesterday's effort has probably succeeded in ensuring that he will spend the rest of his life behind bars in a Spanish prison."

"I think you'd better tell me everything that happened yesterday," Jean-Paul said.

"From what I've been able to gather, Sergeant Cortez, who was mentioned in the file I gave you the other day, got Sofia Torres out of the house before your men got inside. He hid her in a neighbouring house and then drove away from the safehouse, making your men think he had Sofia Torres with him. While one group of your men gave chase, the rest of them continued the fight in the house and ultimately set fire to the first floor before making their escape."

"Did they catch up with him?"

"Yes. I can only assume that when the two groups of your men met up and compared notes, they assumed Sofia Torres had been upstairs in the safehouse and had burned to death in the fire, which would explain the false report you received. I was told the local police are keeping her continued healthy status as quiet as possible in the hope of avoiding any further attempts on her life."

"Well, thank God you heard the annoying bitch is still alive."

"It's what I'm paid for," Dubois said. He didn't care about praise, only that he was paid for the information he supplied. "I have more to tell you. Last night, the remaining men from your assault group invaded the hospital where your man Marc and the other guy caught by the Barcelona Police were being kept under guard."

"What happened?" Jean-Paul suspected things had gone badly since he had not heard anything of the events at the hospital. It was just a question of how badly.

"I don't know all the details. I'd guess I don't know even half of them. But what little I do know is that your men succeeded in getting close to the room where the two men were being protected before they were discovered. At that point a gunfight broke out. When it was over, three of the officers protecting the two men were dead, as was one of the men your men were there to kill. I don't know which one, I haven't got that information yet."

"What of the men I sent?"

"Three dead, one captured, and the other two escaped."

The look on Jean-Paul's face revealed what he thought of that. By anyone's standards it was a bad result.

"What you should be more concerned with is the effect this attack will have on those the Spanish Police have in custody."

"What do you mean?"

"I mean, the decision to have the men killed to prevent them talking to the police will almost certainly backfire. The attempt is likely to convince the men in custody that they owe Mr Noir no loyalty, and that they should make a deal if they can: what they know for immunity or reduced sentences. I would if I were in their position, wouldn't you?" Cousin or not, if he were arrested, Jean-Paul would have to be stupid not to at least explore the possibility of a deal in Dubois' opinion. "Since any deal these men cut will most likely involve selling you out as well as Mr Noir, I believe the time has come for you to persuade your cousin to look outside his organisation for the help he needs to avoid dying in jail."

"Say what you mean," Jean-Paul said sharply. "I'm not in the mood to try and work out what it is you're trying to tell me."

"I mean it's time for Mr Noir to hire a professional hitman, an assassin, someone who can eliminate his problems without the slaughter and failure you've had so far."

"And just where do you think I'm going to find a professional hitman?" Jean-Paul stopped talking abruptly as the lift came to a stop and the doors opened. There was no cause for concern however, they had simply reached the top floor. Realising that, he pressed the button to descend again. "This isn't a movie, you know. It's not like professional assassins advertise openly on the internet."

"I'm aware of that." Bending, Dubois opened the bag at his feet and took out an envelope. "In here you'll find three files. Each man is either a known or suspected hitman, a professional. I know nothing about any of them other than what is in their files, so I can't advise on who to approach. I'm sure you'll make the right decision, though."

"You're not able to make any kind of recommendation?"

Dubois shook his head. "The German is elderly, and it's suspected that he's no longer as active, so you might not want to go with him, but beyond that, no. All I can tell you is that all three men are considered extremely dangerous and are clearly very good since none of them has ever been caught by any police or intelligence agency. If I'm able to get more information on the men, or the situation in Spain, I'll pass it along, but I can't promise anything."

When the lift reached the ground floor again and the doors opened, Dubois stepped out and left, his departure hurried but not incautious.

Only when he was several streets from where his meeting with Jean-Paul had taken place did he relax his search for anyone who might be either following him or conducting surveillance.

29

"Has Yves dealt with that damn witness and the others yet?" Noir demanded the moment he had been escorted into the room where his lawyer waited for him and the door had been shut, with the guards outside.

Olivier grimaced. He wasn't happy that it had fallen to him to deliver the bad news. He would have preferred it if Jean-Paul had been able to tell his cousin what had happened in Spain but that wasn't possible. The only visitor who could speak to Noir without them being recorded was him, since their meetings were legally privileged.

"He failed," Olivier reported, bracing himself for the inevitable explosion.

"What!" Noir surged to his feet, knocking his chair over. "What do you mean he failed?" he demanded. With an effort, he controlled his anger and lowered his voice before the guards came in to find out what was going on.

Olivier quickly recounted everything that Jean-Paul had told him, ending with the recommendation given by Dubois.

Noir was silent for several long moments as he took in what he had been told. Finally, he said, "What do you think?"

"You should do it," Olivier said without hesitation, having had plenty of time to consider the situation and the alternatives open to Noir, who wasn't just a client but also a friend. "Sending your own men to take care of the problem has done nothing but make it worse. I think it's time to hire a professional and make sure things are dealt with."

"How much is it likely to cost?"

"I have no idea. Does it really matter, though?" Olivier asked. "If you don't deal with the maid and the others, you're going to spend the rest of your life in a Spanish prison." *And it might not be as long a life as you expect*, he thought but didn't say.

"You're right," Noir agreed. When it came to keeping himself out of jail, he was prepared to do anything and spend whatever was necessary. "Have Jean-Paul make the arrangements and have him take care of Yves and whoever he has with him as well."

• • • •

WITH GUY, THE ONLY remaining member of the group he had taken to Barcelona, Yves left the airport and made for the taxi rank. There was a long queue of people waiting for taxis but before they could reach the end of it, they were joined by two men who steered them away from the queue.

"Mr Renault would like to talk to you," the man on Yves' left, who was huge in both height and muscle, said, controlling his normally loud voice with an effort, so as not to be overheard by those they passed.

"Where are we going?" Yves asked. He recognised both men and realised he was in trouble — being met by Julian and Louis could mean only one thing — and his mind raced as he considered ways to escape.

"You'll find out when we get there," Julian told him as he led the way to where his car was parked.

• • • •

"WHERE ARE WE?" YVES asked when he was told to get out of the car. The journey had been circuitous, taking them through parts of Paris he was unfamiliar with, and he didn't recognise where they had ended up beyond that they were on a construction site.

"It doesn't matter," Julian said, his voice booming now there was no reason for him to keep it under control.

When the four of them were out of the car, Julian led the way across the construction site to a spot where they could all see that the concrete of the foundations was still wet.

"Where's Jean-Paul?" Yves asked, looking around. He wasn't surprised that Jean-Paul was nowhere to be seen, but he had been hoping that things would prove to be different to how he expected. "I thought you said he wanted to talk to us."

"Don't be naïve," Louis said, speaking for the first time. "You knew Mr Renault wasn't going to be here. He's being watched and can't afford to be seen anywhere near anything like this."

"You've screwed up, not once but twice," Julian rumbled. "Consider yourself lucky you've lived this long."

Yves was about to say something when he heard a loud gasp and saw Guy collapse to the ground, a knife in his heart. Before he could react he felt a sharp pain in his chest, and when he opened his mouth to speak he coughed up blood. Everything went black, and then he collapsed in a heap next to Guy.

For a moment, Julian looked down on the two men, watching for any sign that they might still be alive. When he was sure they were dead, he bent to retrieve his knife from Yves' body. He wiped the blade clean on Yves' jacket and then put the knife away before hauling the body up.

With no apparent effort, he threw Yves into the middle of the wet cement, where his body floated on the surface. Guy's body followed Yves', and with the help of a pole located by Louis they soon disappeared beneath the surface of the cement. In less than two minutes there was no sign that anything had happened.

30

Barcelona

....

UNDER THE WATCHFUL scrutiny of a pair of officers, who showed every sign of being ready to fire at the first hint of trouble, Bright followed Meteiros up the ladder from the speedboat to the deck of the yacht.

Their identities had already been checked before they were brought out to the yacht, but they were still asked for their ID the moment they reached the top of the ladder.

"I feel like I'm meeting a head of state or royalty," Bright remarked as his ID was carefully scrutinised before being handed back.

"I'm not sure I'd go that far," Meteiros said, "but the president has apparently taken an interest in this case. I was told he has insisted this case be given the highest priority. I understand he isn't happy that a French national believes he can get away with killing so many Spanish citizens."

"I don't blame him. I wouldn't be very happy with the idea if I was in his position either. Where's Miss Torres?" Bright asked of the officer who had checked his identity as he slipped his ID card back into his pocket.

"I couldn't say for sure, sir, but I doubt you'll have much difficulty finding her, it isn't a big boat."

"Did you really think it would be difficult to find her?" Meteiros asked.

"No, but I wanted to avoid wandering around blindly if I could," Bright said as he crossed the deck to the hatchway that led down to the cabins. "I'm not sure it would be a good idea given how nervous the security detail is."

His footsteps echoed down the companionway and summoned another officer, who had his weapon aimed in their direction before he even saw them. He lowered his weapon when he recognised Meteiros.

"Miss Torres is this way, sir," the officer announced, indicating the doorway through which he had appeared.

"Are you certain this is the best way to protect Miss Torres?" Bright asked of Meteiros. He hadn't previously questioned the decision to put Sofia Torres on a boat to keep her safe, but now he had seen it, he wondered if it was the right way to protect her. "All an attacker would have to do is set fire to the boat or punch a hole in the hull and then wait for her to either burn to death or drown as the boat sinks." He kept his voice low to avoid being overheard by Sofia Torres.

"They'd have to get close enough to manage either of those things," Meteiros said. "I think that's why Sergeant Cortez came up with the idea in the first place. With four officers patrolling the deck and a radar system that's monitored constantly, it's nearly impossible for someone to get close without being spotted. And if they can't get close, they can't do anything to the boat."

"I suppose that's true. Good morning, Miss Torres," Bright said as he entered the lounge and saw Sofia sitting at a table.

"Agent Bright, DCI Meteiros. Have there been any developments in the case?" Sofia asked. She was torn between eagerness to hear that some positive progress had been made and that she was closer to being able to return to the life she had had before, and concern that any developments would be bad for her.

"We're just here to see how you're doing," Meteiros told her. "Is everything alright? Are you coping with the situation okay? Are you happy with everything?"

"What do you think? The only guy I really trusted to protect me, and someone I thought of as a friend, is dead, I'm stuck out here on a boat that belonged to my dead employer, and someone wants to kill me. You'll forgive me if I'm finding it a little difficult to be happy with anything right now."

"I can't say I'm surprised," Bright said sympathetically. "I don't think I've had a chance yet to tell you how sorry I am that your friend died. I don't imagine it's much of a comfort to know that he did so protecting you."

Sofia was surprised by the sincerity in Bright's voice and kept her head down, her eyes on the table in front of her to avoid showing her tears. "Miguel did what he thought was the best thing he could to protect me. If he hadn't led those men away, they might have figured out where I was. I'd be dead as well as him if that had happened, and you wouldn't have a case anymore. I know that's what you're both really concerned about."

"Yes," Bright admitted with a nod. "Noir's in a cell right now and won't ever get out, we hope, but I'm not prepared to take any more risks with your life than necessary."

"And you think because I'm out here on the water, I'll be safe from the men Noir will send to kill me?" Sofia asked. "For all you know he could send a battleship to make sure I can't testify against him."

Meteiros smiled briefly at that. "If Noir can get his hands on a battleship to send after you, I think we all might as well give up and find other lines of work. I think it unlikely that he'll discover where we have you, so I don't think there's much cause to worry, especially since the boat can be moved whenever and wherever we want, which we intend doing. I suspect that's one of the reasons Sergeant Cortez suggested it."

"Perhaps if you'd listened to Miguel, he'd still be alive," Sofia said bitterly.

"I regret what happened to Miguel as much as you, perhaps even more, but we cannot change what has already happened." Meteiros could tell from the look on Sofia's face that she didn't believe him but that didn't matter. "Is there anything I can arrange to make you more comfortable."

"Some films, or maybe some books. Anything to keep me occupied. Mr Abrantes' library is pretty boring. Or maybe a quick trial. The sooner all of this is over, the better I'll feel."

"I understand that, and I assure you, we are doing everything possible to get Mr Noir into our custody and into court as quickly as possible. Unfortunately, I am told that Mr Noir's lawyer is fighting hard to have the extradition request dismissed. If you give me a list of books and films you'd like, I'll arrange for you to have them."

31

Germany

• • • •

"MR RENAULT."

Jean-Paul started in surprised when the figure joined him. He had been scrutinising everyone who came into the bar, searching for anyone who even vaguely resembled the picture of Luke Caldwell that had been included in the file he had been given by Rene Dubois.

Despite his watchfulness, the figure, who bore no similarity to the man he was looking for — Caldwell was in his mid-thirties and slim, while this man was nearing sixty and overweight — had not only managed to enter the bar without being spotted by him, but had been able to get to the booth where he waited without him being aware of the man.

"Can I get you anything?" The question came from a waitress, who appeared within moments of the figure sitting.

"Whisky, no ice, thank you."

"Red wine," Jean-Paul ordered. "Caldwell?" he asked hesitantly when the waitress had returned with their drinks and then left again.

"I'll be your contact with him," Luke said, adopting a ploy he had used many times before when dealing with a client who insisted on a face-to-face meeting, that of pretending to be a go-between. "You can call me Der Bote. As you were told, Mr Caldwell does not meet clients in person. Your message said you have a job for Mr Caldwell."

Jean-Paul was silent for a few moments while he debated how to deal with this situation. He had expected to meet with Caldwell, despite being told that wasn't possible. Finally, he decided he had no choice but to proceed. "I do. At least my employer does," he said.

"What sort of job?"

"My employer is facing some legal difficulties, which he would like Mr Caldwell to clear up for him."

"I'll need some details to take back to Mr Caldwell," Luke said. "Without information he won't be able to say whether the job is feasible, let alone something he's interested in, and he certainly won't be able to say how much it's likely to cost."

"I'm sorry, but my employer has given strict instructions that I'm to give no information until the job has been accepted," Jean-Paul said. He had voiced his concerns about the instructions, Luke Caldwell was a professional after all, which was why they wanted to hire him, but Olivier had sided with Noir and insisted that nothing should be revealed until it was absolutely necessary, to avoid causing more problems.

"In that case, there's nothing for us to discuss." Luke downed his drink and made to leave the booth. When Jean-Paul stopped him, he went on, "If you're not willing to reveal anything about this job before it has been accepted, which Mr Caldwell won't do without knowing what he's getting into, then you can look elsewhere for someone to help Philippe Noir with his legal problems."

"Wait, please." The use of his cousin's name both surprised and troubled Jean-Paul, though he did his best to conceal it. "Please sit down. You're right, I work for Philippe Noir in France. I assume since Mr Caldwell knows who I work for he has some idea of the legal difficulties he is facing."

"Yes," Luke said as he slid back into the booth, without giving any indication of how much he or his 'employer' knew.

"Good. Well Mr Noir is having some problems with the Spanish authorities. The police in Barcelona are trying to extradite him so they can put him on trial."

"I'd say that's a problem for Mr Noir's lawyers to deal with," Luke said. "Mr Caldwell is a problem-solver for people whose problems can't be solved by more usual methods." He had gathered a fair amount of information on Philippe Noir's situation following the initial contact with Jean-Paul Renault. Because of that he could guess what it was Noir wanted to hire him to do. He wanted to hear it from the man before him, though.

"Mr Noir's lawyers are working hard on his legal defence," Jean-Paul said, "He isn't confident they will be successful, however, and he is not prepared to wait in a cell while his lawyers fight it out with Spanish officials."

"I can appreciate that. What is it Mr Noir would like Mr Caldwell to do to assist him with his difficulties?" Luke asked, again encouraging Jean-Paul to clarify things. He had no reason for thinking the man across from him was an agent for a police or intelligence agency trying to trap him, but he wasn't about to take any chances.

"The Barcelona police have two of Mr Noir's men in custody, and he is concerned that they might be persuaded to testify against him in exchange for immunity from prosecution. They also have under their protection a witness who can place Mr Noir at the scene of a crime."

"And."

Jean-Paul drained his glass and set it down. "This isn't really the place for us to go into details. Is there somewhere more discreet we can talk?"

"Sure." Luke preferred that they talk more privately as well, so he had no problem leaving the bar.

• • • •

"OKAY, MR RENAULT, I suggest you tell me what it is you want from Mr Caldwell so I can relay the information to him, and he can decide whether he is interested in the job," Luke said once they were in his car. He knew it was safe to talk there, the car he was driving then was completely unconnected to Luke Caldwell because he had 'borrowed' it from a couple he knew to be away for several days.

Reluctantly, Jean-Paul said, "Mr Noir wants you to eliminate his problems. He wants you to make certain the witness is not in a position to testify, should he be extradited, and that his men cannot make any deals with the Barcelona police."

"And how would Mr Noir like Mr Caldwell to do that?" There hadn't been enough time for him to research Jean-Paul and his employer as thoroughly as he would have liked, but Luke had learned that Philippe Noir's favoured method of dealing with a problem was inefficient, excessively violent, and caused more problems than it solved.

When Jean-Paul said nothing after several long moments, during which his face wore an expression of confliction and uncertainty, Luke said, "If you aren't prepared to say exactly what it is you and your cousin want done, perhaps you should look elsewhere for someone to take care of your problem." He looked significantly at the door at Jean-Paul's side.

Jean-Paul hesitated for a little longer and then accepted that he would have to be explicit if he wanted Luke Caldwell to accept the job and help his cousin.

"Mr Noir wants Mr Caldwell to kill the witness and the two men the Barcelona Police have in custody. He needs them dead before he can be extradited and before they can testify against him."

"What's the timeframe for accomplishing this?"

"That's hard to say. As soon as possible for sure, but how long there is before Mr Noir might be extradited and put on trial is uncertain. His lawyer is doing his best to get the extradition request quashed, but it's vital that Mr Caldwell deal with the problems as quickly as possible in case he's unsuccessful."

"He hasn't agreed to take the job yet," Luke reminded him. "What protection is there around the people Mr Noir wants taken care of?"

"One is in a police cell, so Mr Caldwell will have to go through a police station to get to him. The second is in hospital and will probably have several armed officers protecting him at the least, though I have no idea how many. As for the witness, I think it's safe to say she'll have a large number of officers protecting her, and they'll be prepared to open fire at the first sign of trouble. I don't currently know where the witness is being kept, but I have a source working to find out."

"Do you think your source will be able to get the information?"

"I have every confidence in him. He hasn't failed me yet. Will Mr Caldwell take the job?"

"I couldn't say. He'll decide that after I've relayed to him what you have told me. I imagine you'll have an answer within a day or two."

Jean-Paul was frustrated that he couldn't get an immediate answer, and he knew his cousin would be unhappy to hear the outcome of the meeting, but there was nothing he could do about it. He couldn't order Caldwell to take the job, nor could he intimidate him into doing so, especially through an intermediary, and to attempt either would only increase the chances of him refusing it.

Reluctantly, he got out of the car and headed down the road to where he had parked his rental car, so he could head for the airport and the late flight back to Paris he was booked on.

32

P ARIS

• • • •

JEAN-PAUL'S HAND SLIPPED inside his jacket when the living room light failed to come on. It wasn't that he really thought there was trouble waiting for him in the darkness, but he had too many enemies to take chances. Before he could get his gun out, he felt something cold press against his temple and his heart leapt into his mouth. He calmed quickly as he realised that if the person who had been waiting wanted him dead, he already would be.

Luke Caldwell pulled Jean-Paul into the room, spun him around, and shoved him into a chair. He then quickly ran his free hand over him, discovering the knife and the gun Jean-Paul carried, both of which he tossed across the room so they were out of reach.

When he was certain Jean-Paul was no longer armed, Luke turned on the lamp on the small table at the side of the chair. The light was weak, only sufficient to illuminate the pair of them and a small area of the room around them, but Luke was okay with that.

"I think there's a few things you neglected to mention when you spoke to my associate, Mr Renault," he said, stepping back to the edge of the light while keeping his gun on the man before him.

"What are you talking about?" Jean- Paul asked, doing his best to conceal the unease he felt at discovering that the intruder was the assassin he was trying to hire, and that he was not happy.

"You failed to mention that you are under surveillance by Interpol," Luke said. "They're very keen on knowing what you do, where you go, and who you speak to. They even have your apartment bugged. Or I should say they did have it bugged." He indicated several small items on the table next to the chair. "Fortunately, they have no idea that Der Bote is connected to me, and I am adept at spotting surveillance operations and evading them, so they have no idea that we have been in contact. Nonetheless, you should have made Der Bote aware that you're under surveillance so I could factor it into my considerations."

Jean-Paul shrugged. "It's an occupational hazard. I'm sure you can appreciate that. Are you here to kill me or take the job?"

"That depends on how much you're willing to pay."

"Mr Noir has authorised me to pay you one million Euros," Jean-Paul said without hesitation.

"And does Mr Noir think that a fair price for everything he wants me to do?"

"Yes. It's far more than he pays any of his men, even me. It's a very generous offer." If he thought Caldwell was going to be impressed by that, Jean-Paul was mistaken.

"The rest of his men," Luke said, "have so far failed to do anything more than kill a lot of Spanish police officers and some Interpol Agents. And in several cases get themselves caught. Whatever he pays them, it's too much. So, tell me, what exactly is it Mr Noir wants me to do for one million Euros?"

"I already told your man that in Berlin."

"Things could have changed since then. If I agree to take the job, I want to be certain of what is expected of me since there will be no further contact between us until the job is completed, so there can be no changes to what I'm hired to do. Be explicit."

"Very well." Jean-Paul eyed the bugs nervously, not convinced that they were no longer working. "In return for one million Euros, Mr Noir wants you to kill the two men the Barcelona Police have in custody and the witness, Sofia Torres, who, according to my source is being kept on a boat in Barcelona Harbour. Now, are you willing to take the job or not? If you aren't, I need to know so I can find someone who is."

"Do you honestly think a million is a fair price for this job? Because I don't. I have a different price in mind, and it's a lot higher than yours. Five million, sterling, not Euros, and that price is not open for negotiation." Luke took a slip of paper from his pocket. "Half is to be paid up front into this account. I'll be back tomorrow night, if the first payment has been made, to collect the information you have on the targets. One last thing," he said. "I choose where, when, and how the targets are eliminated. If you or your cousin have any problems with that, you'd better go ahead and look for someone else to take care of your problems."

He left then, disappearing so swiftly and silently that if it hadn't been for the disabled bugs and the slip of paper, Jean-Paul would have doubted he had been there at all.

The main light in the room blazed on after about thirty seconds, startling Jean-Paul, who hadn't moved. He remained in the chair for a while longer, until he had recovered from the shock of Caldwell's visit, and then he got to his feet.

Crossing to the window, he pulled aside the curtain just far enough for him to look out. He didn't know where the Interpol surveillance team was watching him from, whether they were in a vehicle or one of the buildings across the street, but he knew they were out there. It made him wonder how Caldwell had managed to get in and out of his apartment without being seen by them.

• • • •

AFTER WHAT HAD HAPPENED the day before, Jean-Paul was unsurprised by the bout of nerves he was struck with when darkness fell. He tried to keep himself distracted and relaxed while at the same time keeping alert for the arrival of Luke Caldwell. Even so, he was startled when the hitman spoke.

"Have you got the information I need?"

Jean-Paul jumped violently. "You scared the crap out of me," he said with an annoyed look at the wine he had spilled.

"You should pay more attention to your surroundings," Luke said. "You're in trouble if you can't tell when someone is less than ten feet from you in a quiet room. You should have known I was here the moment I entered the apartment."

"I'm sure if you were an ordinary killer, I would have, but you make a living from being able to sneak up on people," Jean-Paul remarked.

"True. Have you got the information?" Luke asked.

"Yes. I hope there's enough to satisfy you." Jean-Paul retrieved the envelope he had been given by Rene Dubois and handed it over. "This is all the information my source has been able to find."

"If I need anything else, I'll be in touch, but don't expect to hear from me until the job's done unless there's a problem." Tucking the envelope inside his jacket, Luke left the apartment as silently as he had entered it. He had been there for barely a minute.

33

Barcelona

. . . .

THE AUTOMATIC DOORS slid open at his approach and he joined the small queue of people at the reception desk. The officers on duty were efficient and he soon reached the counter.

"How can I help you, sir?" the constable asked.

"Agent Leclerc, from Interpol, I've been ordered to report to Agent Bright," he said in English with a heavy French accent.

It quickly became clear the constable hadn't understood him. Fortunately, the sergeant working alongside him had and she switched places with her subordinate.

"Good afternoon, sir, may I see some identification please."

"Of course." From the inside pocket of his jacket, Leclerc took out an identity card and handed it over.

"Everything seems to be in order," the sergeant said once she had examined the card. "If you'll excuse me a moment." Handing the card back, she moved away to a nearby phone, where she made a quick call before returning. "If you'll come through, sir," she said, opening the security door at the side of the counter so he could enter the station proper. "Special Agent Bright isn't available at the moment, but I'll take you up to the office he's using, you can wait for him there."

"Thank you."

Leclerc waited in Special Agent Bright's office for five minutes without any sign of the man, at the end of which time he left. "Could you tell me where I can find the restroom?" he asked of the first person he encountered.

He followed the directions he had been given until he was out of sight of the officer, and then he made his way down to the ground floor and along to the holding cells, the route to which he had memorised during the five days he had spent planning how to get to his targets.

"Special Agent Leclerc of Interpol, here to speak with Roland Baptiste," he told the duty officer when he reached the custody suite.

"Yes, sir. Interview room three is available, I'll have Mr Baptiste brought to you."

"Thanks, and could you arrange for a couple of coffees as well."

The coffees arrived at almost the same time as Roland Baptiste, who was pushed into a seat on the far side of the table.

Leclerc thanked both officers but said nothing to the prisoner until they had been left alone. "Whitener or sugar?" he asked of Baptiste, taking a packet of each from his pocket as he slid one of the drinks across the table.

"Who the hell are you?" Baptiste asked as he snatched up both packets, tore them open, and poured the contents into the cup nearest him.

"Special Agent Leclerc, Interpol. I'd like to ask you a few questions," Leclerc said.

"I already spoke to you guys, and I've got nothing more to say," Baptiste said.

"How can you be sure of that when you haven't heard what I want to ask you?" Leclerc asked as he watched Baptiste gulp at his coffee as if he hadn't had a drink in hours, which he supposed was possible.

• • • •

"WE'RE FINISHED HERE," Leclerc told the officer who opened the door to the interview room. "You can take Mr Baptiste back to his cell."

"Yes, sir." The officer moved to lead Roland Baptiste from the room.

Leclerc ignored the contemptuous look on Baptiste's face, which had been there throughout the short interview as he made it clear he wasn't about to cooperate, even if it meant a reduction in whatever sentence he eventually received, and with a nod to the duty officer as he passed him, he made his way out of the station and round to the parking lot where he had left his car.

It wasn't until he was several streets from the police station that Luke allowed himself to relax and smile, amused by the ease with which he had completed the first part of his contract. All it had taken was a disguise — a false moustache, white-blond hair, and a birthmark just above his jawline, all of which he had applied before leaving his hotel room — a false ID card, a phone call to get Bright out of the building, and a drug mixed into the packets of whitener and sugar he had given to Roland Baptiste. That and the courage to walk into a station full of police officers and security cameras.

A glance at his watch revealed that there was still half an hour to go before Baptiste would begin to feel the effects of the drug he had unknowingly ingested. That was more than enough time for him to make Agent Leclerc disappear as if he had never existed, which he hadn't, before anyone had a reason to look for him.

34

With a heavy sigh, Pizarro dropped into the seat across from Bright.

"I take it you've seen the report," Bright said, noting the look of dejection on Pizarro's face, which he could hardly blame him for.

Pizarro nodded. "I've read it, but I don't believe it. It's ridiculous that just because someone flashed an Interpol ID card, which should have been picked up on as fake, they were able to not only see a prisoner but be left alone with him so he could poison the guy." He shook his head disbelievingly. "Someone's going to lose their job over this, several people probably. We can't even be glad the guy who killed Baptiste was caught on multiple cameras because it's almost guaranteed that he was wearing a disguise. He'd have to be the biggest idiot in history to come in here and kill a guy without wearing a disguise."

"I think it's safe to say this guy isn't an idiot, and certainly isn't the biggest idiot in history," Bright said. "If I had to guess, I'd say Noir's hired himself a professional, and it wouldn't have mattered how carefully the ID he presented was scrutinised. Whoever Noir's hired would have made sure to have an expertly made false identity card. He would also have managed to poison Roland Baptiste even if he hadn't been left alone with him."

"What do you mean? How could he have done that? Surely if there had been even one officer in the room with them, he wouldn't have been able to poison Baptiste."

"You must have missed the part in the report where it said the poison was in the coffee Baptiste drank. It probably wouldn't have taken more than a second or two for the fake agent to slip the poison into the drink, and I imagine he's adept at doing such things without being noticed."

"Okay, so Noir's hired a professional hitman, and he's already knocked off one target. What happens now?" Pizarro asked. It chilled him to think that someone could make it all the way through the station to the custody area, slip poison to a prisoner, and then leave again without anyone suspecting a thing until it was too late.

"We increase the protection around Sofia Torres and Marc Delcroix, and we do everything we can to find the man Noir's hired before he can get to either of them. I gather your forensics people have fingerprinted and checked for DNA every inch of this station that he could have even looked at and are processing all of that data." Bright didn't say as much, given how dejected Pizarro looked already, but he doubted the forensics team were going to get any results from the wealth of fingerprints and DNA they were likely to gather.

Pizarro was silent for a few moments before saying, "We could move Delcroix to a different hospital, perhaps a private one, and increase the number of protection officers around him. It would probably be easier to protect him at a private hospital, where the staff are likely to be more discreet, as are any patients who are aware of the security operation, and there will be fewer people around to worry about. I have no idea what more we can do to protect Miss Torres, though. She's already on a boat that's being moved every twelve hours, with half a dozen protection officers, and the number of people who know where the boat is at any time is being restricted to only those who absolutely need to know. Short of putting her on a battleship and surrounding her with marines, I don't see what else we can do."

"If I thought you could arrange that, I'd suggest you do so. I hate to think what sort of hoops you'd have to jump through to get permission to have a civilian witness given protection on a naval ship, though." Bright suspected it would require permission not only from someone high up in the navy, but also from someone of ministerial rank in the government. "Putting Delcroix in a private hospital is a good idea, though. As you say, it will probably be easier to protect him there."

 . . . .

"DO YOU WANT TO TELL me how the hell this happened, Agent Bright?" Meteiros demanded.

The two of them were down the corridor from the room in Barcelona Royal Hospital where Marc Delcroix, Noir's killer, had been protected while his transfer to a private hospital was arranged.

"First Baptiste is killed in the middle of the day while in custody, by someone masquerading as one of your agents, and now Delcroix has been killed by someone masquerading as the doctor in charge of this case. Both times he's just walked in and killed one of Noir's men and then disappeared as if he was never there. How is that possible?"

"As I told Sergeant Pizarro earlier, Philippe Noir has almost certainly hired a professional hitman. That's why he was arranging for Delcroix to be transferred to another hospital," Bright said as he watched the trolley bearing Delcroix's body being wheeled away. "It's a pity he wasn't able to arrange things a bit quicker. Whoever Noir's hired, I imagine they're expensive. Someone this good has to be, but I don't suppose that matters to Noir right now. He's probably prepared to pay almost anything to keep himself out of jail. If you're looking for something positive, and I'm sure you are, there's only about half a dozen people across the whole of Europe good enough to have done both jobs, and Interpol takes a keen interest in their movements. With luck we should be able to figure out who is responsible for this, and soon."

"I'll believe that when I see it," Meteiros said pessimistically. "You guys apparently know who they are, yet they're still out there, that says a lot."

"Things don't work any differently for Interpol than they do for you guys," Bright said. "There are plenty of people right here in Barcelona that you and your officers know are criminals, of one sort or another, yet they continue to walk around free. These people didn't get where they are by being sloppy or incautious. We know who they are, we just haven't been able to get enough evidence against them yet. I've requested the latest information on the people most likely to be responsible for this. We should have it soon. In the meantime, you need to warn the men protecting Sofia Torres. They need to be as alert as possible after this."

"I'll warn them. I'll also give them orders not to let anyone on the boat if they're alone, even if it's you or me. This guy's clearly able to make himself look like other people, so I'm not taking any chances."

"That's a good idea. It might be better to take things further, though, and tell the protection detail not to let anyone on the boat at all, and to take into custody anyone who tries to get on, no matter who they claim to be. If no-one's allowed on the boat, it won't matter who Noir's killer tries to disguise himself as. Or perhaps organise a password to identify people with permission to board the boat."

Meteiros nodded. "Good idea. I'll call them immediately and give them their new instructions."

While Meteiros took out his phone so he could make the call, Bright turned to Pizarro, who had been standing a short distance away during the conversation.

"Has Doctor Ramirez been able to provide any useful information?"

Pizarro shook his head. "He's still in shock. He hasn't said much at all. When I asked who attacked him, he said, 'it was me, it was me'. I assume he meant the person who attacked him was disguised to look like him, not that he attacked himself. I don't think we're going to get anything more out of him until tomorrow at least. What I don't understand is why Noir's hitman didn't kill him. Why did he leave him alive to be a witness?"

"Professionals rarely kill people they don't have to," Bright said. "And there was no reason for this guy to kill Doctor Ramirez. It's possible he'll remember something that will help us once he gets over his shock, but I doubt it. I imagine all he'll be able to tell us is that the guy who knocked him out and tied him up looked exactly like him, which we already know. It's possible your forensics team will be able to get something from the areas we know he was, but I can't say I'm hopeful.

"Sorry, I don't mean to be so pessimistic, especially since I said I wished Noir would hire a professional so we wouldn't have so many random and unnecessary deaths, but right now I think our chances of catching this guy are pretty low unless he does something sloppy, and I don't think that's likely. All we can do is hope we get lucky and do everything we can to make sure Sofia Torres stays safe."

"Just what do you think the chances are of us managing that?" Pizarro asked pessimistically.

Bright chose not to answer that question.

35

The night after successfully dealing with Roland Baptiste and Marc Delcroix, Luke crouched at the edge of Barcelona marina, a pair of powerful night-vision binoculars pressed to his eyes.

Two miles out was the yacht on which Sofia Torres was being kept. He had been watching it for over an hour as it dropped anchor at its new position and the protection team settled back into their routine.

When he had determined, as best he could, that there was nothing new for him to worry about, he lowered the binoculars and stuffed them into the waterproof bag attached to his belt. He then pulled down his facemask and picked up the mouthpiece of his aqualung. He sucked on it for a few seconds to be sure the air was flowing before slipping over the edge into the water. He bobbed there for a moment before slipping beneath the surface.

The swim out to the boat was strenuous, but nothing he couldn't deal with, and after almost forty minutes he reached the anchor chain. Treading water, he removed his aqualung and secured it to the chain for his return swim. With that done, he brought his bag to the surface so he could take out his gun, spare clips, stun grenades, and his night-vision goggles. He clipped the bag onto the aqualung strap when he was done and focused his attention on the deck above him.

He trod water for over a minute while he watched and listened for any sign that his presence had been detected but saw and heard nothing to worry him. When he was sure the officers on deck had no idea that he was there, he slowly and silently climbed up the chain. He stopped when his eyes were above the level of the deck so he could scan for the two officers on duty in the aft section. It only took him a moment to find them, and a moment more to take care of them with two quick shots.

As they slumped to the deck, he climbed over the railing and made for the bow with silent steps and his senses alert for trouble, so he could deal with the two officers there. He managed to drop the first of the pair without a problem, but the second officer was evidently more alert than the others. He managed to fire off a three-round burst from his weapon as he collapsed to the deck. The bullets were no danger to Luke for they went up into the sky, but the noise shattered the silence of the night.

With a muttered curse for the vagaries that could ruin the most carefully thought out of plans, Luke hurried back towards the stern. He was almost there when an officer, who was either a lighter sleeper than his colleagues or had still been awake, appeared from below deck.

Luke reacted instantly, firing an unaimed shot that struck the officer high on the chest and sent him tumbling back down the stairs. His gun clattered noisily against the floor of the companionway as it fell from his grasp, ensuring that anyone on the boat who hadn't been alerted to trouble by the gunshots now knew something was up.

When he reached the hatch the officer had appeared from, Luke crouched and peered around the edge of it. He drew back quickly as a burst of gunfire splintered the wood inches from his head. Another burst sent more splinters flying from the hatch and he retreated further.

From his belt he took a stun grenade, which he tossed through the hatch to bounce down the stairs. It exploded after a few seconds, filling the companionway with enough noise and light to render anyone within twenty feet who wasn't behind cover temporarily incapable.

He followed that by poking the muzzle of his gun around the hatch and swinging the weapon from side to side as he squeezed the trigger. He sprayed the companionway until a dull click announced the gun was empty. He ejected the magazine and shoved a fresh one in its place, cocked the weapon, and then risked a peek through the hatch. The two officers who had been firing at him lay unmoving in a tangle of limbs, clearly no longer a threat, which left only two officers for him to deal with according to the information he had.

Luke kept an eye out for Sofia Torres' remaining guards as he descended the stairs and cautiously checked each cabin on that deck. It was a nervous job for he knew each time he entered a cabin that one or both officers could approach him from behind and catch him by surprise, despite his alertness. Thankfully, that didn't happen.

It wasn't until he reached the last cabin, the stateroom that had been used by Tomas Abrantes, that he found the officers and Sofia Torres. He knew they were in there, and that they knew he was coming, but he wasn't daunted by that because he was prepared.

Standing to one side of the door, he pushed it open with the muzzle of his gun and tossed his second stun grenade into the cabin. The moment the grenade went off, he kicked the door wide and dived through, straight into a sustained burst of gunfire.

How the officer could see well enough to get his shots anywhere near him, Luke didn't know. That didn't matter though, what did was that he was hit multiple times, in the side and left arm. Two of the four bullets found the bulletproof vest he was glad he had worn, even if it had made the swim to the boat more strenuous, minimising his injuries. The air was forced from his lungs in an explosive gasp, and he felt as though he had been punched by a heavyweight boxing champion. The pain from that was minimal compared to the pain from the other two bullets that hit him, however. That was almost enough to make him black out.

With an effort, he fought back the darkness that threatened to overcome him and dragged himself out into the companionway, where he slumped against the wall to one side of the doorway once he was out of danger.

There was no time for him to assess the extent of his injuries, which he could tell were serious — his left arm hung useless at his side, and he could feel blood pooling under him from where the other bullet had managed to find a gap at the side of his bulletproof vest — for he could hear someone approaching.

Gritting his teeth, he raised his gun and aimed it at the doorway so he could shoot the approaching officer the moment he appeared. He then struggled to his feet.

Awkwardly, he took out one of his spare clips and tossed it through the doorway. He followed the clip into the cabin and was relieved to see that the trick, simple as it was, had worked. The last remaining officer had glanced away from the door.

With only one hand on his gun, his aim wasn't as steady as it could have been. At that close range, though, it didn't matter. It was almost impossible for him to miss, and his shots struck the officer in a diagonal from hip to shoulder.

Ignoring the officer, who slumped slowly to the floor, Luke turned to Sofia Torres. He watched her for a moment, his expression blank, as she surreptitiously tried to edge past him and out of the cabin, and then he fired once, hitting her in the chest. She fell sideways onto the bed before sliding off it to the floor.

His job finished, he allowed the pain of his injuries to wash over him. Slowly, he lowered himself to the floor, where he let go of his gun and reached into his pocket for his phone, which fortunately hadn't been damaged by the bullets that had struck him.

"The job's done," he said in a voice that trembled with the effort of talking through the pain when his call was answered. "You can come in now. I hope you know a good hospital that can keep quiet because I need..." He passed out from pain and loss of blood before he could finish what he was saying.

36

"Luke, are you there?" Bright listened in vain for any indication that his friend was alright but could hear nothing. "Damn. Get us there quick."

"Yes, sir," the coastguard officer at Bright's side said smartly. "You have the heading, Chief, full speed ahead," she instructed the chief petty officer at the helm. "Everything alright, sir?"

Her orders, which had come from high up the chain of command, were to do whatever she was told by Special Agent Bright without question, but curiosity was a hard thing to control.

"We'll find out when we get there," Bright told her, concealing the worry he was feeling.

Leaving the wheelhouse, he got the men and women waiting on the deck ready. He then leant on the railing in the bow as he searched the darkness ahead for a glimpse of the boat that held Sofia Torres while his mind wandered back almost two weeks to when he had received an unexpected visit from a former friend and comrade-in-arms.

• • • •

TEN DAYS BEFORE

• • • •

BRIGHT GOT THE SURPRISE of his life when he walked into his hotel room. Seated in the chair by the window, as casually as if he were at home, was a man he hadn't seen in more than a decade. He had served in the British Army with Luke Caldwell for five years, and though they had been friends, they had lost contact after he left the army and joined Interpol.

"Luke! Jesus, what are you doing here?"

"Hello, Ben," Luke said with an amused smile for the reaction he had received.

"What are you doing here?" Bright repeated his question after he had closed the door and moved further into the room. "I haven't seen or heard from you in years. I didn't expect to hear from you again."

"I think you'd better order us some drinks. You're going to need one when you hear what I have to say."

"I don't like the sound of that," Bright said, crossing to the phone on the bedside cabinet so he could call room service. "What'll you have?"

"Whisky, and you'd better make it a bottle."

"Okay, we've got drinks, so why don't you tell me what you're doing in my hotel room," Bright said once the bottle of whisky and two glasses had been delivered and the room service waiter had left.

"Is the name Jean-Paul Renault familiar to you?" Luke asked.

"Yes. He works for Philippe Noir, a big-time drug dealer in France. What's he got to do with you being here?" Bright asked. He had an idea, since he was aware that his former friend was suspected of being a hitman for hire, though he had made sure to avoid getting involved with the investigation, but he hoped he was wrong.

"He approached me the other day with a job from Philippe Noir."

"Given everything that's happened here over the past month, and what you apparently now do for a living, I can probably guess what he wanted to hire you to do. Are you going to do it?"

"I've accepted the job, and I've been paid half the money for it, but if I was going to do the job, I wouldn't be here, I'd be out planning the best way to get at the targets Noir wants me to eliminate."

"If you're not going to do the job, why did you accept it?" Bright asked, confused.

"A couple of reasons: you, and Sofia Torres," Luke told him. "I still owe you." He tapped his chest, indicating the spot where Bright had taken two bullets intended for him, bullets that would almost certainly have killed him, and had nearly killed Bright, resulting in his retirement from the army on medical grounds. "And Sofia Torres is an innocent. I've never been keen on killing innocents, it's unprofessional, as are the efforts Noir and his men have made to get to her."

"That doesn't explain why you accepted the job. Noir's not going to be happy when he discovers you've taken his money but don't intend going through with what you've been paid to do. He'll most likely send his men after you, both to get his money back and to send a message to anyone else who might think about ripping him off."

Luke shrugged. "He can be as unhappy as he likes, and he can send as many men after me as he wants. Given how well his men have done so far, I won't have anything to worry about. Besides, as I said, I owe you, and being hired by Noir gives me an opportunity to pay you back. I'm going to kill Sofia Torres for you, and Roland Baptiste, and Marc Delcroix."

Bright's confusion deepened. "You're not making any sense. First you say you're not going to do the job Noir's paid you for, then you say you're going to pay me back for saving your life by killing the people Noir wants you to kill. How does that pay me back? I've been trying to keep them alive so they can testify against Noir."

"I know." Luke refilled his glass and held the bottle out to Bright. "But if I don't kill them, Renault will hire someone else to do the job, and it might be someone who operates in a similar fashion to the men previously sent to kill Sofia Torres. That would mean more unnecessary deaths. Of course, when I say I'm going to kill them, I mean I'm going to fake their murders. If Renault and Noir believe that all three are dead, they won't send anyone else to kill them. And by the time they know they're still alive, it'll be too late."

"I guess that would work," Bright said. "I assume you have a plan for faking their murders."

"Not yet," Luke admitted. "I haven't had enough time to come up with one yet, I only agreed to take the job yesterday. Whatever plan we come up with, it can't involve any of the people currently part of the case against Noir, or part of Sofia Torres' protection detail. I'm sure it's not something you want to hear, but someone connected with this case has been bought. They've been telling Noir's people where to find your witness and what protection she has."

"I've suspected as much," Bright said, though he wasn't happy to have his suspicions confirmed. "The trouble is, I don't have a clue who it is."

"Renault told me he has a source in Interpol, but whether that's the only source he has, I don't know. He could have bought off someone from the local police as well, I doubt it would be hard. Since that's the case, the only person I can trust is you. I might not have seen you for a while, but I know you won't have been bought, so you need to find someone who hasn't previously been involved with this case to help us. Someone with the authority to arrange anything we might need, and someone you're sure can be trusted."

"I'll make a few calls," Bright said, downing his whiskey.

· · · ·

"I WASN'T TOLD THERE would be two of you at this meeting," Chief Superintendent Martinez said when Bright and Caldwell were shown into his study.

"That's because Agent DiMarco was not aware that my friend would be with me," Bright said, his Spanish heavily accented by tiredness and alcohol.

"Please, Agent Bright, your accent is butchering my language," Martinez said with a grimace. "I speak English."

"The accent doesn't improve any when he speaks English," Caldwell said in flawless Spanish. "He's a Cockney lad."

"You speak very good Spanish, but I do not think you are Spanish. Who are you, and what is your involvement with Special Agent Bright and this top-secret meeting?"

"My colleague is the reason for this meeting, sir," Bright said, settling into the seat he had been gestured to. "He prefers to remain nameless at this time, but he has brought a situation to my attention, and an opportunity, one I couldn't take to Detective Chief Inspector Meteiros."

Martinez was silent for a moment as he studied the men before him. "You have aroused my curiosity," he said finally. "What is this situation you cannot take to Meteiros? I assume this has something to do with the Abrantes-Noir case."

"Yes, sir," Bright nodded. "How much do you know about the massacre at Tomas Abrantes' estate, and everything that's followed?"

"I would guess that I know almost as much as you. Since the second attack on Miss Torres, I have insisted on receiving daily reports on the situation. I'd say I know everything that has happened up until four hours ago, when Meteiros delivered today's report."

"That will make things easier," Bright said, relieved that he didn't have to explain everything that had happened. "In the last couple of hours, thanks to my colleague here, I have been made aware of a very serious development."

"What sort of development?"

"Philippe Noir's cousin has hired a professional hitman to kill Sofia Torres and the two men your officers have in custody," Luke said.

"How can you be sure of that?" Martinez asked.

"Because I'm the hitman he hired."

"My associate is an undercover operative," Bright said when Martinez looked in concern from Luke to him. "Which is why he prefers not to reveal his name at this time."

It was a few moments before Martinez responded to that. "So, Philippe Noir's cousin believes you are a professional hitman and are going to kill the people who can put his cousin in jail for the rest of his life," he said finally. "That doesn't explain the need for this meeting, or the insistence on it being kept secret."

"Normally it would be a relatively simple task for Ben to arrange things so we can fake the deaths of Sofia Torres, Roland Baptiste, and Marc Delcroix. Unfortunately, Jean-Paul Renault, Noir's cousin, has indicated to me that someone on the inside of this investigation has been bought off. I know he's had dealings with someone inside Interpol, but I can't be certain that's the only person connected with this investigation who's been bought off.

"Faking the deaths of three people is not something that can be done by just Ben and me, we need help. That help needs to come from someone with authority, and someone we can trust not to be in the pay of Philippe Noir."

"And you think I'm that person."

"Yes."

"What is it you think I can do to help you?"

"You can arrange things. You have the authority to make whatever arrangements are needed to help us make this subterfuge work. We don't yet have a plan, but we will need everyone, especially Philippe Noir, to believe that all three targets are dead, and that means keeping them somewhere out of the way once their deaths have been faked. It also means running this operation without the help of anyone who has currently been involved with either the investigation or the protection of Sofia Torres. Will you help us, sir?" Bright asked.

Martinez thought about what was being asked of him for a few moments before nodding. "Do I really have a choice? The murders that have taken place here are headline news around the world and are making us look incompetent. The situation would be bad enough if a Spanish criminal was responsible for it. It is unacceptable that a French national believes he can act in such a way within our borders."

• • • •

SIX DAYS PREVIOUSLY

• • • •

"THANK YOU FOR SEEING me again at such a late hour, sir," Bright said as he was shown into Chief Superintendent Martinez's study.

"Given the situation, I could hardly ignore your request for another meeting," Martinez said. "I gather you have made some progress with your plans."

Bright nodded. "Yes, sir, we have the beginnings of a plan. There are arrangements that need to be made, but I think it's a good plan, despite its risks."

"Tell me about it."

"My colleague, whom Philippe Noir believes is going to deal with his problems, will infiltrate the station where Roland Baptiste is being kept using a false Interpol ID and administer a drug that will make it seem as though Baptiste has died. Once the drug takes effect Baptiste will be out of it for approximately twelve hours, during which time he will be declared dead. The doctor at the station will have to be in on the operation to be sure he doesn't reveal that Baptiste is alive.

"We'll need a safe place for both prisoners and Sofia Torres to be kept once their murders have been faked, somewhere that can provide the medical treatment Marc Delcroix is currently receiving.

He mostly just needs monitoring, but he could take a turn for the worse, so we have to be prepared for that. Have you been able to come up with somewhere yet, sir?"

"Yes. The headquarters of the Third General Subinspectorate of the army is not far from here, I believe it fulfils all your requirements. It's close enough to be reached in just a couple of hours by car, has medical facilities for the injured prisoner, and is secure enough to ensure that not only will the prisoners be unable to escape but Noir won't be able to get at them should he discover they are still alive. I think your prisoners and Miss Torres will be as safe there as they will be anywhere. In fact, having thought of using the base, I can't help wondering if it's necessary to fake their murders. All three of them could simply be transferred to the base for their protection, they would be safe there."

"They would only be safe from Noir's regular thugs. There are professional hitmen out there who could get to them even on an army base. It wouldn't be easy, but they could manage it, and Noir has the money to hire all of them if he needs or wants to, and I'm sure he's determined enough to stay out of prison to do that if it becomes necessary. At this point, I'm not sure there's anything he won't do to keep himself out of prison. That aside, there is an additional reason for going ahead with the plan to fake their deaths," Bright said. "The evidence against Noir is weak, especially if his men can't be convinced to testify against him, and they have proven unwilling to be convinced so far. Everything we have at the moment is either circumstantial or weak enough that Noir's lawyer can easily argue against it. Faking the deaths of Sofia and the other two provides an opportunity to get a solid conviction against Noir."

"How?"

"When everyone believes Sofia Torres and the other two are dead, his lawyer will get the extradition request dismissed. Once he's out, Noir will almost certainly want to meet my colleague, in his guise as a hired hitman."

"Why would he want to do that?"

"Either to offer him more work in the future; trying to get Sofia Torres has cost him a lot of men, or, more likely, to kill him so he can avoid paying the rest of the money his cousin agreed to. Whatever the reason, my colleague will be able to use the meeting to get Noir on tape admitting to the hiring of a hitman, and possibly ordering the other attempts on Sofia Torres' life, and that will be enough to put Noir behind bars for the rest of his life."

"You're right," Martinez said after thinking his way through what Bright had said. "Your plan will give us the best opportunity to secure a conviction against Noir. I just hope nothing goes wrong. There's a lot of interest in this matter at the highest levels of the government, and a failure to secure a conviction after everything that's happened could see all of us out of a job."

It didn't surprise Bright to hear that. Things had gone badly enough with the Abrantes-Noir case to date. If they weren't able to secure a conviction soon, he was sure the Spanish people would want an inquiry into the situation, and the government would give them one, and would find people to hold responsible.

37

Bright was startled out of his recollections of the events of the past week and a half by the shouts of the ensign as she ordered the launch lowered in preparation for the transfer of the first group to the yacht.

When he looked up, he saw the yacht bobbing up and down barely a hundred yards from the coastguard cutter. Pushing away from the railing, he made his way across the deck so he could climb down and join the group in the launch.

The trip over to the yacht took no time at all, and within five minutes of the first shouted order, Bright and the people with him were on board.

A quick search of the deck revealed that Luke wasn't up there, so while two of the army medics he had brought along checked the guards to be sure they were suffering no ill-effects from the tranquiliser darts they had been hit with, he descended into the interior of the yacht. He moved quickly, driven by concern from the abrupt end to the phone call from his friend, the third of his team of medics on his heels.

When he found him, he was alarmed to see Luke slumped on the floor of the last cabin in a pool of blood. "You'd better get in here," he called out urgently to the medic, who had stopped to check on the two unconscious officers in the companionway.

"I'll be there in a minute, I need to finish checking these guys out," the medic called back.

"No, get in here now," Bright ordered sharply. "There's an injured man in here. How bad is it?" he wanted to know when the medic appeared in the doorway of the cabin.

"I'll need to examine him before I can tell you that."

Bright waited anxiously a short distance away, his eyes never leaving his friend, as the medic checked him over. His concern increased with each passing second as the expression on the medic's face became ever more sombre.

"Well? Is he going to be alright or not?" he asked when the medic finally stood.

"I can't be certain. It's definitely serious. One bullet got past the side of his vest, and I think it's still in there. His arm's been shattered as well, and he's lost a lot of blood. If he doesn't get into surgery soon, things might not go well for him."

"That's going to be difficult to arrange," Bright said, as if the medic wasn't aware of that already. "It'll take some time to get back to shore. Ensign," he said into the radio he was carrying.

"Morales here, over," the ensign answered from the bridge of the cutter.

"How long to get back to base?"

"Thirty minutes or so," came the reply. "Is there a problem? Over."

"We have a guy here who needs emergency surgery."

"I can radio for a chopper. It could be here in fifteen or twenty minutes. It could get the patient to hospital before we could reach base, over."

"No!"

Bright was startled by the sudden exclamation. He had thought Luke was out of it. When he turned to his friend, he found him attempting to push himself up and being held down by the medic.

"No chopper," Luke said slowly and carefully, forcing the words out.

"We don't have a choice, you need surgery," Bright told him. "A chopper is the only way to get you into an operating theatre in time to save your life."

Luke continued to try and sit up, despite the pressure on his shoulder from the medic. "No chopper," he said with a slow shake of his head. "I've survived shit like this before. I'll be alright."

"You have a bullet somewhere in your lower abdomen, your arm is badly damaged, and you've lost a lot of blood. You need the bullet removed and your arm dealt with, that means surgery. A chopper can be here in twenty minutes, maybe less, and you can be in surgery in about ninety minutes," Bright told him. "If we don't get a chopper it'll take at least three hours to get you into surgery. You could bleed to death in that time."

"I'll take the risk," Luke said with a groan.

"You've already taken enough risks," Bright said. "Tell me again why we couldn't have handled this differently. There was no reason for you to put yourself at risk like this. If we'd told Sofia's guards what was going on, you wouldn't have been shot."

"You agreed that we can't be sure one of them hasn't been bought by Noir or Renault, or that they might let slip what was going on to someone who has." Every word was an effort for Luke to get out, but he kept going. "We did this to protect your witness. She's what's important, not me, that's why we did it this way. If you call for a chopper and have me rushed to hospital, it could blow the entire operation. We've got no way of being certain Noir wouldn't find out, and then this will have been a waste of time. Any surgery I need will have to wait until we get to the base. The surgeon there can sort me out."

"I'm not willing to take a chance on you dying because you're stubborn."

"I get paid to take chances like this. If I don't make it, you'll just have to forget about the second part of the plan. Just do what I say, Ben, we're doing things my way," Luke said in as firm a voice as he could manage when it looked as though Bright was going to argue further.

"Fine, it's your call," Bright said after staring hard at his friend for several long moments. "But I'd better not regret this. Ensign Morales, come in, over."

"Morales here, over."

"Cancel the chopper," he told her reluctantly. "We're not going to need it, over."

There was a brief period of silence, followed by, "Are you sure, sir? Over."

Bright was tempted to say no, and have her request the chopper despite Luke's determination, but he didn't. "Yes, I'm sure. But keep it on standby in case the situation changes."

38

"**I**s he going to make it?" Bright asked of the army surgeon who appeared as he was about to follow the bed bearing Luke down the corridor.

He had been waiting for news since Luke was taken in into the operating theatre, and the sight of his friend, still breathing after more than eight hours of surgery, was a relief, though he craved reassurance from someone with medical training.

He remained unsure that following his friend's instructions and taking him to the army base for surgery, instead of diverting to one of the hospitals in Barcelona, was the right thing for him to have done. He wouldn't be sure until he heard that Luke was going to be alright.

Several times during the long boat ride to shore he had been tempted to call for a rescue chopper. Why he didn't, he couldn't say, except that it was what Luke wanted. Not that his concerns had been lessened by that thought.

"Your friend seems to be a very tough individual. He survived the journey here, despite the blood loss, and he made it through surgery without any complications. I'd say he has a good chance of recovering, perhaps as high as sixty percent. The odds would of course be higher if he had made it into surgery sooner."

"Thank you." Bright sank tiredly against the wall. He was relieved to hear that the odds of his friend making it were over fifty percent. That was higher than he had expected. "When will I be able to see him?"

"He'll be in recovery for a few hours, and then he'll be moved to a ward if everything is okay, but when he'll wake is anyone's guess. If I were you, I'd get some sleep and check back later. Someone will contact you if anything happens. You'll excuse me, it's been a long time since I was woken during the night for an emergency bullet removal."

Bright remained where he was for a short while after the captain left, allowing his relief to wash over him, and then he pushed himself away from the wall and made his way out of the hospital.

The morning sun left him squinting after the artificial light he had just left but the fresh air was welcome, waking him enough to make necessary phone calls. He completed his calls during the walk to the barracks building that had been assigned to the Noir operation and he put the phone away as he stepped inside.

There wasn't much to the building: a communal entertainment area with a television, a couple of computers and games consoles, and some tables and chairs, a large sleeping area, a shower area, and several private rooms. Ordinarily the private rooms would have been used by NCOs and officers, but just then they were being used by Sofia Torres and the officers assigned to keep watch over the people 'killed' by Luke.

Bright looked around for any of the people brought in during the night but saw none. He figured they were still sleeping off the tranquiliser Luke had shot them with, which didn't surprise him since it was supposed to last for twelve hours.

"Morning," Bright said, dropping into a chair at the table where Special Agent Gonzalez, who was in charge of the group at the barracks, was playing cards with two members of his team. "How have things been?"

Gonzalez shrugged. "As good as they can be. Baptiste is still causing problems," he said with a glance at the Frenchman, who was sitting alone, "but Delcroix is behaving himself, not that he has much choice given his injuries. He's still over at the hospital under guard. The most he can do is bitch from his bed; he's done a bit of that apparently, but for the most part he's been pretty accepting of his situation. I guess he understands there's nothing he can do but accept things."

"What sort of problems is Baptiste causing?"

"Nothing major, just general bitching. He's not happy about being here. He doesn't like the food. There isn't enough for him to do. He doesn't like not being able to contact anyone. Blah, blah, blah. He gets whatever meals he wants from the kitchens, and he spends most of the day on one of the consoles, that helps to keep the complaints to a minimum. Don't worry, it's nothing I can't handle."

"Are you ready to deal with the new arrivals when they wake up?"

"Yes. The first of them should be up in the next couple of hours. With a bit of luck they'll wake up one at a time, so we can deal with them individually. It'll be easier than dealing with them in a group."

"Good. At least there shouldn't be anything else for you to worry about after today. You'll have no-one else coming to join you, last night's op was the final one, so all you've got to do now is keep everyone happy until we get Noir to trial. If Baptise causes you too much trouble, tell him if he doesn't like it here, he can always be relocated to solitary confinement in the stockade. I'm sure he'll like it there a whole lot less."

Gonzalez grinned at the thought of that. "I'll be sure to tell him. Are we actually able to put him in solitary confinement?" he asked.

"I'm sure it can be arranged if necessary. Do you need anything before I get going?"

"No, I think we have everything we need for the time being. If I think of anything, I'll let you know."

"Okay."

• • • •

"ARE YOU AT THE STATION yet?" Bright asked when Marie answered his call.

"Almost. I should be there pretty soon. What's up?" Marie asked. "I hope you've got something for the team to do today, we've all been pretty bored the last few days."

Since Roland Baptiste had been 'killed' in his cell, the Interpol team had been stood down from the Noir investigation while an internal review was conducted to determine if any of the team was responsible for passing information to Philippe Noir and his organisation.

"There is something for the team to do, but I'm not sure you should be glad your boredom is over," Bright told her sombrely. "I'm sorry to say that Sofia Torres was killed during the night."

"What! Are you sure?" Marie asked. She knew Philippe Noir had hired a professional to take care of his problems, but she still found it hard to believe that someone had managed to reach the yacht and get past the officers on board to kill Sofia Torres.

"Very sure. There's no way she's going to be able to testify against Noir, which I'm sure will make him very happy when he hears about it, since it means he's going to walk free." Bright had worried that Marie might see through his lies, but it was clear that she believed him, which was a relief. "I'd prefer it, and I know Inspector Alvarez feels the same, if Noir doesn't find out that Sofia has been killed. I'm sure he'll find out soon enough, whatever steps are taken to keep the news from him, but the longer we can keep him from finding out the better."

"Surely whoever Noir hired to take care of Sofia will get the message to him, if he hasn't already. And the moment he knows she's no longer around to testify against him, Boucher will get the extradition request dismissed."

That was what Luke's plan called for, but Bright wasn't sure how the plan was going to be affected by his hospitalisation.

"I don't think there's any way we can prevent Noir finding out what's happened. It's just a question of how long it takes for the information to get to him," Marie said.

"The longer it takes," Bright said, "the better for us, since we now have to hope that some physical evidence is found to link Noir to the Abrantes massacre, which is looking less and less likely. Either that or we need to find someone new to testify against him, which is where our team comes in. Inspector Alvarez and his task force believe the assassin, whom they have yet to identify, was injured during his assault on the yacht last night."

"Do they have a good reason for thinking that?" Marie asked. She had seen many officers latch onto an idea simply because it gave them hope, and something to do, and in the process they wasted time and resources.

"Good enough. From what I've been told there's a trail of blood leading through the yacht to the cabin where Sofia Torres was shot, and then back up to the deck and the railing. It doesn't match the position of anyone on the yacht, so the assumption is it was made by Noir's hitman."

"Sounds reasonable. Is there any indication of how he got on and off the boat? He should have been spotted long before he was in a position to get on board."

"If he has an answer to that, Alvarez hasn't told me."

"Okay, so, what is it he wants us to do?"

He'd like our team to make the rounds of the hospitals, medical clinics, and even the vet surgeries, to see if anyone has come in requiring treatment for gunshot wounds since midnight. I don't imagine he expects us to get a result any more than I do, but we can't ignore the possibility, even if it is more likely that Noir's assassin will have sought treatment from someone who's off the grid, assuming his injuries are serious enough to require treatment."

"I'll work up a list of locations to send the team to just as soon as I get to the station. I'll try and come up with some alternatives to the usual locations as well. I'm sure someone at the station will know where the local criminals go to get fixed up. Are we doing this with Alvarez's task force or are we on our own? I don't want to have to worry about us doubling up on the work."

"You don't need to worry about that," Bright assured her. "Alvarez has his team doing other things. I'll get to the station as soon as I can, but I have a few things to take care of first, so it might be a while. Once I get there, I'll help you coordinate the team." He ended the call then and settled back, his eyes closed, to doze through the rest of the drive to Barcelona. He was glad Gonzalez had been able to spare someone to drive him so he could doze, he wasn't sure he'd have managed to stay awake if he had had to drive himself.

39

Paris

• • • •

"I TAKE IT NO-ONE'S joined him in the lift," Agent Ney said. He had been sitting in the front seat of the surveillance van for over a quarter of an hour, with no sign of any activity outside the apartment building that was being watched.

"No, sir, the lift's still empty aside from Renault," Agent Artois, who was positioned inside the building replied softly. "He's just riding the lift to the top floor and back down again. He's definitely waiting for someone. Wait a minute..."

The agent fell silent, and Ney found that he was holding his breath in anticipation of something, anything, happening.

"He's making a call," Artois reported quietly from the top of the apartment building's only lift as he listened to what was happening below him, using a powerful microphone to capture every sound.

"Are you picking up the call?" Ney asked, twisting in his seat to speak to the agents who were monitoring the surveillance equipment in the rear of the van. He saw that the pair were busy adjusting their equipment, so he waited.

"We've got him, sir," Agent Soult said after a moment. "And the signal's clear."

"What's he saying?" Ney wanted to hear what Renault was saying, but he also wanted to keep an eye on the front of the building, so he stayed where he was and had a set of headphones passed through to him.

"*...been here for over fifteen minutes already. I'm not going to wait much longer.*"

Jean-Paul Renault's voice came through the headphones. There was a pause then, which Ney took to mean Renault was listening to what was being said by the person on the other end of the call.

"Fine, but if you're not here in the next five minutes, I'm leaving. I've got other things to do today."

Ney continued to listen in case Renault was going to say something more. When he didn't after almost a minute, Ney concluded the phone call was over.

"Okay, everyone, listen up," Ney contacted all the members of his team. "Renault is intending to leave in five minutes if his contact doesn't show, so keep your eyes peeled. The chances are his contact will be hurrying to get here, so let me know the moment you see a possible target."

The affirmatives came back from his team in quick order. They were all as disgusted as Ney by the thought that one of their fellow agents was selling information to a criminal organisation, and as eager to find out who the corrupt agent was so he or she could be stopped.

"I've got a possible target," one of the agents watching the apartment building and the nearby roads reported after nearly five minutes. "He's stopped at the corner and is looking around. I think this is the guy. He's definitely looking around for something or someone."

"Which corner?" Ney asked as he searched for the figure who had been spotted.

"Northeast. He's looking around the street and the surrounding area. I think it's safe to say he's looking for us."

"Any chance he'll spot you?" Ney asked worriedly.

There was silence for a moment, then, "I don't think so. He's going to need a healthy dose of luck to spot me."

"Can you get a shot of him?"

"Yeah. I've got about a dozen shots, including several good ones of his face. If we can't identify him from these pictures, we never will."

Ney was relieved to hear some good news. "Keep watch in case he leaves the same way."

• • • •

"IT'S ABOUT TIME YOU turned up," Jean-Paul said irritably when he was joined in the lift by Dubois. "Another couple of minutes and I'd have left."

"Like I told you on the phone, I got held up by traffic," Dubois said. "Hardly my fault."

"Fine. You're here now. So, what is it you want to see me about?" Jean-Paul was glad of the information Rene Dubois supplied him with, but he disliked the time and effort he was forced to waste every time the agent wanted to meet with him.

Dubois ignored Jean-Paul's tone. "I thought you'd like to know that the professional you hired has completed his work. He dealt with Sofia Torres and the officers protecting her last night."

Jean-Paul was silent for a moment. He was too surprised to say anything. "I have to admit," he said finally, "I never thought he'd actually succeed in getting all three of them. Mind you, considering what he insisted on being paid, he certainly should have, so I'm glad to hear he did."

"How much?" It made no difference to Dubois what Jean-Paul had agreed to pay but he was curious.

"Five million pounds. Five bloody million." Jean-Paul shook his head in disgust, still unhappy with the price Luke Caldwell had insisted on.

"Worth every penny, I'm sure, to get your cousin out of jail and keep him out," Dubois said. "Which of the three did you end up hiring?"

"Caldwell, the Brit, he was the only choice I had in the end. If you'd taken the time to check the three of them out before you gave me their files, you'd have known that he was the only one available."

"What do you mean?"

"I mean the Italian is dead and the German is retired. Of the three options you gave me, Caldwell was the only one I could hire. Anyway, the job's done now, he's got them all, thank God. Did he have any problems?"

"I take it he hasn't been in touch yet," Dubois said, reaching out to hit the button for the ground floor as the lift stopped at the top of the apartment building.

Jean-Paul shook his head. "If he had, I'd have known already that he got that damned witness last night. So, did he have any problems?"

Dubois shrugged. "The inspector in charge of the case believes your assassin was injured during the attack on the boat, but that's unconfirmed. The team in Barcelona is checking hospitals and similar places for anyone with gunshot wounds but, as I said, it hasn't been confirmed that he was injured, so they could be on a wild goose chase."

• • • •

THE CONVERSATION IN the lift continued for a while longer, with Ney listening through the headphones he had pressed to his ears. To his dismay, nothing was said to help identify the corrupt agent, though they did get plenty on tape to assist their case once they identified him.

"Okay, he's leaving," he informed his team. "Keep an eye out. Team One, you stay with Renault, Team Two, I want you to focus on his contact. Follow him and see where he goes and who he talks to. I doubt we'll be lucky enough to have him lead us to his desk, but he might make it easy for us to identify him."

40

Ney crossed the office and came to a stop in front of the desk. "You asked to see me, sir," he said. He couldn't help feeling nervous at having been summoned by his superior's superior. It was not a common occurrence for someone of his rank to be called in by the deputy director, and he worried that it meant he was in trouble, though he couldn't imagine what for.

"Have a seat, Alain," Lejour said before falling silent for a short while as he examined his subordinate.

Ney wasn't sure what to make of the use of his first name. On the one hand it suggested he wasn't in trouble, if he was Lejour would have been more formal with him, but on the other Lejour had obviously taken the time to find out about him, which indicated an unusual amount of interest.

"I'm sure you're wondering why I asked to see you," Lejour said after a moment. "It's about the request you made to Special Agent in Charge Courtois for permission to detain Agent Dubois for questioning — permission will not be given at this time."

Ney did his best to contain his disappointment. "May I ask why, sir? And why you're telling me and not Special Agent Courtois?"

"I'm telling you because it is my decision to refuse permission, and I thought it only right that you should hear it from me, as well as the reason," Lejour said. "There is another operation running intended to secure a conviction against Philippe Noir. While I don't say it will, there is a possibility that bringing in Agent Dubois will cause problems for the other operation. That is something I wish to avoid. With that in mind, I want you to leave Agent Dubois alone for the time being."

"But, sir, waiting runs the risk of Dubois realising we've found out about him and giving our surveillance operation the slip."

"I'm counting on you and your team to ensure that doesn't happen," Lejour said, his tone suggesting that if it did happen, he wouldn't be happy. "As for your belief that Agent Dubois can help secure a conviction against Noir, I'm not sure I agree with you. Based on the information in the file you compiled, I think it likely that the most Agent Dubois can do is testify that he sold information to Noir's cousin, and I'm not convinced he will be persuaded to testify to even that much. In contrast, the other operation that is in progress has the potential to see Noir behind bars, and to see him there for the rest of his life."

"If we don't bring Agent Dubois in, sir," Ney said in as calm a tone as he could manage, "he might discover the other operation. If that happens the operation will be wrecked, and Noir will get away."

"You may be right," Lejour said, "but it's a risk we have to run. The other operation has to be given a chance, otherwise a lot of time and effort will have been wasted. The people involved deserve the opportunity to see their operation through."

Ney ground his teeth in frustration. He hated the thought of having to put his operation on hold for the sake of another, especially when doing so meant his operation might end up being a bust. "I won't take the blame if Agent Dubois finds out he's under surveillance and gets away because I have to wait for this other operation."

Though he didn't approve of how Ney was speaking, especially to someone so senior to him, Lejour could understand how he felt, and that left him worried that Ney might decide to, if not disobey his orders, then create a situation that allow him to do what he wanted. "I'll make a deal with you," he said, leaning forward in his chair. "There is a possibility the other operation has gone sour, I'm still waiting to hear; if that is the case, you can bring Dubois in." He held up a hand to forestall Ney when he saw he was about to speak. "Not only that..."

• • • •

"GOOD EVENING, SIR," Bright answered his phone.

"Bright. How's the situation in Spain?" Lejour asked, in no mood for pleasantries.

"Hard to say. The doctor told me Luke needs to remain in bed for at least a fortnight, otherwise he risks ripping his stitches out, or worse. Luke disagrees, though." Bright had been reluctant to tell his superior who his friend was, given his status as a suspect in multiple serious crimes, but without doing so he doubted he would have got Lejour's cooperation. "He called me earlier and insisted that I tell him as soon as Noir is released, so he can put the final stages of his plan into operation."

"That presents us with something of a problem," Lejour told Bright. "Special Agent Ney, he's in charge of the surveillance operation watching Jean-Paul Renault, has discovered the identity of the agent who has been supplying Renault with information. Ney wants to bring him in for questioning, as well as Renault. He believes he can persuade Agent Dubois to testify against Renault, and then get Renault to sell out his cousin."

"He might be right about the first part, but I doubt he'll have much luck getting Renault to turn on his cousin."

"I agree, and I've told Ney as much. He wasn't happy, nor was he happy when I told him he would have to wait to detain Agent Dubois because of another operation. I was forced to make a deal with him to be sure he doesn't do anything hasty. Ney will continue his surveillance operation for five days, while you try to get Noir on tape admitting that he killed Tomas Abrantes and gave the order for Sofia Torres' murder. If you can't conclude your operation successfully in that time, Ney will be given permission to take whatever action he feels appropriate given the evidence in his possession at that time. What do you think the chances are of you being successful in that time?"

"As I said, sir, the doctor doesn't think Luke should be out of bed for at least a fortnight, but he thinks differently. I'm going to the base tonight. I'll talk to both Luke and the doctor then and explain the situation. I'll let you know what decision is made. There's another problem," Bright said. "To the best of my knowledge, Noir is still in a cell, and his lawyer doesn't yet know to make another motion to get the extradition request dismissed. We need him out for the last part of the plan to work. If he doesn't get released, it won't matter what shape Luke is in."

"You don't need to worry about that," Lejour said. "Agent Dubois told Renault that Sofia Torres, Roland Baptiste, and Marc Delcroix are all dead. If Noir's lawyer hasn't already started the paperwork, I'm sure he will have by tomorrow morning, so there shouldn't be any problems on that end of things."

• • • •

THE MOMENT HE ENTERED the room, Bright saw it was empty. He checked to be sure he had the right room, he did, and then he made his way back down the corridor to the nurse's station he had passed only a few moments before.

"Excuse me," he said when neither of the nurses at the station showed any sign of having noticed him. "Can you tell me what happened to Mr Caldwell? He was in room ten, but he's not there now."

"He's no longer here, sir."

"I saw that. Where is he?"

"He left."

"What do you mean he left? Where did he go?"

"I don't know, sir," the nurse said apologetically. "All I know is that he left. I'll see if I can find Captain Bilbao," she said quickly when Bright opened his mouth to speak again. "He might know where Mr Caldwell went."

Bright was left to wait, impatiently, for more than half an hour before the doctor appeared. With every minute that passed he became more frustrated. He was tempted to leave and go searching for his friend, but he knew that wasn't a good idea. Not only did he have no clue where Luke might have gone but wandering randomly around a military base was likely to get him into trouble.

"Agent Bright, isn't it?" Captain Bilbao said as he hurried up, his hand outstretched. "I'm sorry it's taken me so long to get here. Sometimes a patient takes longer than you expect. I'm sure you understand." He spoke hurriedly, as if eager to get the conversation finished. "I understand you want to know where Mr Caldwell has gone."

"Yes, I do." Bright did his best to keep his annoyance in check, realising that making a fuss with a captain in the Spanish army would accomplish little. "The nurse said he's left. I assume she means he has left the hospital, but I don't see how that's possible when I was told he needs to be here for at least a fortnight."

"The nurse is correct," Captain Bilbao said. "Mr Caldwell has left the hospital. He did so against my advice," he went on. "I was called to his room just before lunch, and when I got there, I found him out of bed and half dressed in the clothes he had remaining from his arrival. I attempted to persuade him to return to bed, making it clear that he was in no condition to leave, but he was insistent. He said he had a job to do."

"So you just let him walk out of here, even though he had surgery in the early hours of yesterday morning." Bright couldn't believe what he was hearing. "How was he even able to get out of bed so soon after surgery?" He knew how tough his friend was, but it still seemed inconceivable to him that Luke was mobile again within forty-eight hours of getting shot and having an operation.

"I don't know," Captain Bilbao admitted. "I wouldn't have thought it possible. The injury to your friend's side was serious, and the slightest movement could cause him serious problems. I explained that to him, but he insisted on leaving. Short of having him arrested by the MPs, or securing him to the bed, there was little I could do to keep him here."

It was clear that Bilbao was just as unhappy that Caldwell had left as he was, but that didn't make Bright feel any better.

"Okay, so you weren't able to keep him here. I'm sure even MPs would have had a hard time keeping him here, despite the surgery. That doesn't explain why I wasn't informed that he released himself."

"I couldn't say why you weren't informed. The nurse was supposed to call you. I would have called you myself, but I had other patients to deal with. Perhaps she got sidetracked by something and forgot, I couldn't say."

Bright sighed. "Do you at least know where he went?"

"Yes," Bilbao said, relieved to be able to provide some positive news. "I was concerned that he would tear out his stitches and start bleeding again, or simply collapse from the effort of walking around, so I had one of the orderlies follow him with orders to bring him back here, by force if necessary, if he showed any signs of trouble. Mr Caldwell went to the barracks being used by the other members of your task force. I believe he has remained there since, though I hope you'll understand that I can't say that for certain."

"Thank you." Without another word, Bright turned and walked away so he could find his friend.

When he reached the barracks, he found Luke playing cards with Sofia Torres in a corner of the recreation area.

"Evening, Ben. I was wondering how long it would take you to find me here," Luke said, surprising not only Bright but Sofia.

"How did you know who was there?" Sofia asked. She had no idea how Luke could have known who was approaching given that his back was to the room.

"I could feel angry eyes boring into the back of my head," Luke said. "And Ben is the only person who would be angry with me right now." He shrugged as though it was no big thing, though the movement made him grimace. "Besides, I saw his reflection in your glass." He gestured to the drink in front of Sofia. The look of disappointment on the faces of the other two made him laugh.

"What are you doing here?" Bright asked as he reached out to pick up his friend's drink so he could take a sip, suspecting that it was more than just orange juice. "And why are you drinking alcohol?"

"I've been trying to get him to answer that question for the last hour," Sofia said, putting her cards down.

"You were asking a different question entirely," Luke said as he too abandoned his cards. "You wanted to know why I chose to come to Spain and arrange all of this." He gestured around the barracks. "You can't understand why I went to the effort to fake the deaths of everyone here when I don't know you, especially when doing so could have cost me my life. Ben on the other hand wants to know why I'm sitting here playing cards with you when I'm supposed to be in a bed over at the base hospital, being checked on every half an hour by a coldly impersonal lieutenant dressed as a nurse."

Bright picked up Luke's glass again. "Don't forget this. I also want to know why you're drinking vodka."

Luke took the glass from his friend and lifted it to his lips. "That's an easy question to answer," he said after a long swallow. "Vodka's a great pain reliever, and a lot more enjoyable than the pills and morphine they were giving me at the hospital."

"Okay, so that explains the booze. What about you leaving the hospital less than thirty-six hours after having surgery? You had to have a bullet removed from your abdomen for God's sake, not to mention having your arm pinned back together." His gaze went to Luke's arm, which was heavily bandaged and strapped to his chest to keep it immobile.

"I've never been particularly fond of hospitals," Luke said. "Once the surgeons have done their work, there really isn't much reason to stay in a hospital, not unless there's something seriously wrong with you."

"And a bullet in the abdomen and a badly messed up elbow isn't something seriously wrong?" Bright asked. "I was under the impression that you're in a lot of pain, and your injuries are too severe for you to be up and out of bed, let alone out of hospital."

"Well, I won't deny I'm in some pain, hence the pain relief," Luke held up the glass, "but it's at a level I can tolerate. Being out of hospital helps. I've always found that just being in a hospital makes me feel worse, no matter what's wrong with me. Since that's the case, I left as soon as I felt able to. I'm a lot better off here. Besides, I need to get myself mobile and ready for when Noir is released."

"That brings me to the reason I came out here to see you." Bright hadn't been sure how he was going to bring the conversation around to the phone call he had received from Lejour, and he was relieved that the opportunity had been presented to him. "Is there somewhere we can talk privately?"

"I guess we can use one of the NCO rooms." Holding his glass in the hand of his strapped-up arm, Luke pushed himself up. He had to stop for a moment once he was on his feet as pain stabbed through his lower abdomen, making him grimace.

Once the pain subsided, which took a few moments, he led Bright through to the dormitory and then into the closest of the private rooms.

"Okay, what's going on?" Luke asked as he settled himself on the bed, leaving the room's chair for his friend.

"We have a problem," Bright said. "It seems that we are now working to a deadline. We've got just five days to get Noir on tape admitting to everything. If we can't manage it in that time our operation will be terminated, though obviously everyone will have to remain here on the base until the trial is over to ensure their safety."

"Why do we now have a deadline?"

"The surveillance team watching Jean-Paul Renault has had some good luck."

"And how does their good luck translate to our bad luck?" Luke asked.

"Because their good luck means they've identified the agent who has been selling information to Renault, and there is concern that if he isn't taken into custody soon, he might become aware of the surveillance operation. Lejour has agreed with the agent in charge of the surveillance operation, that if we can't conclude our operation in the next five days, he can arrest Agent Dubois and Renault."

Luke shrugged, though he immediately regretted the move for his alcoholic pain relief wasn't a hundred percent effective. "So what if he does. How does that stop us going ahead with our operation? If anything, having his cousin and the agent who's been selling him information behind bars is going to make him more likely to want to meet with me, so I can take care of his new problems."

"Our operation isn't exactly a standard one," Bright said. "We might not be breaking the rules in working with someone from the most wanted list, but we are skating close to them, and I think that's making Lejour uncomfortable. He authorised the operation, so if anything goes wrong with it, he'll be the one carrying the can. I'm not sure he likes that thought. While our operation was the best chance of getting a conviction against Noir, he was happy to go along with it, but now there's another option, and one that doesn't put his position at risk, he'd rather go with that. He doesn't want to just abandon our operation, though, so he's given us this deadline of five days to get Noir on tape or we're done."

"But Noir hasn't been released yet, and he won't be until tomorrow at the earliest. That won't leave us with much time to get the job done."

"I suspect Lejour is counting on that. If we say the operation can't be completed in the time he's given us, and he already knows you're injured and are supposed to stay in hospital for a minimum of two weeks, he'll tell us to wrap the operation up and give the go-ahead for Renault to be arrested."

"I guess we're going to have to hope I continue to be as lucky as I always have been. You can tell Lejour we'll have the operation finished in the time he's given us. We'll have Noir on tape admitting that he told his cousin to employ me to kill Sofia Torres and the others, and everything else he's done, inside of five days."

"You're crazy. How can you even think about going ahead with this? You're in bad shape, you could rip out your stitches and bleed to death with the slightest movement. I know you're doing this because you think you owe me, but I've never felt like that, and even if I did, what you've done so far is more than enough to repay the debt."

"It's not about that anymore. It's about the job. I started this, and I'll be damned if I'm going to give up on it before it's finished just because of a few injuries. I don't give up until a job is done. If you think about it, me getting shot actually helps us."

"Care to explain that?" Bright asked.

"It will help to convince Noir that I'm genuine, and I really have killed the people he wanted dead," Luke said. "In fact, now I think about it, it would look suspicious if I turned up without any injuries, especially given how many people I'm supposed to have killed. I'm good at what I do, but not that good."

"I'm glad you can find something positive about you getting shot," Bright said acidly. "But I still think you're crazy for being out of hospital so soon after being operated on. And there's something you seem to have forgotten; this is an Interpol operation, and I'm in charge of it, if I decide your health would be too much at risk, and I'm sure you realise I already think that, then the operation won't go ahead."

"Don't be daft. You can't keep me on this base, and you know it, so if you decide not to finish this operation, I'll just go and do it myself. One way or another, our operation will be over in five days, and I don't plan on exerting myself any more than necessary in that time, so just relax and let me get this finished."

Angry, and concerned, Bright tried to think of a way to convince his friend to be sensible. He could think of nothing, however. He doubted that anything he said or did would stop Luke doing what it was he had set his mind on.

"Fine. If you want to kill yourself for the sake of putting Noir away, then go right ahead," he said, getting to his feet. "Just remember, this is your decision. As far as I'm concerned, you've already done everything you need to, and more."

41

P ARIS

. . . .

PHILIPPE NOIR FELT relief wash over him as he stepped through the heavy door and out of prison, Olivier at his side. He had only been in prison for a month while the hearings to decide the extradition request against him took place, but it had seemed much longer.

Despite having a single cell and being afforded the respect of both the guards and most of the other inmates, thanks to his name and reputation, the experience had not been a pleasant one for him. The food, and the general level of comfort, was far below what he was used to, and he was not happy that a price had been put on his head by Roberto Abrantes, which two people had tried to collect on.

Revelling in the first truly fresh air he had breathed in four weeks, Noir made his way to the BMW where his cousin was waiting for him. He immediately climbed into the back, where he was joined by Olivier, and relaxed.

. . . .

"OKAY, JEAN-PAUL, TELL me about this hitman you hired," Noir said once he was sitting comfortably in the leather chair behind his desk at the vineyard with a glass of wine. He had said nothing during the drive from the prison, not wanting to take any chances on Interpol having managed to bug his car.

"His name's Caldwell, he's in his mid-to-late thirties, and he was trained by the British Army," Jean-Paul summarised, though he quickly expanded on that when he saw his cousin looking at him expectantly. "According to the file I was given, he spent time with

British Special Forces. He's been under suspicion by Interpol and police agencies across Europe for years, but they've never been able to get enough to charge him with anything, let alone get a conviction."

"How much did you agree to pay him?" Noir asked. "Olivier told me it was a significant amount but not how much. I assume from his résumé that he's a man who knows his value."

Jean-Paul hesitated for a moment before answering. He had hoped he wouldn't be asked that. "Five million pounds," he said finally. "And he insisted on being paid half up front."

"Was there no-one else you could have got? Someone who was willing to work for a more reasonable fee?"

Jean-Paul shook his head. "My source was only able to give me the names of three people known by Interpol to have the skills we needed. One of them is dead and another is retired, Caldwell was the only one available, and he knew I was desperate. You told me to do everything I could to get you out of prison and clear up your problems," he reminded his cousin. "That is what I had to do. I think you should consider the price cheap. It would cost you a lot more than five million pounds if you ended up in a Spanish jail."

Noir could hardly disagree with that. "Did this Caldwell character have any problems getting rid of Roland, Marc, and that bloody witness?" he asked, changing the subject to avoid thinking about how much the man's services had cost.

"That's hard to say. Caldwell hasn't been in contact since he collected the files on the three targets, so I haven't been able to find out if he had any problems. My source did tell me it's believed that Caldwell was injured during his last job, when he killed Sofia Torres," Jean-Paul said. "There's no confirmation of that, though, and I imagine there won't be until either Caldwell contacts me or the Spanish Police report his capture or death." He was relieved that Noir seemed to be taking the size of the fee calmly. "On the plus side, he hasn't been paid the second half of his fee yet, and I don't intend paying it until I hear that he's alive and not in custody in Spain."

"Good." Noir nodded approvingly. "There's no point paying him the rest if it isn't necessary. Of course, that still leaves the question of what I'm going to do about him."

"What do you mean?"

"Well, I have a few options," Noir said. "I can hope he was injured and dies from his wounds, so I don't have to pay him. I can wait for him to turn up and then refuse to pay him. I can pay him and hope he goes away and doesn't get caught by either the Spanish Police or Interpol. Or I could have you kill him, so I don't have to pay him, and we don't have to worry about him revealing anything to anybody."

"I don't think you should do anything," Olivier said. "The most sensible course of action is simply to wait and see what happens. If Caldwell is dead then great, you don't have to pay him what he's owed, and you don't have to worry about anything. I don't think you'll have to worry if he gets caught either; I saw the file Jean-Paul was given, and nobody has come close to catching this Caldwell, but if they somehow do this time, he's professional enough not to speak."

"And I definitely don't think you should attempt to kill him, not unless you have a very good reason," Jean-Paul added his opinion.

"Why not?" Noir asked. He was in a good mood after his release from prison and hearing that his problems were over, otherwise he would have been annoyed by the opinions being offered.

"He was trained as a special forces soldier, and is now a professional hitman. The chances are good that he will expect you to try and kill him, rather than pay him what he's owed. He'll be ready for something like that, and it will be us rather than him that gets killed," Jean-Paul said. "Let's not forget that he's just succeeded where more than a dozen of your best men failed. He's clearly very good at what he does, and I don't fancy having him hunt us down because you're not willing to pay him what was agreed." He saw his cousin's face darken and he hurried on. "You have to remember that he's professionally trained, while we're more used to dealing with people who, at best, can be called gifted amateurs. There is another reason not to kill him."

"Really, what might that be? You like him and think he'd be a laugh to hang out with?" Noir asked sarcastically.

"No. I think he might be useful in the future. He's clearly a lot better than the rest of our men, even if he costs more. It's pretty much guaranteed that you will find more people you want dead in the future, and some of them may be as well-protected as Tomas Abrantes was. It might be better to use Caldwell to eliminate those problems, rather than using your own men. He can do it better, quicker, and with fewer risks to you."

"You might be right," Noir conceded. "There's little point in having a fortune if you aren't able to enjoy it." That was something that had occurred to him during his stint in prison. He was silent for a few moments while he sipped at his wine and thought about what Jean-Paul had said. Finally, he said, "If he contacts you to get the rest of his money, arrange a meeting. Maybe if I see him, I'll make up my mind what to do about him. Is there any other business I need to worry about?" he asked, looking from Jean-Paul to Olivier.

42

BARCELONA

. . . .

LUKE WAS IN THE MIDDLE of a game of poker when his phone rang. It was on the table in front of him and the vibrations made the chips dance across the table.

"Afternoon, Ben," he answered the phone after a glance at the screen to see who the caller was.

"Are you sober?" Bright asked without preamble. He knew his friend hadn't been drunk since he left the base hospital, but neither had he been completely sober.

"Close enough for it not to matter. Why, what's up?"

"Noir was released a few hours ago. He was picked up from prison by Renault and his lawyer and they drove straight to his vineyard," Bright told him. "If you still insist on going through with this idiocy, you have about sixty-five hours to get to France, meet with Noir, and get him on tape. I was able to persuade Lejour to give you until nine a.m. two days from now. It gives you a bit of extra time, but not much. No-one will blame you if you decide to leave the assignment and let Ney and his team bring in Dubois and Renault and do things that way."

"We've been over this already. I'm going, so stop trying to dissuade me." Luke surrendered his hand in the game and pushed his chair away from the table, leaving his chips to be divided amongst the remaining players. They weren't playing for money, so it didn't matter. "I should be able to get to the airport in about three hours, so get me a booking on the first flight to Paris after that. I'll need a hotel booking as well."

He could make the arrangements himself, but he figured Bright could manage it quicker and easier since he could use his position with Interpol to push the arrangements through in the face of any trouble resulting from booking at the last minute.

. . . .

PARIS

. . . .

WHILE HIS LUGGAGE WAS being loaded into the boot, Luke slowly manoeuvred into the passenger seat of the taxi. He would have preferred to hire a car and drive himself, but with his arm so heavily bandaged and strapped up there was no way he could manage it.

Throughout the drive to his hotel, he kept an eye out for any sign the cab was being followed. It was a force of habit for him to be so cautious, he had no real concerns about being tailed just then since he was working with Interpol. It was a strange situation for him, but he was used to strange situations, so he didn't let it trouble him.

The first thing he did once he was alone in the room Bright had booked him into was dig out his painkillers. He downed a couple of them with whisky from the minibar and then, his immediate needs dealt with, he settled on the bed with the room service menu.

The sandwiches he ordered served to quiet his rumbling stomach and once he finished them, he changed his bandages. It was a difficult task to manage on his own and with only the use of one hand, but he got the job done after a couple of false starts, and when he was finished, he put his head down for a nap.

. . . .

THE MOMENT HIS WATCH beeped, Luke's eyes flew open and he awkwardly pushed himself up, swinging his legs around so he was sitting on the edge of the bed. He sat there for a moment while he breathed through the pain the sudden movement had provoked, and then he groped on the bedside table for his phone and dialled from memory the number Bright had given him.

"Olivier Boucher?" he asked when the call was answered.

"Who is this?" Olivier asked, blinking rapidly in the darkness as he tried to focus on the luminous numbers of the clock on his bedside cabinet. He didn't recognise the voice and he felt a twinge of concern at being woken in the middle of the night by someone he didn't know, someone who had his private number, which so far as he was aware was known to only a handful of people.

"I'm the man Jean-Paul employed to deal with your boss' problems in Spain. I want you to deliver a message to Jean-Paul for me, tonight."

"Why don't you give him the message yourself?" Olivier asked. He was annoyed at having been woken but also a little cautious about upsetting the hitman. "I know you know where he lives."

"He's being watched, as I'm sure you know. It was difficult enough to contact him the first time without being seen. I'm not about to take the risk again. You are a known associate of his, though, and can contact him without arousing additional suspicion. I want you to tell him that I'm waiting for the money I'm owed, and he is to go to the Hotel De Vere tonight to explain why I haven't been paid. If he doesn't have a good reason, or he doesn't turn up, I'll be paying him a visit, regardless of the surveillance team watching him. I'm sure he won't like it if I have to do that." He was bluffing, he was in no shape to even think about doing anything to Renault just then, but he didn't imagine either Boucher or Renault knew that.

He gave one last instruction and then he hung up.

• • • •

CURSING, JEAN-PAUL all but fell out of bed and sleepily stumbled from the bedroom so he could answer the ringing of his doorbell.

"What the hell do you want, Olivier?" he demanded when he saw who was at the door. "Do you have any idea what time it is?"

"Of course I do," Olivier said tiredly. "I'm here to deliver a message. Can we go inside? We don't want anyone to hear the message I've been given for you." As soon as Jean-Paul stepped back he entered the apartment.

"So, what's so bloody urgent?" Jean-Paul asked after closing the door behind Boucher. "Has Philippe got a new problem he needs sorting?"

"Don't you think Philippe would have called you himself if the message was from him?" Olivier said more sharply than he intended. He was barely awake and in danger of falling asleep on his feet.

"Okay, so your message isn't from Philippe. Who the hell is it from, and what is it?" Jean-Paul asked irritably.

Olivier looked around cautiously, as if he expected to find an Interpol agent hiding in a corner of the room, before he said anything. "I got a call a while ago from your hired killer, Caldwell," he said finally. "He wants you to meet him at the Hotel De Vere, tonight."

"Did he say why, or why he didn't come here, or even why he contacted you instead of me?"

"Try asking one question at a time," Olivier said. "I'm too tired to deal with a barrage. He said he doesn't want to contact you directly because of the surveillance team watching you, and he insisted that you meet him tonight to explain why he hasn't been paid the rest of his fee. If you don't go and see him, he implied that he'll kill you, and I'm not sure he'll settle at just you. I don't know about you, but I value my life at more than two and a half million pounds."

"You're used to tricky verbal manoeuvring, what do you suggest I tell him? What do I give him as a reason for not paying him?" Even if he had been more awake, Jean-Paul wasn't sure he could have thought of a reason good enough to satisfy Caldwell.

"Why don't you tell him the truth," Olivier suggested as he smothered a yawn. "I'm sure he'll understand not being paid until you and Philippe knew he was alive and not under arrest. I know if I was in his position I would."

"That's a great comfort," Jean-Paul said acidly. "Where did you say he wants me to meet him? The Hotel De Vere? What time?"

"He didn't say. He just said you're to go there tonight, and if you don't, he'll come looking for you and you won't like it."

"I don't imagine I would. Given what he managed to do in Spain, I don't want to piss him off."

"Oh yes, he told me to give you this." Olivier handed over his mobile phone. "I guess he wants to contact you on a number he's confident isn't being monitored." He knew that Interpol and the police would have loved to be able to monitor his phone number but getting a warrant for that was tricky, if not to say nearly impossible, because of his position as a lawyer and the legally privileged nature of phone calls between his client and him.

• • • •

JEAN-PAUL HAD GONE no more than a couple of steps across the lobby of the Hotel De Vere when Olivier's phone rang. Certain that it was Luke Caldwell, and not sure what to expect, he answered the phone cautiously.

"Hello."

"Take the left-hand lift to the seventh floor."

How Caldwell knew he had arrived at the hotel, he didn't know, but he followed the instructions he had been given without hesitation. He kept the phone to his ear as he rode the lift to the seventh floor, but it wasn't until the doors opened and he stepped out that he received further instructions.

"Walk round to the stairs and take them down to the third floor. When you get there, call for the lift and get into the one on the right."

Bemused, and feeling more than a little stupid, Jean-Paul gave serious thought to forgetting the whole thing and going home. If it hadn't been for the ease with which Caldwell had managed to get into his apartment on two separate occasions, and what he could have done to him had he been of a mind, he might well have left. Instead, he turned and headed along the corridor, following the sign that pointed to the stairs. He guessed Caldwell was having him go up and down the hotel to make sure he wasn't being followed, but he couldn't help thinking that the precautions were over the top.

"Take the lift to the top floor and get out."

The order came the moment he stepped into the lift on the third floor, leaving Jean-Paul to wonder how Caldwell could possibly know his movements. It was obvious the hitman knew exactly where he was, but he didn't see how that was possible.

The phone in his hand went dead as the lift approached the top floor, and Jean-Paul took that as a sign that there would be no more manoeuvring. He hoped he was right for he was too tired to spend any more time going up and down the hotel to avoid people he couldn't see and wasn't convinced were there.

When the doors slid open, he stepped out and found himself face to face with Caldwell, or rather with the gun Caldwell was holding. With an effort he looked past the gun, the muzzle of which was pointed right at his face, and saw that Dubois' information had been accurate, as it always was. The arm not holding the gun was heavily bandaged and supported by a sling.

The corridor was too dark for him to see Caldwell's face clearly, but he didn't need to. The gun was enough to make him stand still and wait for the hitman to say or do something. He couldn't even bring himself to ask a question, he simply stood there, frozen to the spot.

Caldwell waited until the lift doors closed and then he said a single word, "Strip."

43

Barcelona

. . . .

WITH THE DOOR OF HIS office closed, Bright returned to his chair behind the desk and picked up the phone.

"I heard from Luke a short while ago, sir," he informed Lejour when his call was answered. "He made contact with Renault during the night, and a meeting has been arranged between him and Noir for tonight at nine. They're meeting at Noir's vineyard outside Paris."

"I guess you were wrong about your friend," Lejour said. "He seems to be doing alright so far, despite his injuries. I'll begin making preparations for tonight. How do I get in touch with Caldwell? We'll need to wire him up for the meeting, so we can get Noir on tape."

"He's at the Hotel De Vere, room seventy-three," Bright said. "You're to send along one tech this afternoon at five to sort that out." He had already discussed the situation with Luke, who was understandably reluctant to have any more dealings with Interpol than was absolutely necessary. "I don't think we should take any action until he's left the meeting and is safely away, sir. If your teams move in while he's there, he'll be at risk if Noir and his people decide to make a fight of it, which is likely. He's already taken bullets for this operation, there's no reason for him to have to risk taking more."

Lejour agreed, though he remained unhappy that the operation relied so heavily on someone who was almost as high on Interpol's wanted list as Philippe Noir. His only consolation was the fact that Caldwell had not requested any kind of immunity or protection in exchange for his assistance, which meant there was still the possibility of prosecuting him in the future, either for one of the murders he had already committed or for one he was yet to commit.

"Something might go wrong, though, and the assault team might have to go in before Caldwell can get out of there. It might be best if you're here so you can go in with the team to protect Caldwell," Lejour said. He was tempted not to worry about the possibility of Caldwell getting himself injured further, perhaps even getting killed, but it seemed wrong to allow that to happen when the man had volunteered his help, and that help was likely to lead to the arrest of a criminal as significant as Philippe Noir.

"Yes, sir." Bright was glad Lejour had suggested it. He wanted to be there in case Luke ran into problems, but he hadn't wanted to either suggest or request it in case Lejour would think he was more concerned about a suspected criminal than he was in doing his job. "I'll make some arrangements and book a flight."

* * * *

"WHAT'S GOING ON?" MARIE asked from the passenger seat as Bright drove them to the airport. "Why are we flying to Paris?"

"Now we're away from the office, I think it's safe for me to tell you," Bright said. He hadn't wanted to say anything of what was going on before then because he didn't want to be overheard by anyone who might be in the employ of Philippe Noir. "Firstly, Sofia Torres, Roland Baptiste, and Marc Delcroix are all still alive."

Bright heard Marie gasp and took it for surprise.

"How?" Marie asked, doing her best to keep the fear and worry she was feeling from her voice. "I thought the hitman Renault hired killed them all. How did you manage to trick him?"

Bright took his eyes off the road for a moment to smile at Marie but didn't notice anything out of place. "Renault made a mistake when he picked his hitman," he said. "The man he hired is a former colleague of mine from the British Army." He couldn't help feeling pleased with the way things had turned out, even if he knew he could only claim a part of the credit for it. "I'm sure if he'd known that, Renault wouldn't have hired him, but his mistake is our good fortune."

Marie was silent while Bright filled her in on everything that had happened since Luke Caldwell was approached, but the moment he stopped talking she voiced the questions on her mind. At the same time, her hand crept towards the gun she had in a holster at her right hip.

"Where's Sofia now? And the others? Where did you find to keep them that Noir's people wouldn't find out what you did?" Not only was she afraid of what Noir would do when he found out the truth, for she was Rene Dubois' partner, and had supplied him with some of the information he had sold to Jean-Paul Renault, Marie was afraid of the steps she might have to take to fix everything. "Was Caldwell really injured, or was that just a story you put out to help his credibility?"

Bright couldn't help laughing at the questions, thinking they came from astonishment at what he had done without her knowing, rather than fear of what it might mean for her.

"I can only answer one question at a time," he told her. "Yes, Luke is injured, it isn't just a story that was put out there to help him. We couldn't tell Sofia's protective detail what was going on in case one of them sold the information to Noir or let something slip to the wrong person, so they thought Luke was really trying to kill her and shot him. Luke got hit a few times but is mostly okay and was able to knock out everyone on the boat with tranquiliser darts. Delcroix, Baptiste, and Sofia, along with her protective detail, were taken to an army base, where they will remain until the trial. It's the safest place for them."

"I assume Caldwell is at the base as well, recovering from his injuries." Marie unclipped the catch on her holster, wincing at the, to her, loud sound it made, and began easing the gun free. Out the corner of her eye she watched Bright to see if he was aware of what she was doing, but he was oblivious as far as she could tell.

"No," Bright said. "I wish he was, but he insisted on continuing with the plan he came up with. He's in Paris for a meeting with Noir and Renault tonight. The plan is for him to get Noir on tape admitting that he ordered the murders of Sofia, Baptiste, and Delcroix, which will enable us to arrest Noir and Renault and guarantee convictions. We're on our way to Paris to take care of Luke after the meeting, or when the meeting is raided if things go wrong."

She would have to act, Marie realised. Given what she had been told, she had no choice. "Is there anything else I need to know?" she asked, annoyed that she had been backed into a corner where she would have to give herself away as a corrupt agent, even if Bright didn't yet know that that was what he had done.

"Yes. As well as the luck we've had with Luke, we've been able to identify who's been leaking information about our progress here in Barcelona."

Marie's heart stopped for a moment. She thought she had been discovered and was being driven into a trap.

"The surveillance team watching Renault was able to catch him meeting with his contact a few days ago. It's an agent by the name of Rene Dubois from the communications department at the Paris office."

"Do they know how he got hold of the information he sold to Renault?" Marie asked, keeping her voice as calm and casual as she could, while clenching her gun in a grip so tight she was surprised she didn't break it.

"Before he transferred to the communications department, Dubois worked in the records department and took a number of courses in various aspects of computing. It's suspected that he's been hacking into files to get the information he's been selling. The surveillance team watching him is under orders to keep their distance to avoid alerting him until they're ready to make their move, so they haven't been able to confirm that yet." Bright took yet another turn then, starting down a long road that led out of the city and passed a sign that revealed the airport was two kilometres away. "Once Noir's in custody they'll bring Dubois in, then they'll make certain of how he's been getting his information."

Marie had heard enough for her to make up her mind. It sounded as though they didn't yet know that she and Rene were a couple, and that she was involved in supplying him with at least some of the information he had been selling, but it was only a matter of time before they found out.

She lifted her gun from where she had been hiding it at her side. "I'm sorry, Ben, but you've left me no choice. Take the next turn," she ordered.

Bright's jaw dropped in shock when he looked around and saw the gun. "What the hell?" His voice trembled in a way that surprised him. He had never reacted like that before, not even when under fire while in the army.

"Take the next turn," Marie repeated. "If you force me to, I'll shoot you here and now. The road's straight enough that I can get the car under control before it crashes."

Bright wasn't so sure about that, but the look in Marie's eyes told him she would shoot him if he forced her to. He ran through his options in his mind, but it only took him a fraction of a second to realise that he would have to follow her instructions, for the time being at least.

Nodding slowly, to show that he was going to do as he had been ordered, he moved his hand to the indicator stick so he could let the traffic behind him know what he was doing. He continued to keep his movements slow, so as not to startle Marie into shooting him, as he turned off the main road.

• • • •

"STOP HERE," MARIE DIRECTED a couple of minutes after ordering Bright to turn onto a narrow track, which appeared to be a service path of some kind that led towards the airport. "Give me your gun." She held out her free hand for the weapon.

When he handed over his weapon, Marie put her own away and then swapped his into her right hand. "Get out of the car."

Slowly, Bright obeyed, uncomfortably aware that although Marie had opened her door, she hadn't moved from the passenger seat and was pointing his own gun squarely at his back.

When he heard the car shift, indicating Marie was getting out on the other side, Bright took his chance. He darted away from the car, making for the nearest of the bushes. He knew it wasn't going to hide him completely, nor would it protect him from any shots Marie aimed at him, but he hoped it would at least make it harder for her to see him well enough to hit him with any shots she fired, and perhaps give him enough time to get to the backup weapon he had at his right ankle.

Marie was quicker than he expected, however. Before he could make it halfway to the bush, he was struck twice by bullets that threw him forwards and into the dirt. He wasn't sure if bullets hurt worse than they used to, or if he had simply forgotten how much it hurt to get shot, but the pain was incredible. He wanted to roll over so he could get to his backup gun and return fire but his body wouldn't respond to the commands his brain was giving it.

He could hear Marie approaching, but her footsteps faded as darkness slowly overcame him, robbing him of consciousness, and perhaps life as well.

The gun in her hand at the ready in case Bright was faking, Marie cautiously knelt at his side. She nudged him, and then nudged him again. When she didn't get a response, she reached out to check for a pulse, relaxing when she didn't find one. Satisfied that Bright was dead she got to her feet and returned to the car, where she cleaned her fingerprints off Bright's gun before negligently tossing it away. She then slid behind the wheel and reversed the car down the path until she reached a space where she could turn around.

As she drove her mind raced. Foremost in her thoughts was the problem of how she was going to reach Rene to let him know what had happened. With him under surveillance that was not going to be easy. She had to, though, he had made plans against the possibility of one or both of them being discovered as traitors to Interpol, and she didn't know all the details of those plans.

44

P ARIS

. . . .

FROM HER POSITION SEVERAL streets away from the main Interpol building in Paris, Marie had no problem spotting Rene's car as it went past. Having seen him, she searched the traffic that followed for the surveillance team she had been told was watching him. It didn't take her long to spot it, but that was only because she knew to look for it and had had enough dealings with surveillance operations to recognise the vehicles they used.

Following the non-descript van with the plumber's logo on the side at a distance, Marie parked around the corner from Rene's building. She had only spotted the van initially, but halfway to the building a BMW had taken over tailing Rene, and was then replaced by a battered old Citroen. She saw the BMW again, parked down the road, as she walked towards the apartment building.

Discreetly, Marie looked around for the two agents from the BMW. She couldn't see them, and had no clue where they had gone, but she guessed they were somewhere with both a line of sight to Rene's apartment and a view of the street outside the building. Thinking of that she tried not to dwell on the eyes that might be on her as she walked down the street.

"It's me, buzz me in," she said quickly when Rene answered the intercom in his apartment. The moment the lock clicked, Marie pushed open the door and hurried inside so she could make her way up to the second floor.

"What are you doing here, honey, I thought you were in..." Rene began when he opened the apartment door. His words were cut off as Marie crushed her lips to his.

Marie was glad to see Rene, whom she had been away from for a couple of months now, but she hadn't kissed him for just that reason. "Be careful what you say, you're under surveillance. They might have the apartment bugged," she whispered in Rene's ear after breaking off the kiss. Out loud, she said, "I missed you, so I decided to come home early."

She followed Rene down the passage and then pulled him into the kitchen when they reached it, instead of heading into the living room. There was no window there, so no reason to worry that the surveillance team would be able to see them, and once she turned on the taps full blast, she felt confident that they couldn't be heard by any bugs that had been planted.

"Are you sure?" Rene asked, having stayed silent until then.

"Positive."

"How did you find out?" Rene kept his voice low, despite the running water. He trusted Marie and was sure what she said was true but he was still curious.

"Ben Bright told me," Marie said, standing close to Rene so she didn't have to speak any more loudly than was absolutely necessary, just in case the bugs the surveillance team had almost certainly planted were more sensitive than those she was used to. "He only told me today as we were on the way to the airport to come back here, but apparently they've had you under surveillance for several days. You're going to have to get away, get out of the country. They're going to arrest you soon, possibly this evening. They'll arrest me soon as well, or at least bring me in for questioning. I killed Bright after he told me what was happening."

"What did you do that for?" Rene didn't mind selling information to Renault, but killing a fellow agent was something else entirely. He ignored the fact that the information he had sold had led to the deaths of multiple agents, and numerous other people. He didn't consider himself responsible for those deaths. What was done with the information he provided was none of his business, at least that was how he rationalised things.

"I didn't have a choice," Marie said. "Noir's being arrested tonight, and once he's arrested, you will be too. I needed to get away from Bright so I could warn you. We need to warn Noir as well, the hitman Renault hired is a friend of Bright's, and all the people he's supposed to have killed are still alive. They're on an army base outside Barcelona."

"Shit!" Rene swore. "I gave Jean-Paul the file on Caldwell. He's going to blame me for this. Noir's going to blame me for this. Shit! He's going to kill me for this." His voice rose as the realisation of just how bad the situation was for him set in and he began to panic.

"Don't worry, I've got a plan," Marie told Rene, who didn't look the slightest bit reassured.

45

"Good evening, Mr Noir." Without waiting for an invitation or asking for permission, Luke crossed the room and settled himself in the chair opposite Philippe Noir in his office at the vineyard with a grimace. His decision to limit the pain relief he was taking to keep his mind as sharp as possible was causing him more discomfort than he liked.

"Mr Caldwell," Noir returned the greeting, while hiding the annoyance he felt at the man's casual attitude. "I was told you were injured." His gaze went to the sling that held Caldwell's bandage encased arm. "Given what you did, I'm surprised you got off so lightly. I applaud your skill. I would not have thought it possible for one person to deal with one of the targets, let alone all three, without receiving serious injuries. I confess, when you didn't contact Jean-Paul immediately after dealing with Sofia Torres, we were concerned that you had either been caught or killed."

"I gathered as much from your cousin when I spoke to him last night," Luke remarked. "And that that is the reason you failed to pay me promptly after I eliminated the last of your problems. That, and you being unhappy with the price he agreed with me."

"You're right," Noir said. "I was unhappy with the price Jean-Paul agreed to pay you. When I told him to find me a professional who could deal with my problems," he wasn't the sort to admit that it was his cousin who had brought the idea to him, via Olivier, "I didn't expect it to cost me anything like five million pounds. Of course, I was in jail when he made the deal, and by the time I got out I'd had time to think, and you had killed that bloody witness and my useless employees, so Jean-Paul was able to convince me that he had done the right thing."

"I get the impression you're now glad you had your cousin employ me to kill Sofia Torres and the others," Luke remarked, relieved that Noir was making it easy for the surveillance team, who were listening to the signal from the tiny microphone hidden in his bandages, to get him on record incriminating himself.

D ubois waited for an hour after Marie left and then he made his move. He hadn't expected her to contact him, so he wasn't surprised not to hear how her efforts to warn Renault and Noir had fared, though it did leave him worrying.

He wasn't idle while he waited, he had plenty to do to keep him occupied. Most of his arrangements had been made shortly after he began selling information to Renault, but he still had last minute things to take care of.

The first thing he did was pull the curtains to keep the watching surveillance team from seeing anything of what he did. He then sat at the powerful desktop computer system he had built, where he used a back door he had built into the system when he worked there to access the Interpol Records Department. Once he was in, he uploaded a program he had prepared, a program which altered his and Marie's personnel files; the program made minor alterations to the photos, fingerprints, DNA, and other identification records contained within both their files, which would make it more difficult for his colleagues to catch or identify them.

While the program did its job, he retrieved a memory stick he had taped to the underside of his desk. The memory stick held a virus, which he had paid someone else to write since it was beyond his programming skills, and it went to work the moment he plugged it in.

He left the virus to do its deadly work, destroying every file and scrap of information it encountered, both on his system and on the Interpol database, and made his way into the bathroom, where he got on his knees so he could reach under the tub to remove one of the floor tiles. From the cavity he revealed he took out a wrapped package.

After replacing the tile, not that he needed to, he carried the package into the living room, where he pulled off the waterproof wrapping. Inside was a pair of pistols, with extra ammunition clips, two passports, with matching drivers' licences and credit cards, and a large bundle of Euros.

The small collection of items was only a fraction of what he would need to successfully evade Interpol and the efforts they would inevitably make to find both him and Marie long term. The rest of what he needed was kept in a locker at the airport, with similar bundles, differing only in the names used, in other places. Arranging everything had been costly and time-consuming, but he hadn't wanted to take a chance on having only one escape package in case it was compromised.

Dubois emptied his wallet of the cards it currently contained, all in his real name, and replaced them with the ones in his false identity, Helmut Kroeger. He then stuffed the Euros, spare ammunition, and Marie's false identification into his pocket. The guns, which were unregistered and untraceable, went into the waistband of his trousers, one at the front and the other at the back. He didn't anticipate needing to use either weapon, let alone both, and he hoped he wouldn't have to resort to them, but he wanted them available, just in case.

Marie raced down the road towards Philippe Noir's vineyard, wondering as she did where the surveillance team was hiding. She knew they had to be somewhere nearby if Caldwell was there, their equipment only had a range of about half a mile. Not only that but they needed to be close so they could move in to arrest Noir and anyone else at the vineyard once they had his admission of guilt on tape.

She didn't know for certain that Caldwell was at the vineyard, but she did know that Renault and Noir were either there or on their way there.

After failing to get hold of Renault using Rene's usual method of making contact, she had gone to both Renault's and Noir's homes to warn them, despite the danger to herself from the Interpol surveillance operations. She hadn't found either man, but she had been told where they were going. Marie was sure that both Renault and Noir were already at the vineyard since they had left before her, and she could only hope she got there before Caldwell.

The gates to the vineyard appeared more suddenly than she expected as she raced around the last bend, and she slammed her foot on the brake. She came to a skidding halt just before the gates and looked around until she spotted the intercom box.

"Vin du Noir Vineyard, how may I help you?"

It was more than a minute before the voice sounded from the intercom, and when it finally did it made Marie jump in surprise. Her attention had been on the woods surrounding the property as she searched for any sign of the surveillance team and the officers waiting to arrest Noir. She was sure they had to be there somewhere, even if Caldwell hadn't yet arrived.

"I need to speak to Jean-Paul Renault, I've got an urgent message for him," Marie said once she had recovered.

"I'm afraid Mr Renault is busy and cannot be disturbed."

Marie swore in frustration. It was possible Renault was busy with something else, but she thought it more likely that he was busy because Caldwell was already there. If that was the case, it was even more important that she get in there to speak to him, before either Renault or Noir said or did anything to incriminate themselves.

"I'm Special Agent Marie Hapsburg with Interpol," she said sharply. "It's imperative that I speak to Mr Renault immediately. Please tell him I have an urgent message from Rene Dubois, and that it concerns Luke Caldwell."

There was a long moment of silence and then the voice, which Marie assumed belonged to a butler or similar employee, spoke again, "I will tell Mr Renault you are here."

Marie was left to wait, and while she waited her mind dwelled on the possibility that Bright's body had been found and she had been connected to his murder. She suspected she was okay for the time being, his body was in an out of the way location and she didn't suppose anyone was going to go there without a good reason, but it was surely only a matter of time before he was found, and suspicion was bound to fall on her. She also wondered if Rene had eluded his surveillance team and was safely on his way out of the country. She hoped he was, and that he would have no problems reaching the safe location he had told her was the rendezvous he had chosen.

"Please follow the drive to the main house," the voice said from the intercom as the gates swung open. "Someone will meet you when you get there. Please be careful as you drive up, there are guard dogs loose in the grounds."

Returning to her car, Marie shifted into gear and sped through the gates, which swung closed behind her. She tensed when a dog appeared alongside her, she didn't want to run it over if it darted in front of her, but it simply kept pace with her until she reached the house.

Marie drove between two ornamental posts and into a semi-circular area at the front of the house, where she saw a man in a guard's uniform. The dog saw the man as well and loped over to stand at his side, where it remained until she left the car and approached. When she was half a dozen feet from the guard, the dog moved forward and began sniffing at her, clearly trying to decide if she was a friend or an enemy. After a few moments it decided she was a friend and returned to its previous position at the side of the guard.

48

"What do we do now?" Tête asked of his fellow agent as the two of them sat in their BMW outside Charles de Gaulle airport, having followed Rene Dubois there.

"I think we need to get instructions," Agent Schneider gave his opinion. "Dubois could be waiting for a flight so he can get out of the country. If he does that, we're in trouble. We don't have permission, let alone the resources, to continue surveillance if he gets on a plane. And arranging for him to be picked up at the other end might take longer than the flight does."

"Sir, it's Agent Schneider," he said when Special Agent Ney answered his phone. "We've got a problem with Dubois."

"What sort of problem?" Ney asked from his position in the operations room at Interpol's Paris office where, along with Deputy Director Lejour and a variety of other staff, he was overseeing the operations taking place that night.

"Dubois left his apartment this evening and drove to Charles de Gaulle airport, where he retrieved a case from a locker. He's now sitting in the main departure lounge. Agents Martin and Laurent are watching him, but we need to know what you want us to do."

"One moment." Ney put Schneider on hold while he discussed the situation with Lejour. The conversation didn't last long. "Okay. For now, you're to continue as you have been, observe and follow, that's all. Do you think he's aware of your presence?"

"That's unclear, sir. He's given no indication that he knows we're watching him, but his coming to the airport has us concerned, especially with him retrieving a case and not leaving again straightaway. He could be waiting for someone or something, but we have no idea what. He might also have got wind of what is going on and be planning on doing a runner."

"You might be right, but for now, continue as you are. If he makes any attempt to board a flight or an obvious attempt to evade you then bring him in, even if you have to stop the flight on the runway." Ney hoped that wouldn't be necessary. Stopping a commercial airliner to apprehend a corrupt Interpol agent would attract a lot of trouble and unwanted publicity.

"Yes, sir, I understand. I'll keep you informed of any developments." The phone went dead in Schneider's hand then and he turned to his partner. "You'd better join Martin and Laurent inside," he said. "We've been given orders to bring Dubois in if it looks like he's trying to ditch us or he tries to board a flight."

"Let's hope it doesn't come to that," Tête commented as he opened his door. "Things could get very messy if we have to try and grab him here, especially if he makes a fight of it. I'd rather wait until he's somewhere with fewer people to make our move."

"Amen to that," Schneider said as his partner shut the door and started across the car park.

49

"Where's Caldwell?" Marie demanded the moment Jean-Paul strode up to her in the entrance hall of the house. "He's already here, isn't he?"

Jean-Paul dismissed the guard, who returned to his patrol, before he responded, "Calm down, Agent Hapsburg, take a deep breath." It was advice she didn't take. "You said you have a message for me from a Mr Dubois concerning a Mr Caldwell."

Marie realised Renault was being cautious to avoid incriminating himself in front of a stranger, but she doubted there was time for that.

"Yes. I'm the one who gives Rene most of the information he sells you. I'm how you knew where Sofia Torres was being kept in Barcelona. Now, where's Caldwell? There's no time to waste." She saw that Renault wasn't going to budge without an explanation of some sort and ground her teeth in frustration. "Caldwell's working with Interpol. He never killed Torres, she's still alive," she said urgently.

Jean-Paul's face drained of colour. He had difficulty breathing and his mouth went dry. "Are you sure?" he finally managed to ask.

"Yes. I was told this afternoon by the agent in charge of the operation in Barcelona. He's a friend of Caldwell's. Caldwell faked the deaths in Barcelona. He's..." Marie didn't have a chance to say any more than that for Renault turned away and raced upstairs, yanking out his gun as he ran. She guessed that Renault was heading to where Caldwell was with the intention of killing him and she hurried after him.

When he reached the first floor, Jean-Paul sprinted along the corridor to the large office at the rear of the house. With his gun in hand, he burst through the door almost before he was able to get it open. Out the corner of his eye he saw his cousin rise from his chair in surprise at the abrupt invasion, but Jean-Paul was focused on the assassin who had deceived them. He realised how quick Caldwell's reactions were, even with one arm in a sling and a bullet wound to the lower abdomen, when a gun appeared in his hand as if by magic.

Jean-Paul felt a bullet crease his thigh as Caldwell surged to his feet, spun around, and fired all in one, almost impossibly fast, move, managing to get off a shot before he could fire his own weapon. He saw his first bullet hit Caldwell in his heavily bandaged arm, while his next three struck the man in the chest, knocking him backwards over the chair so the last two shots missed him.

"What the hell are you doing?" Noir demanded as Jean-Paul moved forward to kick away the gun Caldwell had dropped.

Jean-Paul was about to turn to his cousin when he spotted movement in the doorway out the corner of his eye. He turned quickly, ready to deal with whatever trouble had arrived. His hand was on the gun he had only just put away when he realised the movement was Agent Hapsburg.

"What's going on?" Noir said sharply, startled by both the murder and the sudden arrival of a strange woman in his office.

"Not here," Marie said, taking in the shot assassin, Renault's bleeding leg, and Noir's look of stunned incomprehension in a single glance. "We can talk outside, but not here. I said not here," she repeated sternly when she saw that Noir was about to speak again.

When Jean-Paul limped after the woman, Noir was forced to follow them to find out what was going on. He glanced briefly at Caldwell's body as he passed it but didn't stop. It didn't bother him that the assassin had been killed, especially since it saved him two and a half million pounds. What did was that Jean-Paul had killed the man without first telling him he was going to do so or why.

"Okay, Jean-Paul, who the hell is this? And why the hell did you kill Caldwell?" Noir demanded once he was out in the passage.

"My name's Marie Hapsburg," She didn't know how Noir felt about Caldwell's murder, but she was disturbed, mostly because of how it had happened, and the fact that it meant they would have to move even more quickly than before. "I'm an agent with Interpol and, indirectly, one of your cousin's sources." She saw a look of concern cross Noir's face as he realised that an Interpol agent had just witnessed his cousin murder someone in his office, and that he could be considered an accomplice to that murder. "We need to get out of here right now."

"I asked you a question," Noir said to Jean-Paul.

"We don't have time for this, Mr Noir," Marie told him. "Your cousin shot Caldwell because I told him Caldwell's been working with Interpol, he never killed Sofia Torres, nor any of the others." She was gratified to see Noir go as pale as a man kept underground his whole life. He also shut his mouth on whatever it was he had been about to say. "If your cousin had been a little more patient, I'd have had time to tell him that Caldwell's wearing a wire, which means that murder was overheard by the surveillance team that's nearby. We've got to get out of here now. Interpol teams with local officers are going to come bursting through the gates any time now."

"Shit!" Jean-Paul swore, wishing he had waited a little longer before rushing off to kill Caldwell. "She's right, Philippe, we've got to get out of here," he said when he saw that his cousin was frozen to the spot by indecision and uncertainty.

"We don't just have to get out of here, we have to get out of the country," Noir said, coming to his senses. "If that bastard was wired, they've got me on tape admitting to murder and conspiracy to commit murder, and ordering you to do the same. They've got enough on both of us to put us away forever." He thought of something then and turned to Marie Hapsburg. He was about to say something when he changed his mind, instead he snapped, "Kill her," to his cousin as he hurried back into his office and over to where his safe was hidden.

"Okay, let's get out of here," Noir told Jean-Paul when he re-joined him in the passage, stepping over the fallen body of Marie Hapsburg.

Rene was glad the Charles de Gaulle airport was busy, it meant he only had to sit around for ten minutes before the passengers from a recently arrived flight came through the main lounge. He joined the crowd as they made their way towards the exits and then split away to follow a small group of men who diverted to enter the nearest toilets. By moving quickly, he was able to secure himself a cubicle just ahead of one of the men and the moment he had the door locked, he put down the lid on the toilet so he could rest his case on it and open it up.

Stripping off his jacket and shirt he shoved them into a corner of the case and took out a white t-shirt and a light brown pullover, both of which he pulled on. After that he took out a box, from which he removed a fake moustache and a wig. He affixed the moustache to his upper lip and slipped the wig on over his own hair, he then took out a pair of glasses, the lenses of which were ordinary glass. The last thing he did before leaving the cubicle was apply several stickers to the outside of his case, so it looked different from the plain case he had carried into the toilets.

As he walked away from the toilets, he looked around and was pleased to see that neither of the agents he had spotted gave him more than a casual glance. It was clear that his disguise had fooled them.

Instead of making for the booking desk for one of the airlines, as he was sure the surveillance team would be expecting him to, he made for the nearest of the car rental agencies.

"**S**hit!" Lejour swore, echoing the feelings of the rest of the people in the room as the sound of the gunshots died away.

Ney was the first to break the silence after his superior's exclamation. "Perhaps it isn't as bad as it sounds," he said hopefully, straining his hearing to pick up something from the tiny microphone Caldwell had been fitted with.

"I think it's safe to say that things are as bad as they sound," Lejour said unhappily. "In fact, I think I can confidently say that they're worse than they sound. Caldwell's been shot, judging by what we just heard, Bright is missing, and for some reason Agent Hapsburg has turned up at Noir's vineyard. I think we can safely assume that Dubois was not the only person Noir had on his payroll."

"Caldwell might be alright," Ney said, trying to sound positive. "He is wearing a bulletproof vest. I know you said he's already been shot, but he's clearly tough."

"That isn't something we can take a chance on," Lejour said. "It's time for you all to send your men in," he directed the various teams in the operations room. "Bring in Noir, Renault, and anyone else at the vineyard." He knew that most of the people who were brought in would be released almost immediately because they had nothing to do with Noir's criminal activities, but there was always a chance they might know something that would help them. Every scrap of information they gathered would help to make their case more secure. "And bring in Dubois as well."

· · · ·

BARELY FIFTEEN MINUTES after the orders were given, six vans, containing a mix of Interpol agents and Paris police officers, smashed through the vineyard gates and raced up the drive.

When they reached the front of the house, the first three vans skidded to a halt, while the fourth sped around to the rear, and the last two turned away from the drive to search the grounds and round up the guards and anyone else they found.

Agents Dubreton and Soult jumped out ahead of the others and raced for the front door. They moved aside when they got there so the officer carrying the portable battering ram could smash open the door, which he did on the second swing. The moment the door flew open, almost in the face of the butler, the assorted agents and officers all of whom were armed with a variety of submachine guns and pistols, swept into the house.

The butler was immediately handcuffed and led away to be placed in the back of the third van by one of the officers, while the rest of them dispersed through the house. Everyone they encountered, no matter who they were, was handcuffed and led outside to the van by either an officer or an agent.

* * * *

"SIR, AGENT SOULT HERE."

The radio in Lejour's hand came to life sooner than anyone in the operations room had expected and they all looked around in surprise and concern, uncertain whether it heralded good news or bad. They soon learned that it was both.

"What's the situation?" Lejour asked.

"We've secured the estate and arrested everyone we found here, but there's no sign of either Noir or Renault. Apparently, they drove away about 10 minutes before we got here."

"Damn!" Lejour swore, echoing what everyone in the room was thinking. "What about Hapsburg and Caldwell, what's the situation with them?" he asked of Soult before turning to the room at large and saying, "Get everyone you've got looking for Noir and Renault, I want them found. They're going to be trying to get out of the country, so check airports, ports, any way they could conceivably escape. And lock down every scrap of money and every connection either of them might have access to. I don't care how many people you have to wake up to get authorisation, do whatever it takes to catch them."

Everyone in the room quickly turned away from Lejour to get on with the job of finding Philippe Noir and Jean-Paul Renault and make it as hard as possible for them to get away or to get help. All of them offered up prayers and wishes for sizeable chunks of luck that would enable them to catch the fugitives as quickly as possible.

"Hapsburg's dead, sir," Soult reported. "We found her body in the passage outside Noir's office. She had her hand on her gun but evidently didn't manage to get it out or protect herself. She was shot twice in the chest."

"What about Caldwell?" Lejour asked. With a degree of reluctance that he felt guilty for, he hoped the news on Caldwell was positive. Fortunately, it was.

"He's alive," Soult answered. "He took three shots in the chest, but they were all stopped by the vest he was wearing. He might have some cracked ribs, and he's almost certainly going to have some pretty major bruising that will make breathing uncomfortable for a while, but he should be okay apart from that. We've got an ambulance on the way to take him to hospital."

"Okay, keep me informed on the situation," Lejour said before signing off to leave Soult and his team, now they had secured the vineyard and everyone they had found there, to begin the painstaking task of searching the property for any evidence to link Noir to his criminal activities.

They had Noir on tape admitting to killing Tomas Abrantes, his family and the others at his estate, and ordering the attempts on Sofia Torres' life. They also had Renault on tape committing the attempted murder of Caldwell and could easily link both him and Noir to the murder of Agent Hapsburg. The more evidence they could get, though, the easier it would be to secure convictions against not only Noir and Renault but also against everyone in Noir's organisation.

52

Without a backwards glance from either of them, Noir and Jean-Paul raced away from the house in the Range Rover they had taken from the vineyard's garage. It wasn't the fastest of the vehicles they could have picked, but it was the one best suited to the unpaved paths that led through the grounds of the vineyard.

They knew that Interpol and the police would be smashing through the gates of the estate soon, looking to take them both into custody, but they hoped to get away through the vineyard itself. There were multiple ways out of the estate on the other side of the vineyard, and not all of them were obvious, so there was a good chance that Interpol and the police wouldn't have them all covered.

"This is all your fault," Noir told Jean-Paul for the third time since they had rushed out of the house and jumped into the vehicle. "I trusted you to keep me safe and you put me in this position. What the hell happened?"

"I don't see how you can blame me," Renault said, responding for the first time. "Dubois' the one who failed to discover Caldwell was working with Interpol." He felt aggrieved by the way his cousin was blaming him when he had done everything he could, always, to help him. "You should be thankful the information was discovered before it put the two of us away. You should also be thankful that I planned ahead and arranged fake papers for us." Even if his cousin wasn't glad of his foresight, he was. He had no desire to spend the rest of his life in jail. He much preferred the idea of remaining free, even if being free meant never being able to set foot in France, or any part of Europe, again.

"Don't get me wrong, I'm glad you planned ahead," Noir said, though he didn't sound it. "But you haven't yet told me how far ahead you planned. It's one thing for us to get away before the estate is raided, but what's our next step? What do we do now?"

"We do the sensible thing," Jean-Paul said as he steered the Range Rover along the path that led through the vineyard to the nearest of the hidden exits that he was sure neither Interpol nor the Paris police had a clue about. "We get out of the country as quickly as we can. We've got at least a quarter of an hour lead on Interpol, probably more, and we've got fake IDs. We should be able to get out of the country before they have a clue where we are."

"I'll take your word for that. I just hope you aren't as wrong about that as you were about Caldwell," Noir said with a bite to his voice. "You're the one with all the plans, so I'll trust you for now. What exactly is the plan?" he wanted to know.

"Just what I said. We're going to get out of the country as quickly as we can. I'd say South America is our best choice, at least to start with. Once we're there we can take the time to think about what we're going to do long term. Be thankful you had the foresight to put the bulk of your money into untraceable accounts that Interpol can't block. Wherever we end up, you'll still be able to access it and live whatever type of life you want. What do you want to do about Olivier?" he asked, changing the subject. As far as he was concerned Olivier was a good friend and he didn't want to see him in jail, which was bound to happen if he was picked up by Interpol or the police. More than that, though, Olivier knew about at least some of the accounts Noir had set up to hide his money, and there was always a chance that the prospect of jail would encourage him to trade that information for his freedom.

"Sir, it's Agent Tête," said one of the agents handling communications in the operations room. "He says they've lost Agent Dubois."

For several long seconds Lejour simply stared at the agent, not able to believe what he had just heard, then he stalked over and snatched the radio from him. "What the hell happened?" he demanded. Nothing was going the way it should have, and he was far from happy.

"We lost Dubois," Tête admitted. "He must have realised he was being watched. I don't know how, we were very careful," he said almost defensively. "Anyway, he sat around the airport until a bunch of passengers went through from a flight and followed some of them into the toilets. I realised he might be trying to evade us, but I couldn't be certain, and I didn't want to tip him off, so I didn't send anyone in after him. When he didn't reappear after a quarter of an hour I sent my men in. There was no way he could have escaped through any of the windows, they're too high, too small, and all the catches were secure. And there's no other way out of the toilets except the way he went in." Tête wasn't happy with the ease with which Dubois had eluded his team. It suggested that they, and by extension he, had messed up somehow.

"And your men didn't see Dubois leave the toilets?" Lejour asked, fighting to keep his voice level.

"I suspect he put on a disguise. His car is still here, and no-one's approached it, so we're investigating the other ways he could have left the airport. I've got my people checking all the flights that have left or are due to leave, the car rental agencies, taxi ranks, and every other way he could possibly have left. No luck so far."

Lejour grunted. "It's doubtful he'll go back there but send someone to his place. Have it searched thoroughly for anything that might suggest where he's going, and while you're at it, see if you can find anything that links Dubois to a Special Agent Marie Hapsburg." He signed off then before Tête could say anything. He was too annoyed by events to want to deal with any unnecessary questions.

. . . .

THE RINGING OF ONE phone, amidst the cacophony of phone calls, radio messages, and discussions went unnoticed by Lejour. He had no idea of the importance of that one call until the excited voice of a communications officer cut through the noise.

"Sir, we've got an intercept of a phone call from a monitored number. It's Noir, he's on his mobile, talking to his lawyer."

"Can we hear the call?" Lejour asked eagerly, hoping the intercept was going to be the breakthrough they had been waiting for.

"Yes, sir."

Everyone fell silent as Noir's voice filled the room.

. . . .

"WHERE THE HELL HAVE you been?" Noir demanded of Olivier when his call was finally answered. "I've been trying to get hold of you for an hour."

"I've been taking care of a few things," Olivier said. "What's wrong?"

"We're in big trouble, that's what's wrong. Caldwell was an undercover agent. A bloody plant," he all but yelled. "He never killed those people in Barcelona, they're still alive, which means they can still testify against me. Worse than that, the bastard has us on tape talking about everything, from me killing that bastard, Abrantes, to everything that happened after. He almost certainly has Jean-Paul on tape hiring him to kill the witness as well. We're screwed. All of us. Especially since Jean-Paul decided to shoot the lying son-of-a-bitch while he was wearing a wire. Interpol has us committing murder on tape."

"Jesus!" Olivier breathed, unable to think of anything more to say for a few moments. "How did you find out?" he asked finally.

"Jean-Paul's contact turned up to warn us that Caldwell was working for Interpol. Too late as it turned out. By the time she warned Jean-Paul, Caldwell already had everything he needed from me." Noir wasn't sure what he was most angry about: that Caldwell had turned out to be working for Interpol, that his cousin had hired someone who worked for Interpol, or that he had been stupid enough to let himself be recorded talking about his criminal activities after years of being so careful to avoid it happening.

It took Olivier only a fraction of a second to appreciate how serious the situation was for Noir and Jean-Paul. It was as serious as things could be.

"Are you in custody?" Olivier's mind raced as he tried to think of a way to get Philippe out of the trouble he was in. He suspected it was an all but impossible task, but he was paid well to at least make the attempt.

"No, we left the estate as soon as we knew what was going on. Interpol probably isn't far behind us, though, with local help, but Jean-Paul's confident he can lose them once we reach the city."

"Especially since we haven't seen any sign of them since we left the estate," Jean-Paul spoke up, loud enough to be heard by Olivier.

"Where are you planning on going?" Olivier asked. "You realise neither of you can go home, not if Interpol has as much on you as you say. Neither can you go any place that Interpol or the locals might be able to connect to you. They'll be searching for you everywhere. Family, friends, businesses, Interpol will have people checking all of those places on the off chance you'll go there." As he said that he realised that his house was probably one of the first places that would be checked, which meant he had to get home before the authorities arrived and scared his family. "You need a plan, a very good plan."

"We have one," Noir assured him. "We've arranged for a private jet to take us out of the country, it's waiting for us at Charles de Gaulle under the name Briand. We should be safe once we reach South America. Then we can find somewhere quiet where we can make long term plans."

Olivier had to admit the plan had merit. There were still plenty of countries in South America that provided a safe harbour for criminals, especially criminals with the kind of money that Noir had stashed away.

"I'm sure you're right. South America will be safe for you as long as you pick the right country. How far from the airport are you?" The lawyer in him tried to work out the legalities of the situation. He couldn't be certain, since he had never dealt with such a situation before, but he believed Noir and Jean-Paul would be safe once they were in the air and over the Atlantic.

Noir looked around. "An hour, maybe an hour and a half," he said. "It depends on the traffic when we get closer. That gives you an hour and a half to get you and your family to the airport. The jet we've chartered is with Eagle Aviation, you'll find us there. I wouldn't advise wasting any time packing, you'll have to leave your stuff behind. If you're not there when I get to the jet, you're too late. I won't be waiting for you." He had known Olivier a long time, and considered him a good friend, as well as a valued associate, but he wasn't about to risk his freedom waiting for him.

· · · ·

"WE'VE GOT THE BREAK we've been waiting for, ladies and gentlemen," Lejour announced once it was clear the phone call between Noir and Olivier Boucher was finished. "We need to act quickly if we're going to stop Noir getting away, though. Ney, I want you to get a group of agents to the airport so they can arrest Noir and Renault when they show up. I want you there to take charge personally. If possible, you're to wait until they're away from any crowds before making the arrests. I don't want to have to worry about a hostage situation. Inspector Joubert, I'd like you to provide some officers to assist, and to take charge of Noir and Renault once they're in custody." Since Interpol was primarily an investigative force, they had no choice but to work with local law enforcement agencies when the time came to make an arrest, no matter what country they were operating in. "I would advise extreme caution," he said unnecessarily.

"I'll make sure there are plenty of officers around," Joubert said. "They won't be able to try anything. And they'll be put in the most secure location I can find. What about Boucher? Do you want him brought in as well? That phone call makes him an accessory to multiple crimes."

"I think we should bring him in," Ney offered his opinion. "He's a good lawyer, and will probably be able to get himself off most, if not all, of what he might be charged with from that phone call, but if we apply the right amount of pressure, and maybe offer him immunity, he might agree to testify against Noir. Even if that doesn't work, bringing him in will make it impossible for him to represent Noir, which means Noir will have to get himself a new lawyer, who is unlikely to be as willing to take chances as Boucher has been in the past."

"Doesn't Boucher have a wife and two kids?" Lejour asked. When Ney nodded, he said, "Good, we can use that. He won't want to be away from them, and I'm sure he's smart enough to know that he's going to have a very hard time fighting the amount of conspiracy charges he's going to be looking at. I think you're right. He may well agree to testify in return for immunity, especially if we sweeten the deal and offer to put him and his family in witness protection. Bring him in."

"I told you two to hurry up!" Olivier yelled up the stairs to his children, annoyed that they hadn't paid attention to the instructions he had issued upon his return home. He supposed he should be glad they had been home, and he hadn't had to try and find them, which would have taken precious time. "There isn't time to pack everything. Just grab the essentials and get your asses...shit!" he swore as the sound of sirens, distant but getting closer, reached him.

He had made it home fifteen minutes before, and had hoped to leave five minutes after that, having called his wife while he was racing home so she could have the kids ready to go the moment he arrived. Unfortunately, while his wife had accepted the urgency of the situation and responded to it, his children hadn't.

Storming up the stairs to the sound of the approaching sirens, Olivier rushed into his daughter's bedroom, where he found her sitting on the end of her bed, her mobile phone pressed to her ear. "You were told to pack one bag and get downstairs, not call all your bloody friends!" he shouted angrily. He snatched the phone from his daughter's grasp and dropped it into the open bag he picked up from the bed. With the bag in one hand, he took his daughter's arm and dragged her to her feet and out of the room. When he reached the head of the stairs, he tossed the bag down them, to the horror of his daughter.

"You'll break all my stuff," she wailed as she hurried down the stairs so she could check her things and make sure they were alright. "If you've broken anything, you're replacing it."

"I don't care if it's all broken," Olivier told her. "Just get out to the car. If you're not in the car in one minute, Louis, we're leaving without you!" he shouted in the direction of his son's bedroom before he hurried down the stairs.

A minute and a half later, Olivier shifted into gear and gunned the engine as he raced out of the drive. In the passenger seat was his wife, she was concerned but as calm as she could be under the circumstances, while from the back seat his children expressed their feelings on the situation, which ranged from confusion, to unhappiness, and was mixed with wishes for him to die so he couldn't ruin their lives.

Olivier ignored the shouted comments from the back seat and focused on his driving. He was halfway through a turn to the left at the end of the road when he saw the flashing lights of an approaching police car. Hurriedly, he spun the wheel to turn the car the other way, mounting the curb as he pressed his foot down on the accelerator. For a few seconds the police car seemed to be almost on his rear bumper, and then the superior acceleration of his Mercedes pulled him ahead and he began to inch away.

All of Olivier's focus was on the car behind him, and he wasn't aware of the other police car, which pulled out of a side road ahead of him until his wife screamed for him to look out. Twisting the wheel sharply, he found himself in the headlights of an oncoming car. His eyes closed, and his hands braced on the steering wheel, he uttered a silent prayer as he pressed down on the brake so hard he thought it would break.

When he opened his eyes, he saw that he had stopped barely an inch from the other vehicle. That was good, but that fortune was offset by the six police officers who were rushing towards his car, all of them with handguns at the ready, and all of them wearing looks which suggested they were ready to use their weapons at the slightest provocation.

"Everybody out of the car!" an officer wearing the stripes of a sergeant yelled, while his men aimed their weapons at Olivier and his family.

Olivier was not a brave man. He had never been involved in the violent side of Noir's business, except in the most remote of ways. Even if he had been, the knowledge that the guns were aimed at his family, as well as at him, would have stopped him doing anything stupid.

"What's going on, daddy? Why are they pointing guns at us?" Angelique sobbed. Unlike her brother, who was trying to act as though there was nothing to worry about, she had no problem showing that she was scared. Tears of fear rolled down her cheeks.

"Don't worry, honey, I'll sort it out," Olivier said reassuringly. "For now, let's just do as they say." Slowly, so as not to provoke a response from the officers, he released his seatbelt and swung open the door at his side.

The moment he was out of the car, Olivier was spun around, pushed roughly up against the side of his car, and ordered to place his hands on the roof and spread his legs. The same orders were given to his family when they got out, which prompted a scream from his daughter.

"Is this really necessary," Olivier asked of the sergeant as hands were run quickly and roughly over his body to check for a weapon. "It's okay, honey, everything will be alright," he said when Angelique gave another scream, this time in reaction to the search that was being made of her. "What's the meaning of this?" he demanded of the sergeant, who didn't answer, but instead watched his men as they conducted their searches. "I insist you tell me why you are arresting me and my family," he said when his hands were twisted behind his back and he felt the cold metal of cuffs on his wrists. "I'm a lawyer and I have well-connected friends. You can't arrest us without cause."

By that time several cars had been forced to stop because of the blocked road and there were numerous witnesses to his arrest. Olivier didn't care about that, though; he didn't even care that one of the onlookers was the mother of one of his daughter's friends.

"I'm merely doing my job, Mr Boucher," the sergeant said finally. "I was told to arrest you, and that's what I'm doing. I believe the charge is to be conspiracy to commit murder, but I'm sure you'll be given all the details when you get to the station. I know there are several people from Interpol who are keen to talk to you."

Olivier wasn't surprised to hear that, though it did make him worry, despite his best efforts to remain calm. "You have no reason to arrest my family," he said. "They've got nothing to do with any of this."

"I have orders to arrest you, and anyone with you, Mr Boucher," the sergeant informed him, doing his best to ignore the sobs from Angelique Boucher, and the reproachful look being directed at him by Helene Boucher. "I'm sure you'll be able to sort all of this out at the station and arrange for your family to be released. Load them into separate cars," he ordered his men, though the fact that they only had three cars and four people to transport meant the two children had to be put in a car together.

55

After driving through the gates and stopping at the small security and customs checkpoint, as was required of them, Jean-Paul found the first available space in the car park that belonged to the charter airlines.

When he got out, he left the keys in the ignition. Since neither he nor Noir were planning on ever returning to France, there was no reason for either of them to care if the vehicle was stolen. He thought it would actually be to their benefit if the vehicle was stolen, as it would throw the police and Interpol off their trail, which would increase their chances of getting away.

With no luggage to burden them, Jean-Paul and Noir walked empty-handed across the car park to the offices of Eagle Aviation. When they reached the building, Jean-Paul opened the door for his cousin, who strode inside and over to the counter, where a smartly dressed young woman stood.

"Good evening, the name's Briand," Noir informed her. "I have a jet chartered for a flight tonight."

"Yes, sir, the Gulfstream," the woman said immediately. "I understand you wish to leave as soon as possible."

"That's right, is the jet ready?" Noir/ Briand asked. He hoped it was, he didn't want to wait around any longer than necessary. Every delay increased the chances of Interpol and the police finding out where he was and stopping him escaping.

"I believe so, sir. If you'll follow me, I'll take you through to the lounge." The woman stood up and came around from behind the counter. She opened a security door and led the way down a short passage to the small but comfortable lounge, where they found someone in a pilot's uniform waiting for them.

Jean-Paul looked around the lounge as they entered, but there was no sign of either Olivier or his family.

"Mr Jaures, this is Mr Briand and his associate, they are your passengers. Mr Briand, this is Mr Jaures, the co-pilot for your flight."

"Thank you," Noir/ Briand said absently as the young woman turned away to return to the reception area. "Is the jet ready?" he asked of the co-pilot.

"The pre-flight checks are just being completed. Everything has been arranged to make your flight as comfortable as possible. If you would care to come with me, I'll take you out to the hangar so you can board the jet," Jaures said. "Is your luggage in reception?"

"No, we haven't brought any with us," Jean-Paul said, hoping no questions would be asked of their lack of luggage because he wasn't sure he could provide an answer that wouldn't make the co-pilot suspicious.

"Very well then, it's this way."

"What about Olivier?" Jean-Paul asked as they followed the co-pilot out of the lounge and the building to where a cart was waiting to transport them to the hangar, and the jet that would take them out of the country.

"You heard what I told him. If he wasn't here with his family when we get here, we'd be leaving without him. He isn't here. I'm not about to wait for him. We'll get in touch once we're safe, if we can, and he can join us wherever we are, assuming he hasn't been arrested."

It wasn't a long journey across the airport, and they soon reached the hangar belonging to Eagle Aviation, where they saw the Gulfstream jet Noir had chartered. It was sleek and looked fast, which was just what they wanted, and the stairs were already down, so they could board without delay.

Jean-Paul swung out of the cart the moment it stopped and hurried over to the jet, where he waited at the foot of the stairs for his cousin and the co-pilot to catch up. He hadn't paid much attention to Jaures before then, but now he did, and he noticed that the man's uniform didn't quite fit him properly: the jacket was a little tight across the shoulders and under the arms, and the trousers dragged on the ground at the heels, all of which aroused his suspicions. He was sure, given how much the charter airline charged, that their staff would be dressed in uniforms that fitted them properly in order to maintain the appearance of a top-class operation. More suspicious than the ill-fitting clothes was the gun Jaures appeared to be carrying in a holster at his left armpit, which was revealed by the tightness of his jacket.

Jean-Paul waited until Jaures had passed him and started up the stairs, and then he grabbed him by the back of his jacket. With a quick jerk he dragged him off the stairs and threw him to the ground, where he dropped heavily on top of him.

"What the hell are you doing?" Noir demanded, staring in surprise at Jean-Paul.

"This guy isn't the co-pilot," Jean-Paul told him.

"Are you sure?"

For answer, Jean-Paul reached under Jaures' jacket and took out the gun. "Do you think a real pilot would be carrying this?" he asked. He turned his attention back to the man beneath him. "What are you, police or Interpol?" To encourage Jaures to answer when he appeared reluctant, he pressed the muzzle of the gun into his eye.

"DROP YOUR WEAPONS!"

The shout came from behind Noir, and he spun around while Jean-Paul dragged Jaures up so he could use him as a shield as he surged to his feet and turned to the front of the hangar. Facing them was an assortment of armed police officers, counter-terrorism officers armed with submachine guns from the main airport terminal, and several non-uniformed men who were holding handguns, whom Jean-Paul and Noir guessed were from Interpol.

"You drop your weapons," Jean-Paul called back. "Drop them or I kill him." He emphasised his point by shifting the gun so it was against Jaures' temple, where all the people in the hangar doors could see it.

His finger on the trigger, ready to fire the moment it became necessary, Jean-Paul's eyes travelled from one end of the line of officers and agents to the other. He counted eight people in the line, all with their weapons aimed at him and his cousin, but he wasn't about to simply give in, despite the odds being stacked against them. He was determined to get the two of them out of the country, no matter how many people he had to kill to manage it.

"Be sensible, Mr Renault, you're outnumbered, you can't get away," Ney called out, doing his best to project a level of confidence he didn't feel. He didn't know how the two men had realised the co-pilot was one of his officers, but that didn't matter just then. He was more interested in trying to deal with the situation at hand and arrest Noir and Renault without getting anyone killed. "Don't make things worse for yourself. You're already in a lot of trouble. If you give yourself up, things will go better for you."

"Don't give me that crap. You know as well as I do that if I give myself up, I'll be in jail until I die. Nothing I..." Jean-Paul spun around at the noise that came from behind him, still with a tight hold on his hostage. He yanked his gun away from Jaures the moment he saw the gun-toting woman on the steps of the jet and fired twice. Both shots hit the woman in the chest before she could react to the danger, and she tumbled down the stairs.

Jean-Paul turned away the moment he shot the woman, without waiting to see the result of his actions, and refocused his attention on the people at the front of the hangar.

"All of you drop your weapons or more people die," he told them, digging the muzzle of his gun into Jaures' temple threateningly.

"We can't do that," Ney said, though he immediately realised that it was the wrong thing to say. He dived to one side as Jean-Paul took the gun from Jaures' head and pointed it at him. The shots missed, thankfully, and he had to resist the urge to shoot back for fear of hitting Jaures.

Jean-Paul realised he was losing control, the look on his cousin's face told him as much, but he didn't seem able to stop himself. "I told you all to drop your weapons!" he shouted angrily, waving his gun around. He was pleased to see everyone in the line of officers and agents flinch and tense themselves in preparation to get out of the way if he started shooting again. "Get everyone off the jet except the pilot. Philippe and I will get on board and fly away. When we get to where we're going, we'll release Mr Jaures, or whatever his real name is, and he can fly home."

"Be reasonable. You know we can't let you go. Even if we let you fly away, you'll be tracked, and there will be people waiting for you when you land." Ney wished there had been time for the police snipers to get there and into position before Noir and Renault arrived. One well-placed shot could have ended things without any further problems.

While his cousin waved his gun around and tried to get them on the jet, Noir was more sensible. It was a reversal of their normal roles, he thought, as he worried that Jean-Paul would start shooting in some mad attempt to fight their way out of there, which, he realised, was something he might have ordered his men to do if they were there, and his life wasn't one of those under threat.

They would never be able to get away in the jet, it just wouldn't be allowed, which meant they need to find another way of escaping. He was confident they could still get away, so long as they kept thinking, didn't do anything stupid, and kept hold of their hostage. While they had Jaures, Interpol and the police would be cautious about making any aggressive moves. That kept the two of them safe, up to a point. If they could get out of the airport and to a vehicle, he believed they stood a chance of evading the authorities, though it wouldn't be easy.

Once they had done that, his organisation would be able to smuggle them out of the country. After all, they smuggled tonnes of assorted drugs into the country every year without them being discovered, so they must be able to smuggle two people out. First, though, they needed to get out of the hangar.

While Jean-Paul kept control of Jaures and watched the group at the hangar's main doors, Noir searched for a way out. At the same time, he searched for any sign that there were others in the hangar, waiting to stop them. He was certain there had to be at least one other way out of the hangar, for health and safety reasons if nothing else. He was equally certain that there were officers and agents hiding in the hangar, waiting for an opportunity to catch them by surprise. He found what he was looking for, a door in the back wall of the hangar, after a minute. He had no idea where it led, but neither did he care. It led out of the hangar, and that was the only thing that mattered to him then.

With a hand on Jean-Paul's arm, Noir slowly guided his cousin towards the door. As he led the way, Jean-Paul holding on tight to their hostage, his eyes darted all around, searching for trouble.

They made steady progress, despite the situation, but the line of officers and agents kept pace, moving further into the hangar after them. He didn't like that. If the door wouldn't open, they would be more trapped than they had been before.

They were twenty-five feet from the door when two men appeared, rising to their feet from behind some machinery and moving quickly to block the door.

Noir fired the moment he saw the men, forgetting that he had intended remaining calm and behaving sensibly. The first man went down after being hit but before he could change his aim to fire at the second man he was spun around by a hammer blow to the shoulder. He was hit again as he fell and then his head impacted with the concrete floor of the hangar, at which point everything went black.

The moment Noir started shooting, Jean-Paul twisted around. He saw his cousin fall but ignored that as he fired at the agent blocking the door. He was squeezing the trigger for the third time when Jaures hooked his foot around the back of his leg and threw himself backwards, knocking him off his feet.

Jean-Paul landed heavily, and then had the breath knocked out of him as Jaures landed on top of him and drove an elbow into his ribs. Surprised and winded, Jean-Paul let go of his hostage, who quickly scrambled to his feet so he could get away.

Jean-Paul raised his gun as he struggled to get his breath back and get to his feet. He was able to get off a shot, which took Jaures in the middle of the back, and then someone dived on top of him. They pinned his arm to the floor and forced his gun away from Jaures before wrenching it from his grasp and throwing it aside.

Moving forward cautiously, their weapons at the ready, Ney and Joubert, along with their team, approached Noir and Renault. It was clear that Noir was unconscious, and not an immediate threat, so they focused their attention and their weapons on Renault. They kept their weapons trained on him until the officer who had put himself at risk to save Jaures rolled Renault over onto his face and cuffed his hands behind his back.

Handcuffs were also placed on Noir, despite him being unconscious, to further ensure he couldn't cause any trouble, and while two Interpol agents kept watch on Noir and Renault, those who had been shot were checked.

To the relief of both Ney and Joubert, and the rest of their team, none of those shot by Noir and Renault had been killed thanks to the body armour they were wearing, and Ney took out his phone to report in while Joubert organised medical assistance.

• • • •

"WHAT'S THE SITUATION?" Lejour asked without preamble when he answered Ney's call.

"Noir and Renault are both in custody," Ney said. "Noir's going to need surgery, he was shot in the shoulder and the stomach, but he should pull through okay. Renault's okay, just a few bumps and bruises, nothing to worry about." He wasn't inclined to worry about any injuries sustained by the pair, he wouldn't have worried even if they had been more serious. They were alive, and that was good, but only because it meant they could stand trial and receive the appropriate punishment for their crimes.

"Any injuries to your team?"

"Nothing to worry about," Ney reassured him. "Everyone who was shot got hit in their vests, so the most they're going to have is bruises, and maybe a cracked rib here or there. They'll be okay in a few days, a week at the most. Things could have gone a lot worse."

Lejour uttered a silent prayer of thanks. Everything had been arranged with such haste he wouldn't have been surprised if the worst had come to pass, and he was relieved that hadn't happened.

"Okay, get Noir to the hospital and get him into surgery. Make sure you have plenty of officers there in case he's stupid enough to try and make a break for it. And get Renault into a cell." He hung up then so he could begin winding down the operation and get everyone back to their normal duties. Things had not gone to plan, and there was bound to be some fallout and a fair number of questions about what had gone wrong, but the thing that mattered most was that they had got the result they were after: Philippe Noir and Jean-Paul Renault were under arrest, and they had enough evidence against them to be sure that no amount of legal manoeuvring would save them from prison.

The only questions that remained was how many crimes they would be charged with and how long would be the sentences they received.

56

T HREE DAYS LATER

. . . .

"GOOD MORNING, MR CALDWELL," Lejour greeted his visitor in a neutral voice, showing no pleasure at seeing Luke Caldwell, despite it being he who had arranged the meeting. "Please have a seat." He indicated the chair across the desk from him.

"Deputy Director Lejour," Luke returned the greeting in a similar tone.

"How are you?" Lejour asked. He hadn't missed the brief flash of pain that had crossed Caldwell's face as he sat, and his eyes went to the heavy bandage on his guest's left arm.

"All things considered, I'm doing good," Luke said. "You didn't ask me to come in and see you just so you can see how I'm doing, did you. I'm sure it's enough for you to know that I'm alive, and I doubt you're all that concerned about that. So, why did you ask me to come in?"

Lejour nodded briefly. "You're right, that isn't why I asked you here. I asked you to come in because of your friend, Agent Bright, Ben."

"Where is he?" Luke asked. "Is he alright? I expected to see him after the operation, but he hasn't even called."

"No, he's not alright. He's dead."

"How? When? Where?" The news shocked Luke. He had suspected that something had happened, which was why he hadn't heard from Ben, but dead hadn't occurred to him.

"We don't have all the answers," Lejour admitted. "And it's possible we'll never have them. What we do know is that Bright was on his way here to Paris with another agent to take part in the operation when he disappeared. He never made it to the flight he was booked on, but the agent with him did. That agent later turned up at Noir's vineyard immediately before you were shot and Noir and his cousin made their escape. We believe that she was in Noir's pay and killed Bright after being told about the operation against Noir that you were involved in, and she then came to Paris to warn Noir. Unfortunately, this is all supposition; since she was found dead outside Noir's office when the vineyard was raided we can't ask her what happened."

"So, how do you know Ben's dead?" It wasn't that he doubted Lejour, Luke was sure he wouldn't have said Ben was dead if they didn't know for certain, he just wanted to know how they knew.

"Because we found his body yesterday morning. When the agent turned up at the vineyard and there was no sign of Bright, we knew something had to be up. We had more pressing matters to worry about at the time, though, so it wasn't until the operation was concluded and we had Noir and Renault in custody that we were able to do anything about Bright's disappearance. We finally found him through the GPS on his phone. His body was off a service path on the outskirts of Barcelona airport. It looks as though he was shot with his own gun.

"She must have surprised and disarmed him after being told about the operation, and then used his gun to kill him." Lejour was surprised by how calmly Caldwell was taking the news that his friend had been killed by a corrupt agent, he had expected an angry outburst at the least, that was how he had wanted to react when he learned what had happened to Bright, but outside of his initial reaction Caldwell was talking as though they were discussing the weather. "I'm sure you can understand that we want to keep this as quiet as possible, at least until we can be more certain what happened. I thought you deserved to know about Bright's death, though, especially since it was your friendship with him that led to you helping us to bring down Noir."

"Thank you." Luke appreciated the consideration, especially when he knew Lejour would rather have seen him in jail than accepted his help. "So, what happens now? You've got Noir and Renault, and I assume you have enough to prosecute them."

"We do," Lejour said with a satisfied nod. "We may not be able to get them on anything drug related at the moment, but we can definitely get them both on multiple counts of murder, attempted murder, and conspiracy to commit murder. There's no chance they're going to walk away from this, nor are they going to get out of jail this side of the grave."

"That's good, but it doesn't answer my question. What happens now? Am I going to be needed to testify?"

"I don't think so, no. We've got everything we're likely to need to secure convictions against Noir and Renault, and it will only create confusion during the trial to have someone like you testifying. We have no idea how much information Renault was given about you, but anything he has could be used during the trial to cause problems."

"And you want to avoid that," Luke said. He was okay with the idea of not having to testify. Doing so was likely to cause him problems he would rather avoid, and he had brought enough problems on himself through helping his friend and Interpol.

Lejour nodded.

"In that case, I think we're done. Unless there's something else you'd like my help with."

"I think we can manage without your help in the future," Lejour said. He had no intention of involving Luke Caldwell in any other investigations, especially when he was sure that any future help would come with a price attached to it.

"I'm sure you can." Luke smiled at what Lejour hadn't said, but which was obvious to him. "I'll be off then. Thanks for letting me know about Ben, I appreciate it."

Lejour waited for more than a minute after Caldwell left his office, accompanied by the officer who had escorted him there, and then he picked up the phone on his desk. His call was answered almost immediately. "He's on his way out of the building," he told Ney. "Make sure your men don't lose him like they did Dubois."

"They won't," Ney said. "We'll tail him wherever he goes."

• • • •

LUKE COULDN'T HELP smiling to himself as he walked down the road and away from the Interpol building. He was sure the surveillance team in their blue Citroen and dirty white Vauxhall van, supposedly belonging to a window repair company, thought they were being discreet, but he had spotted them almost straight away.

He had suspected the moment he was asked to meet with Lejour that it was nothing more than an excuse to get him somewhere they could begin a surveillance operation on him. He would have been surprised if they had just let him walk away without some attempt to keep an eye on him, despite the help he had provided them.

He was more amused than annoyed by the deception, having anticipated it. Interpol, and others, had been doing their best to keep track of him for years, so it was nothing new. It could be irritating when he had a job, but when he didn't he found it entertaining to lead surveillance teams all over the place before giving them the slip.

Thinking of the fun he was going to have while he healed, he strolled down the road.

57

TWO MONTHS LATER

• • • •

PASCAL MONTOYA, SPORTING a deep tan after six weeks under the sun as he sailed the islands of the Caribbean, a close-cropped beard, and several fresh tattoos, made a last check of his boat and then headed away down the dock.

Guadeloupe was the largest island he had stopped at, and he was a little nervous about being there, but he needed to resupply if he was going to continue his aimless wandering of the world's waters. Before he resupplied, though, he decided to get himself something to eat. He had skipped lunch because of how close he was to Guadeloupe, and now his stomach was protesting. He hadn't realised how much work was involved in sailing a boat, especially sailing one single-handed, until he took up the lifestyle. Not that it had been his intention to be living a single life on the seas.

He didn't have to go far to find something to eat, thankfully. At the end of the marina was a fish market, not very active at that time of the day, and about a hundred yards beyond that, with a good view of the harbour, was a bar, a sign outside of which advertised a variety of local dishes. He had no idea what most of the dishes were, despite having become more familiar with Caribbean food during his recent island-hopping, but he wasn't bothered by that. He had always been adventurous when it came to food and was willing to try any new dishes he came across.

No sooner had he taken a seat at a table outside the bar, there was a nice view, but he wasn't concerned about that just then, he was more interested in filling his stomach, when a waitress appeared at his side.

"Welcome to Elizabeth's, first time here? I've not seen you before."

"Yes, my first time. I'm cruising the islands and stopped off for supplies. I thought I'd get something to eat first, though, what do you recommend?"

"We do the best Porc Colombo on the island," the waitress said without hesitation.

"I'll have some of that then," Pascal said. He didn't know what the dish was, but he was sure it would be nice. "And a rum, whatever brand you think best." He preferred wine to spirits, but while in the Caribbean it seemed appropriate to him to sample the various rums on offer.

It didn't take long for either the rum or the food to arrive, and he was soon enjoying the best meal he had had in several weeks. He was a decent cook, and more than capable of preparing dishes from around the world that would satisfy even locals who grew up with them, but the galley on his boat was small and it limited what he could do.

He was halfway through his meal, and debating with himself whether to see if they did desserts, when someone sat down across from him. Annoyed that someone would be so rude as to join him without an invitation, he looked up, and immediately knew he was in trouble. The man on the other side of the table had the appearance of a businessman, or maybe a banker or lawyer, but Pascal knew instinctively that he was none of those things.

"Pascal Montoya?" the man asked. "Or should I say Rene Dubois? You are Rene Dubois, aren't you?"

Pascal Montoya, Rene Dubois before he went on the run, sighed and pushed away his plate, his appetite gone. He had known this day was likely to come sooner or later, but he had thought that his precautions would keep it far off in the future.

His first thought was to utter a denial, and his second was to make a run for it. He abandoned both ideas as soon as they occurred to him, however. There was no point in him trying to deny who he was, the man across from him wouldn't be there if he wasn't certain he had the right man. Making a run for it was equally pointless, he didn't need to look around to know that the man was not alone, and that all avenues of escape would have been discreetly blocked while he was waiting for his food.

"Who are you?" Dubois asked.

"Special Agent Ney, Interpol," the man said, taking out his identity card, though Dubois showed no interest in examining it.

The name was known to Dubois, Ney was considered to be one of the best when it came to surveillance operations and tracking down criminals who were on the run, but he had never thought to look up those who worked in the surveillance department in Paris, and so wouldn't have known him had he passed him in the street. It was a mistake on his part not to have done so, though it was too late to waste time chastising himself for it.

"How did you find me?" he asked. "I thought I'd covered my tracks."

"You tried to, but you didn't do as well as you thought. Your virus was detected almost as soon as it started attacking our system and the safety protocols kicked in, shutting the system down and switching over to the backup. We lost some data, and that caused us some problems, but not as much as you intended, and certainly not enough to stop us finding you."

"Then what took you so long?" Dubois asked. "If my virus didn't work," it annoyed him to think that the time and effort he had spent on arranging the back door into Interpol's systems, and the virus that was meant to destroy them, had been wasted, "shouldn't you have found me sooner?"

"I'd say two months is pretty good going, given that you changed identities twice, travelled across Europe by car, used cash at every opportunity, and then disappeared onto the oceans on a boat. Of course, you were made a high priority, so I was given plenty of resources to track you down with."

"I guess. How did you manage to track me down?"

"There will be plenty of time for us to get into that on the journey home, if you're really interested," Ney said. "I trust you're going to come quietly and not try to resist."

"Yes," Dubois said with a nod. He couldn't see any point in trying to resist when doing so would only make his situation worse, he knew what had happened to Marie, Jean-Paul Renault, and to Philippe Noir, and he had no desire to be shot while trying to escape. "Can I finish my food before we go?" he asked, pulling his plate back towards him.

"You might as well, it's likely to be a very long time before you get to eat anything as good again." Ney was glad Dubois showed no sign of causing any trouble, but he didn't trust the man enough to simply take his word for it that he wasn't going to try and run. He kept his men where they were, positioned to block any attempt Dubois might make to escape, while he waited for the former agent to finish his food.

Dubois took his time finishing his meal, making it last for as long as he could, knowing that the moment he finished it his freedom would be at an end. He could only make it last for so long, however, and when it was finally done he reluctantly got to his feet and allowed himself to be cuffed and led away.

Don't miss out!

Visit the website below and you can sign up to receive emails whenever Alex R Carver publishes a new book. There's no charge and no obligation.

https://books2read.com/r/B-A-BNVD-RLLOB

BOOKS 2 READ

Connecting independent readers to independent writers.

Did you love *The Witness Must Die*? Then you should read *Where There's a Will*[1] by Alex R Carver!

[2]

The kidnapping of a child is every parent's worst nightmare, for the Keatings though it isn't a nightmare, it's a reality.

Inspector Stone is tasked with finding Alice Keating and bringing her home safely. Hard enough under normal circumstances, but between investigating an unrelated armed robbery, family problems, and the machinations of an ambitious underling, it's almost impossible.

Unbeknown to either Stone or Alice's parents, the kidnappers have more in mind than collecting a ransom. And when it turns out that the Russian Mafia might be involved in the kidnapping, things begin to spiral out of Stone's control.

---

1. https://books2read.com/u/bxgXVl

2. https://books2read.com/u/bxgXVl

Can Stone find Alice before the kidnappers make good on their threats? If not it won't just be Alice that becomes a victim to their deadly plans...

Read more at https://alexrcarver.wordpress.com/.

Also by Alex R Carver

Cas Dragunov
An Unwanted Inheritance

Inspector Stone Mysteries
Where There's a Will
An Eye For An Eye
A Perfect Pose
Into The Fire
A Stone's Throw
Under Pressure

The Curious Cousins
The Curious Cousins and the Smugglers of Bligh Island

The Oakhurst Murders
Written In Blood
Poetic Justice